EVOLUTING
Sherman

MICHAEL SHANE

Cover Design: Our Secret Agency
Edited by: Nicola Brown
Book Design, Layout &Typset: Sanya Dockery

Published by: LMH Publishing Limited
7 Norman Road,
LOJ Industrial Complex
Suite 10-11
Kingston C.S.O., Jamaica
Tel: 876-938-0005; 938-0712
Fax: 876-759-8752
Email: lmhbookpublishing@cwjamaica.com
Website: www.lmhpublishing.com

Printed in the U.S.A.   ISBN: 978-976-8202-54-3

This book is dedicated to
Max, Madeleine and Margaret.

I

PROLOGUE

Debauch…

In itself it paints a picture worth a thousand words, doesn't it. It has substance; it's a "woody" word, a word with character, with flavour; an onomatopaeic word, filled with the indication of an inkling of just what you know I'm talking about.

There are people, and I know this intimately now, who live lives beyond the sort of usual social mediocrity; people for whom the laws of the land, of nature, of God and of gravity just don't seem to exist.

And me? Well at least I'm not bored anymore; bleeding as I am from cuts on my face and hands. I'm sitting here beside a road, in the shade of a rustling Sea Grape tree around which the car I was driving is not so neatly wrapped and steaming from and through and around gaping bits of battered bodywork.

Ignore it, I am. I'm instead sitting in the soft white sand looking at the sun come up over this delightful and tranquil piece of tropical water. I think my wrist is sprained and I may have broken my right index finger. My head hurts where I used it to crack the windshield and at least one rib is busted, bent, bruised or just plain battered; I can feel it every time I breathe.

The car is pinging behind me and the Sea Grape is rattling in the breeze like the last Smartie in a box, while the sea is lapping rhythmically against the beach. But, besides these noises, the dawn world is absolutely silent.

I light a cigarette, it's the last one in the pretty gold box, the smoke is like some semblance of salvation, blood gets on the filter, my hands are shaking and I notice that my new white shirt is a shambles and I've lost one shoe. A lizard comes across the sand, it looks at me. Curious, it stares at me and bobs on its front legs three times, then skirting me trots off to look at the car.

I look over my shoulder and can see the battered bleeding body slumped oddly against the dashboard where the passenger side of the car used to be.

'Fuck you,' I think and smile all red and twisted.

1

New York City, the 'Big Apple' about four months ago – I was parked on West 91st between Columbus and Amsterdam, just down the road from the Trinity School, nursing a coffee and this fantastic pastry that I picked up from a Euro-style bakery on Columbus just down from 85th. I've already forgotten the name of the place, but I know I'm going to have to go back.

This isn't my usual neck of the woods; I live in Queens, this is Manhattan.

I'm looking at this yew tree that's just outside my car window; at least I think they're yews (you suppose a guy should know something like this after 20 years of living in a place – but hey!), and I'm thinking that it will die of cancer. They, these Yews, trees in this city, don't look like trees in the country, you know, with that sort of hidden vibrance beneath the grey of their trunks – these trees are all dull all the way through.

It's July, hot, dirty and smelly. I'm sitting in this nondescript Ford LTD with the broken a/c and soiled grey Naugahyde seat looking at the tree and watching Fred McMurphy load his sister's sofa into a pickup truck as if it were made of Styrofoam.

He's not wearing his back brace and he seems to have misplaced his cane, and I've got him on video.

I've also got him on video having sex with his wife and playing fetch with his dog (though not at the same time). Not bad for a guy who 3 months ago got 10.5 million in a PPD (permanent partial disability) physical disability lawsuit, which included damages for loss of the use of his penis.

I'm sweating, wet right through my nice, new, white, cotton shirt from the Gap – it's like I'm standing at the edge of some jungle somewhere, feeling that wall of heat that takes your breath away, it's that hot. As I reach for the Canon Eos with the *'Super Grande Large See Ya From A Mile Away'* lens to snap his picture I suddenly feel like one of those semi-sleazy PI's in the movies – Jake Geddes. – But I'm no Jack Nicholson and this isn't 'Chinatown'.

I'm an insurance investigator (sort of); part of the SIU team (Special Investigative Unit) at the second largest primary insurance group in the world. My name is Chris Sherman.

2

"We can let this guy Sherman handle it," Franklin Carpenter must have said to James Carnegie. "He's one of the men in O'Malley's field SIU team…he's from the islands."

Mr. Carnegie is the CEO, Chairman of the Board of Directors and the company's major shareholder. Franklin Carpenter is his managerial assistant (so to speak) and son-in-law. Both tall and slim, Mr. Carnegie because he's a vegetarian, Franklin Carpenter because he's self-obsessed and wouldn't want to be caught being fat or balding or noncompetitive or…well, or poor. So, both have all their hair, nicely coifed, Carnegie in a nice even shade of grey; Carpenter, with just a touch of grey at his temples.

"O'Malley swears by him." There's a little flick of the head for emphasis. "A stand-up boy, works hard; he's careful…smart!" I like that Franklin added that last word.

"Is he black?" Prejudice peeking its sinister little face from behind the Brooks Brothers fabric.

"No, no," shaking his head. "Where's his file? Ahhh – here's his file. No, no, James, he's white, ahm, here, born in Grenada in 1950, 50, 58. Yes, 58. He might have a bit of Jewish in him."

James Carnegie looks at the file, head tilted slightly back. "He's not exactly…well…is he full white, Franklin?"

"He might have some Mediterranean influence but he is white," Franklin added.

"Good good, but from the islands…Grenada, was it? But not from the Caymans?" He picked up the photo of his daughter absently, turned it around and then set it back down. Franklin followed closely behind to straighten it back into its original place.

"No sir, no. We don't have any investigator on staff from the Caymans!" He always spoke slowly, as if he was considering each word as he said it.

"Well, Grenada will have to do then!" And there's no discussion of credentials – there's no 'hey how about it, can he do the job?' I'm a go just like that because my parents had me in a place on a map that means something to these two in a very generic way, but, which has little to do with any reality.

"Who's at our Caymans office, Franklin?" enquired the old man, looking out the window.

"Staff of six, James…" Franklin is always unsure what to call his father-in-law. "…ahm, Sir. And, well only one who isn't a, a local, Sir. Rebecca Starr is her name. Yes, yes, ahm, yes, Rebecca Starr, she's English, Sir, but with strong ties to the island. She grew up there." Again, as if pleading his case.

But the story is leaping ahead of us again. Tomorrow's news today, so to speak. Let's go back a bit, six months further back…in the Bahamas.

*****

The polished marble *tile floors of the house seem to go on forever, like the surface of a still sea. The row of French doors that lined the entirety of the far wall of the living room certainly added space and light and a fantastic view of the ocean off Lyford Cay, Nassau, the Bahamas.*

In the room are a woman and a man, and the man is tied to a chair.

"Are you comfortable Mr. Luthra?" *She asked the question so pleasantly, as if she might actually care. This tall, very slim woman with fading red hair drawn up in a tight bun at the top of her head, was very attractive at 60 and must have been absolutely smashingly delightful as a young woman. She had the perfect George Hamilton tan and very large white teeth that filled her mouth perhaps just a little too much. Her eyes had that Slavic "oriental-ity" to them and were a lovely blue-green tint. She dusted something nonexistent off the brightly printed 'Mu Mu', a style she wears all the time. She has a closet full of them and three pairs of sandals to match every one. And her feet are perfect feet; long lovely toes pedicured just so. And she almost never wore anything under her Mu Mus but her flesh, and even at 60, naked, she was exquisitely done.*

Mr. Luthra was not comfortable. *He was tied to the chair in the middle of the otherwise empty room; and was bleeding from a cut at the corner of his mouth; the lip around the cut was swollen and bruised.*

"Mummy?" *a voice echoed in the empty house. The smell of take-away food charged ahead of him, following on the waves of his voice, into the large room.*

"Mummy?" He was tall and very handsome, his hair of that strawberry blonde, more strawberry than blonde, that his mother would have had at 29 ... and he is 29.

He walked, loped along really, in that bent-forward, feet and head leading his cock and balls sort of gait that people with large feet seem to have, on his way through to the kitchen. He would have been, as always, expensively, neatly, cooly dressed.

"Baby I'm in here with Mr. Luthra," she called back, laying down the cricket bat.

"Ahh! Do you want a Coke?" She could hear him opening the fridge.

"Love one." She lifted Mr. Luthra's chin, tilted her head first one way and then the other to look at him and smiled oddly...he looked a lot worse now.

"How's he doing?" It came out ' how eez he doowin' ' – all sort of Germanic and clipped.

Mummy had spent 9 years in federal prison, in Nevada, and Karl spent the same in public school in Switzerland.

'Mumsy misses you baby, how was Gstaad?' the echoing call from the jailhouse phone.

Karl came to give his mother her drink without even glancing at the bleeding man.

"I think he'll be ready when he wakes up. How's my baby?" she touched his cheek.

"I'm fine." Karl smiles. *"How are you feeling now?"* remembering her 'episode' of earlier.

"Good, good..." she walked to the glass door and looked down the lawn through the shade of Casuarina pines to the sea. *"I think I'll go for a little swim."* And she lifted the Mu Mu up over her head. *"Coming?"* She turned.

"No, no. No, I'll, I'll just stay here and, and watch Mr. Luthra."

Mother – son certainly wouldn't be the way that I'd choose to term their relationship. It seemed to be filled with equal parts fear and love and a good portion of psychological one-upmanship and something else that was kinda twisted and sick and evil and mean and nasty.

"Okay, suit yourself, but call me if he wakes up." She dusted something imaginary away from her neatly trimmed but still red and fluffy pubic mons and then, opening the door, walked away along the patio. She was very stately, even in her nakedness, when most people are apt to lose their decorum in shyness.

Karl sat heavily on the step that led down from the entrance hall into the living room for a moment and took out a box of cigarettes.

He lit one.

And then stood and walked to the window.

The house site, up on a hill, was surrounded by Casuarina pine trees. At the other side of the pool terrace the lawns stepped down in two stages. The last stage a long green lawn with an avenue of coconut trees, not Royal Palms, ran down to the sea. It was a house from another era, the golden age of the Bahamas – many of its lovers are gone now, replaced by a different class of visitors, the quick and the cheap. Like an old whore whose past glory with the art of her tongue has faded along with the less attractive nature of her physical appearance.

Ava was swimming strongly and as she got to the shallow end she stood and flicked her hair back. She walked to the steps and climbed, swayed, sashayed...she walked, with all sorts of sway and verve and, ooh baby, you hurt me when you do that, slowly out of the pool. There was one lounge chair; she went to turn it to face the sun, dragged it up against the peeling painted concrete balustrade at the edge of the pool deck and lay down on it.

Karl inhaled slowly, exhaled slowly, tilting his chin just a tad up and to the left without ever actually taking his eyes off his mother.

She ran her hands up the front of her thighs and then down the insides, swishing away the beads of water and sweat, and then did the same down the length of the front of her torso; each stroke ending in the valleys where her thighs started the climb back up to the flesh of her vagina.

3

Mr. Luthra was crying, he was whimpering, he was bleeding, *swelling and begging, please please don't kill me, for his life.*

Karl, always careful of his appearance, took off his shirt, folded it neatly and laid it on the kitchen counter before approaching Mr. Luthra. He was wearing a crisp white sleeveless undershirt, the kind some people refer to as 'wife beaters'. He squatted in front of Mr. Luthra, resting a hand on his knee, as you would to a child you wanted to comfort.

"Just tell her what she wants to know, Mr. Luthra and I promise I will kill you quickly and painlessly," whispering, looking over his shoulder to make sure that she had not heard him.

Karl lifted Luthra's head; the face was swollen and badly battered...purple and distorted. Karl glanced at the cricket bat leaning against the table all dented and stained by its work on Mr. Luthra. He was not averse to brutality, not in the least, just that Karl's way was usually far more subtle than his mother's – Ava was the cricket bat type, Karl preferred a nice quiet eye-popping strangulation or perhaps a close up smell-the-last breath abdominal stabbing.

"Would you like some water?" he said with a certain tenderness and concern in his voice that belied the reality of the man.

"Yet-th." Bloodied spittle ran down from the corner of his mouth. Karl looked around. He could still see her lying naked in the sun.

"I will have to go and get her now…will you tell her what she does want?"

"Yet-th." And he was crying.

Karl stopped to wash his hands at the sink and dry them, carefully, before putting his shirt back on and tucking it in – too much mess really.

I don't need the surface of things to tell me what I already know. In the end, Mr. Luthra turned up dead in Eleuthra and from the look of things he hadn't died quickly and painlessly. They found him with a plastic bag tied around his head; his hands, but, not his feet had been tied. He'd been thrown into the sea alive. He had suffocated while trying, in a blind panic to avoid drowning.

"Karl, darling, dispose of Mr. Luthra, would you."

4

She walked into the party like she was walking onto a yacht, *like she owned the yacht. People whispered; those who knew who she was, were the stars of the moment, able to impart the gossip. All this, while Mr. Luthra was probably, just then, quietly washing up on that lonely shore elsewhere in the Bahamas. ('Where were you on the night in question, Ms. Courie?' 'Dahling, I was at a party.)*

"Who's that?" Leaning in for confidence while keeping eyes fixed on the quarry; which, in this case, was Ava and Karl.

"Ursula Ketner, and that dish with her is her son, darling; rumour has it, but I know it for a fact, that she's of royal blood, Czechoslovakia, darling, or was it Hungary? Anyhow, a princess, darling."

"The boy is exquisite. A prince?"

"Certainly. His name is Andreas; lovely, isn't he?"

One elegant man watched *her entrance from near the bar, and as if bored, turned back to order, "A gin and tonic, splash of bitters, please." He pushed the glass with one hand, long fingers* extended. The other hand held a cigarette, casually, as if it were part of the two fingers that encompassed it. He seemed to lose contact with the glass only under duress, watching it leave his fingers resting on the bar, a faint loss at its parting.

He looked back again to Ava and Karl; a little smile crossed his lips. But, if you weren't watching, you might have missed it.

"Thank you." He took the drink, took a large sip, looked out over the rim, took another large sip, then a drag from the cigarette.

He could only have been termed a hunter or maybe a predator; the distinction between the two is somewhat hazy isn't it? It was written in that coldly casual way he observed the Couries.

Ava and Karl were saying their hellos to the hosts – George and Stephanie (his very much younger wife) Stephanopolis, of the Philadelphia Stephanopolises.

The elegant man took one last sip of the gin and set it down. Turning through the crowd, obscured and smoking, he slipped away; like a lion into the tall grass, he sort of blended away in the shading of all the dark suits and salt and pepper hair.

Ava Courie glanced up at the spot where he had been, focused a moment like a nervous antelope at a waterhole, sensing a certain carnivore-ic intention.

"I have this habit of looking at the posters on post office walls," the elegant man said, dropping himself into the lounge chair beside Ava Courie, uninvited, the next morning. The pool was large and artistically unrectangular with faux Greek Doric columns in a semi-circle at one end, where the pool widened and followed the curve of angle set by the columns. "Call it a hobby if you like." He had a nice, soothing, deep voice with that Hollywood actor's lack of accent. He took off his dark glasses a moment and looked at the lenses, wiped them, then put them back on. *"Perhaps it's just vanity, because really it's always my face I'm looking for... How's Las Vegas these days Gretchen?"* without ever looking at her.

"You're a very handsome man; I've always liked a man with longer hair. You know, it especially suits in age, something quite so European about that, darling." She waved a couple of fingers casually about the air. *"I'm delighted to meet you, though we have not been formally introduced. My name is Ava, Ava Courie, and you have obviously mistaken me for someone else."* She, too, kept her eyes looking straight-forward. Then became distracted by a paunchy man whose arms from the shoulders down, his face, a circle around the base of his neck, and his legs below his shorts were bright shocking burnt-flesh pink, the rest of him the white of an Alaskan in March.

The elegant man smiled his version of the Sean Connery smile, which she didn't see, took a cigarette out of a silver case, and offered it to Ava Courie.

"It's lovely poolside here, isn't it?" He smiled again, but the comment sounded sarcastic as he watched the sunburnt tourist pass by.

"Thank you." She took a cigarette, reaching out as a blind person might, without turning her head. *"Well, darling, it used to be. And you are?"*

"I'm Stewart Bryce." He signalled a waiter.

"Mista Chance, good mawnin."

"Morning, Horace; a gin and tonic for me, please, splash of bitters and lime...not lemon."

"Yes sah!"

"Ms Courie? Or is it Mrs.?"

"*Mizz!*" *she said taking the 'liberated' form.* "*I'll have the same please.*"

"*Well there it is, two gins p-p-please.*" *A very slight stutter that could easily* go *unnoticed.*

"*So, where were we? Ah yes, yes! I was mistaking you for someone else. Gretchen Moll, from Las Vegas...and her son, Hubert.*"

There's this crisp whiteness to the sun that makes the pool shimmer, and the blueness of the water become more translucent. And here were these two people having a conversation with each other as if they were talking to themselves.

"*You're too beautiful to be a policeman, darling.*"

"*I'll take that as a compliment.*" *He contemplated his cigarette, seemed to take great pleasure in it.*

"*And too lovely to ask so many questions. The interview is over, Mr. Bryce.*"

"*Okay. Well I'll leave you my card; call me if you want. But don't take too long, I'm off to the Cayman Islands in a couple of days.*" *He handed her a card, plain white, and slightly more square than American business cards, that was engraved in black ink:*

Carroll Chance.
   Fine Antiques
   Jewellery
   Art.

"*Isn't Carroll a girl's name?*"
"*Not today.*"

"**Do we really care** *who Mr. Bryce is, Mummy?*" *Karl Courie asked his mother.*

"Yes, baby, yes I think we have to." Ava explained the story to Karl.

"I'm going to call Elmo Gaunt, darling."

"Ah." Karl ran his fingers down a cigarette to smooth it out before lighting it.

"Let him see what he can find on Mr. Bryce. You don't like Elmo, do you, sweetie?"

"What's to like, Mumsy? A highly unattractive ex-crooked cop with pigeon toes and halitosis and far too much body hair, turned private detective."

"Elmo, Elmo, yes it's Ava, darling; *how are you?" Loudly into the phone. She covered up the mouthpiece. "Get a cool drink for mumsy, please." She was rushed, but not nervous, at least not that it showed. "Elmo, darling, I need a favour; have you got a pen ready? Stewart Bryce." And she spelled it. "I need to find out as much about him as I can…"*

"You could just look on the wall of any post office, sweetie," came the gravelly voice back down the line. "He'll be the fourth poster you come to, the F.B.I.'s ten most wanted. Stewart Bryce. Oh, come on, sweetie! He's the guy who they believe did the Hudson house in upstate. One hundred million worth of art and jewellery, including the Blue India sapphire." He sounded like he had a bad chest cold.

"Oh, how lovely…can you get me a photograph and put it on the email to me?"

"Sure can, sweetie. How is the Bahamas?"

"Lovely, Elmo. Yes, dahling, quite so very lovely." Czechoslovakia seemed a million miles away from the Ava of today.

"How did you find me?" *Ava asked when she found Mr. Bryce sitting at the bar, wearing a handmade polo neck shirt and a pair of blue linen trousers, in the middle of the atrium-like lobby. She eased herself into the seat next to him. The bartender, a guy named Giddeon, served her a drink and wiped the bar between them with a blue towel.*

"Well, let's just say it wasn't chance, Gretchen." He sipped his gin and tonic. "And it wasn't fate... Mr. Luthra seems to have gone astray. They'll be missing him in Antigua shortly." He stirred the drink with his finger and then sucked it for punctuation. Then he turned to look at her and smile.

"They might well. Nice shoes, I like them."

"Do you?" Mr. Bryce seemed genuinely pleased with the compliment. "I just got them in Hong Kong last month." He looked down at them, then back up. "You don't suppose Mr. Luthra will be popping up around here anytime soon, do you?"

"Are you trying to tell me something, Mr. Bryce?"

'Who's that casting devious stares in my direction?'

"Is it time then for a little trip to Antigua?"

"Yes, well I do...we do, Karl and I, we do have to visit our bankers in Antigua."

"The eastern Caribbean is fantastic at this time of year. Mind if I join you?" He turned to watch a tanned young girl walk by, her shirt said 'cupcake' and she had the top of her shorts rolled over.

5

"Mr. Sherman, we want you to go to Miami and then on to the
Cayman Islands," said Franklin Carpenter, with an attitude which
suggested I had no other choice.

I'd never been called into the office of anyone so high up in
the company before; O'Malley, my immediate boss, was there to
keep me company, on the modern leather sofa that still smelled
as if it arrived from the shop yesterday.

O'Malley's a big guy all over, big feet, big hands, big bones.
The red plaid shirt he was wearing seemed filled to its capacity
with chest. Franklin Carpenter and James Carnegie sat in two
large leather chairs opposite us. Because of the way we sank into
the sofa, we had to look up at them.

The view was duller than I'd thought it would be, it was all
roves, which are not particularly exciting – but the height and the
panorama was nevertheless spectacular; I couldn't walk close to
the window without feeling a twinge of both fear and jealousy.

The leather furniture was cold and expensive and Italian and
handmade and squeaky when I sat on it. And I'm sure I've never
even touched a suit that was as expensive as the one old James

there was wearing; here I was in my uniform of jeans and a T-shirt under a heavy cotton shirt… I was out of place; I was out of my depth.

"Sir?" It wasn't really a question, but it wasn't really a statement either.

"Do you remember the Hudson House job of about a year ago, Mr. Sherman? At lease one hundred million in jewellery and art stolen, including the Blue India; a famous sapphire?" Franklin was doing all the talking, slowly, in that way of his; measured, as if anything he said might incriminate him. James must have just been there for effect. At least one hundred million! I would have bet that Franklin and old James both knew exactly, down to the penny, what that heist had cost the company.

Here's the hierarchy – primary Insurer (like us) is who Joe public comes to to get his insurance; they will hold probably about 10%-15% of the risk. The primary will then cede to a reinsurer, who assumes another portion of the risk and who then in turn retrocedes to a retrocessionaire a remaining portion of the risk – this way it's all spread out and major disaster doesn't bring any one company crashing down. So, on a job like the Hudson House, James and his pals would have been in for close to 20 million. The next guys up the line would be even angrier. The retrocessionaire would be pissed.

"Yes," even if I am a bit doubtful.

"The man whom the FBI believes did that heist, a Stewart Bryce, showed up dead in a Miami hotel room 3 days ago." He blew into his hands and then smoothed his tie.

He must have seen the question on my face.

"He died of natural causes, a heart attack."

"Dey want choo to lead the investigation in da Cayman Islands on behalf of da company," interjected O'Malley, who's really really

from Noo Yawk, but would consider himself Irish if you asked him. "They believe that some of the jewellery may have made its way to the Caymans and that he disposed of it dere."

"Mr. Bryce it seems has ...ahm, had a Cayman Islands address and driver's license in a different identity. You're from the Islands, right, Mr. Sherman?"

"Ahm, yes, no, well not really sir; I, I was born in Grenada, sir. But, I ah, I grew up in Queens, sir. I've, I've only ever been back twice...in ahm, twenty-five years. Sir, I've... Sir, this is a big deal, sir; sort of out of my league."

My job isn't really 'investigation' – I'm the guy that they send to take the pictures, the photos, the videos; I set up visual and audio surveillance (and the odd wiretaps). I gather secondary evidence; I don't create it.

I pick up and put down, touch and turn my coffee cup in its saucer but haven't actually drunk any yet.

"Your parents were from Grenada?" Ignoring me, but still trying to find something to do with his hands; finally he puts one in his pocket.

"Yes sir. Well sort of, sir, I mean yes sir but we've been here twenty-five years sir."

"I hear you can speak like an islander?"

"Well, at home sir, sometimes the accent comes out, I guess it's like growing up French or something." I try a smile, but am not sure it works at all.

"We want to send an 'island person', one of their own so to speak. O'Malley feels you can handle this." Franklin again, smoothing his $150 tie as if making sure it was all still there.

"Things are, well, at home things are..." I'm looking for a way out.

"Look." His hands opened wide, welcoming me in. "Don't answer today."

Thank God!

"Think about it talk it over with whoever; it'll be 2 – 3 weeks, Miami, Cayman, all expenses paid, first class of course. The company has a condo on Seven Mile Beach in the Caymans and a car. You'll have an open expense account."

Bribery will get you everywhere!

"I'll, I'll think about it – yes. And let you know…tomorrow?"

"He doesn't look black Franklin." I heard Carnegie say as I was closing the door. (And I'm not. I am, however, 'ethnic'.)

"No sir, no he doesn't." Franklin staring at the door we'd just walked through.

There is something of the Mona monkey about Carnegie (it's a Grenadian monkey), maybe it was the dark pants and rust-coloured shirt with his grey hair, maybe the shape of his face… maybe the way he talked or walked or smelled.

I don't like him.

O'Malley was far more excited than I was. "If you don't take this you'd be an idiot Chrisy; worse than that you'd be doomed here, forget about it."

"It's…this's very big." I fumble a bit. "This isn't just some guy faking injury, Freddy." I'm making a point. "This is 100 million of the company's high profile. This, if I mess this up, I'm gone, history. I've got a kid to support Freddy." I say this to him, but it's just not really the truth. The truth is that the job's a little high-profile for me. It scares me. "And besides, this is, this is big boy stuff, man, I, I'm just a small fry, Freddy, I follow guys around who hock their wife's jewellery and then say someone stole it. I follow them around and I take a few pictures."

"You're selling yourself short again, Chrisy. You're a good investigator, pal." He puts one of those big knuckled large fingered hands on my shoulder and gently squeezes. "This is a big big opportunity for a stand-up guy like you, this is glamour time baby…forget about it, you pull this off you write your own fucking ticket in the company."

"It'll be a bus pass if I screw it up." What am I hiding from? You ask.

My father once said that I was, and I presume I still am, a waste of a good education. Not that he meant it in any grave sense, just that I never used it to become a doctor, a lawyer or an Indian Chief. Early in life I was sent away to school in Barbados. I was six when first I went; we, my brother, sister and I, went to stay at a cousin's house. My father was a fifth generation Grenadian (from a good local family, the antecedents of which had first arrived in the early 1800's), my mother's family had come up from Barbados where they'd been since the mid-1700's. We were, as a family, a mix of intermarried generations of Portuguese Jews, English adventurers, Irish peasants, African ex-slaves, French Protestants and Spanish whatevers. Father was, in my youth, a bank manager at Scotia Bank. Mama's people were farmers. Grenada's a small place and in the 60's had nothing much to offer except its certain special charm and beauty: and nutmeg, lots of nutmeg. If you were in a good position, you sent your kids to Barbados or Jamaica or Trinidad or England for an education. Mama had been away to school, in England and she liked the thought of the glamour and adventure of it. Father had stayed at school in Barbados and then Boston College. So when I was twelve – to get that leg up in life – I left Barbados and was sent to school in Toronto with my brother and my sister. Father's job came with a house, a car and education abroad for the children, the same package as the Englishmen or Canadians who usually held these sort of managerial positions. It was a testament to who my father was, as a person, that he held that position in that time.

Big shoes that we would try hard, always, to fill: Edward, my brother got the master's degree in architecture from NYU, Grace, my sister, the four beautiful children and the successful Jewish doctor from Manhattan as husband. Me, I just wanted something different; I studied English Lit and languages and film. What I really wanted to do was write for movies. If ever a degree can be wasted, I wasted mine.

New York's home now: we moved in March of 1979 when I was thirteen. We, the kids we, actually stayed in Toronto, at school, through that June. I had always wondered why we hadn't just moved to England or Canada; never asked father why until two years ago. We didn't really make a move up in life either, going from the top of Island society to the middle rung of the off-Jewel Avenue. Stepped from the top 2% of the social hierarchy, to the middle 70% of the invisible in the pecking order. They, we, seemed so out of place in NYC. I know that certainly I was out of place.

"We left home too soon, Chrisy." Father had shrugged. The smell of politics was in the air. "So, I, we, didn't come here to Wall Street banking. I was lucky to get the job with the State Credit Union, it was what I knew and there were lots of us to feed ah."

"Why didn't we go to England or Canada? Is this a new cat?"

"Who the fuck knows boy, your mother seems to collect the damn things; every week there's another fucking cat in the house. Anyhow, England, Canada, France, we never had the time, boy. There was a certain political tension building…a power base was being established. If you weren't in, you were out. As the power base became more defined…" he let it trail off there. "We took the first plane out the day I heard they were coming for us. We left everything behind. Some dollars followed a week later, but it wasn't much…" He looked out the window a moment, patted his pocket for cigarettes.

"Wasn't it still an English colony?"

"Internal self-government boy. England was already out; they just hadn't finished packing yet. You want a cigarette?"

"You know I don't smoke."

"I know, I just keep hoping you'll come to your senses." He smiled a smile that I've always liked. "Mix me a nice drink, nuh." He always drank rum and water – Mount Gay, Barbados rum that somebody had to send or 'bring come'.

6

So the next morning, when I walked back into the big office –

"Sir," help me here somebody. "Ahm, look, I have a son and a soon-to-be ex-wife to look about. I…" I was nervous, as I spoke to Franklin Carpenter.

"Soon to be ex-wife, Chris?" He walked to the big window and stopped, then made this almost theatrical 'seen it a dozen times in the movies' turn. "I had one of those once. I know exactly what that's like. Happily married now" which sounded like a lie. "My guess is right now you could use a long holiday." He stopped to touch that picture of Alice.

"Well…" God, the view was big from up here.

"Take it man! It'll be good for you, in lots and lots of ways! It'll be two weeks work and two weeks holiday. Mr. Carnegie'll be watching on this one, you can go places in the company, Chris, big places." New 150 dollar tie, same old fidgeting.

"I…" Then the secretary came in with coffee in china cups, those same delicate Limoges, on silver service just like at mama's (she'd kept the trappings of our Island level of society) and there was that pause in conversation just as there would be at a restaurant when the waiter comes to the table.

"I…" And all of a sudden I couldn't think of any reasons why I shouldn't jump on this – all the old reasons that I might have had were dead. Do something for yourself, Sherman. Maybe I was thinking of the china cups on silver service.

"I'll take… Sir, I'll do the job."

He smiled then. "Good…good."

And I was glad all of a sudden – I felt the weight of a lousy job, a disillusioned life, a misplaced dream and a destroyed marriage all start to dissipate. I could smell my freedom from the daily pain that I was causing myself.

"Good. Listen, Mr. Sherman, Chris…why, why don't you check back with me tomorrow and I'll get you briefed on the situation, get you the files that we have to date. There's an FBI agent assigned to the case…" He leaned over his desk a moment. "Aha! An agent Froeman. And, well, look, just come in tomorrow, anytime and I'll have this all together. Oh and Chris, we want to keep this in house. Hush hush, you understand? The re-insurers have already paid out on this and it'll make us look good if we handle this properly." He paused and fondled something on his desk that I couldn't see. "We've also got a presence in the Caymans. Our captive insurance affiliate. It's delicate stuff, Chris, I mean, you understand?" And he sort of let it trail off there and I couldn't bring myself to tell him that 'well actually I didn't understand a thing he was telling me really.' But my tongue tasted my lips and my eyes saw the bright orange sunsets – the green flash as the sun expired into the sea.

7

"Pass me that rib cage, would ya, Ed," said the pathologist to the detective. He was trying to fit the two opposing pieces of the rib cage back onto a body in the morgue in Miami.

I'd never seen this done, but what they do is they make a "Y" incision straight down from the thorax and then each way along the ribs as they run from the sternum across the top of your 'six pack'. This is how they pop you open so that they can get inside and get out the bits and pieces and chunks and wads of you that they'll weigh and dissect and examine and test.

I wondered to myself, is it a cadaver at this stage? Or is that just in med-school?

"Who is he?" I asked, standing well back from the table, but finding myself drawn to looking at the body. It's grey really and looks less lifelike than a Madame Tassaud's wax statue. And I thank God that the corpse's eyes are closed, because I find that gelatinous opaqueness in the eyes of the dead really creepy.

"No idea. Jaime, who's the body?" says Detective Mallory, offhandedly waving a finger at the corpse.

"Probable suicide." I can't see the destroyed back of the skull from where I'm standing near his feet.

Just six days after my last visit to the big offices, and to Franklin Carpenter, I'd rolled into Miami. I'd never been to Miami before except to pass through the airport and I wasn't getting much of a chancce to see it now. Here I was the next morning after a pretty awful breakfast of cold standing in a pathology lab with two old hands, Detective Ed Mallory and the Pathologist Jaime (that's Hi-may) Furnace. I almost expected Jaime to be eating a ham sandwich, he's so calm about the whole thing, and I was wondering just how long before I throw up.

"Okay…" said Jaime pulling off one bloodied glove and then the other; he'd had another pair of gloves on underneath. He took off the second pair and then he washed his hands as he looked at a file he'd spread out on the marble countertop beside the sink. "Enlarged liver, yellowed with advanced signs of sclerosis, scarred and enlarged heart, it displaced almost twice what a healthy heart might. He'd had at least two prior heart attacks, probably minor enough that he may not have noticed – clogged pulmonary veins and arteries; too much fat in his diet, and and too much alcohol. Your man may have been fit on the outside, tight stomach and taut ass, but on the inside he was 95. There they all are." He pointed to the specimen jars with a latex finger before pulling a glove on. "His brain weighed more than Einstein's but less than Beethoven's… Any of that help you, kid?"

"No." I'm squinting and I really don't know what he's talking about.

The pathologist shrugged. "It's what I know."

"The point is, Mr. Sherman, that he, Mr. Bryce, died of natural causes," said Detective Ed Mallory.

"We know he was dead by the time that he hit the ground as his teeth and nose were broken, showing that he made no attempt to break his fall."

"But he was alone we believe."

"But alone we believe, Detective Mallory is correct."

I must have looked stupid, but I was simply numbed by the fact that they'd removed the man's penis.

"Mr. Sherman, we'll move over to the evidence locker." He rested a hand on my back.

"Thank you. Ahm, Jaime," as if I'd just remembered his name, "Thanks!"

"No problemo kid."

"Here's his Caymanian driver's license in the name of Carroll Chance. The address is a condo at, ahm, what was it…hang a sec." Detective Mallory, perched his eyeglasses on the end of his nose, licked a finger and leafed through some papers in the file "…ahm, yep, right here, Beach Bay. I didn't go down myself so I can't tell you much more than that; except, it was, is, in the name of one Mrs. Jannette Chance. We've got no line on her. She has no Caymanian paperwork; no driver's license. We're presuming that she's a fictitious person." He wrote down the address. "Is it cold in here? I'm cold." He reached for a very late 70's hounds-tooth blazer in dull grey. "It's cold in here."

"Naturally you ran an asset search?"

"Yep, not only here, but Cayman is an English colony (his mistake and not mine – it's a British Dependent Territory) so we ran her through Interpol and Scotland Yard. Fred over there…" He pointed, Fred looked up and smiled. "Did an internet search and we ran her through the FBI VICAP and all their ancillary systems, actually the FBI did that! She's fictitious, I promise. Have you been to talk to the FBI yet?"

"No, no, but they're next though." I sound both hopeful and worried.

"Don't bother, I mean bother if it's just for the paperwork, but don't bother for the info you'll get. They'll give you little or nothing but the runaround and a pain in the ass! That's just the way they are over there. Any-hoo, we ran the investigation here mostly; I mean 'cause it was our crime scene and besides, it was evident pretty early on that it wasn't going to be any sorta big deal, too cut and dry, so the Feds weren't interested more than just a bit. Besides we're friendly over here, ain't we, Fred? We'll tell you all you'll need to know before you go down to the Caymans. What's that fucking thermostat set at, Fred, damn it's cold in here."

"There was a jeweller's business card?" I ask, remembering something that I'd read – and something that I wanted to know.

"I've made a copy for you." Detective Mallory was a star, "…and a copy of his driver's license and his passports, two of them. They're in this envelope with the address and details of the condo, etc." I like Detective Ed a lot actually. We made eye contact and smiled our appreciation at one another.

"…in the last six months he'd been to the Bahamas, the Caymans and we believe he may have been in Antigua, although his passports don't show any entry stamp," Ed continued.

I'm way out of my depth here.

"What, what was he doing in Antigua?" I ask innocently.

8

The First National Bank of Antigua has a nice new office by the airport. *The rumour, and let's just call it that, is that if you're a "good" client you fly in on your private plane, the manager meets you, you skip customs (and that evil little stamp in your US passport) and go straight to the bank. You make your large cash deposit and then go back to the airport and get on your plane and pretend you were never there.*

"I was never there! That's what the bumper sticker should say." Heh heh!

"Do I make you uncomfortable, Hubert?" Mr. Bryce was speaking loudly above the sound of the wind and the airplane to Karl Courie. Peter Dolin, the pilot; one of those tall thin, Ray-Ban wearing aviator types with the pronounced jawline and the grey at his temples, stood at the far tip of the wing, only half paying attention. Ava stood between Peter pilot and Karl arguing with Bryce.

"My name is Karl. And no, no you do not make me nervous at all." He was obviously not nervous.

"I didn't ask you if I made you nervous, Hubert, I wanted to know if I made you uncomfortable. Do you like my new dark glasses? Gretchen, do you like my new dark glasses?" tapping a cigarette on the nail of his thumb.

"Mr. Bryce you are being annoying." She was watching a short undistinguished black man cross the hot tarmac from a taupe Mercedes Benz.

"If we're going to fuck, you might as well call me Stewart," he said, not looking at her, but also watching the short black man make his way across the tarmac.

Ava ignored Bryce and walked off from under the shade of a wing toward the approaching Mr. Grainger, her scarf trailing like a windsock off her right shoulder.

"Mr. Grainger, how are you? Ava Courie, do you remember me? We met with Mr. Luthra. This is my son, Karl, and my lawyer, Mr. Chance. Thank you so much for coming to pick us up. Have you heard from Mr. Luthra?" she added after the slightest pause.

"No no 'e has been out of touch for some days now. He is still off-island."

A customs agent peeked a head around the corner of one of the support columns of the shaded colonnade that ran along the front of the airport building. It seemed he had no intention of making his way out into the hot sun, so they waved at one another and that seemed to suffice any perfunctory needs of semblance of a duty performed.

"Everything is alright; shall we go to the car ... do you have any more bags?" He glanced around.

"What gives you the impression that we'll be, ahm, fucking Mr. Bryce." Ava suddenly said, pushing the Chanel glasses, back onto her head. They drove along the tree-lined road in view of the American's

*impressive array of gigantic white parabolic dishes – Bryce wondered
if a dish in Antigua could be considered 'American territory'.*

"*Confidence,*" *he answered, not looking at her. Then slowly
he turned his head and smiled.*

"We're not breaking into *the vault here, we're just breaking
into the manager's office." Stewart Bryce looked out the hotel
room window, he glanced at his watch, already 12:30. They'd
been on the island for almost five hours.*

"*What does that mean?" Karl was sitting uncomfortably in a
yellowed rattan and floral cushioned armchair; he seemed worried
that if he relaxed into it his tasteful clothes might catch whatever
ugly disease it was that had slaughtered the chair's fabric.*

"*Well, Karl, that means that it should be relatively easy. May
I have one of your cigarettes, please, and if you don't mind fixing
me a gin and tonic. What time is your plane, Gretchen?"*

"*I really do prefer Ava, Mr. Bryce, and it's in two hours."*

"*We'll meet in Martinique, Ava?"*

"*How long will this take you?"*

"*Two weeks, may be less, depending on how quickly certain
people can move." He sat on the edge of the bed, tested it with
his hands and then lay back.*

"*Right, well, we don't want to be here when Mr. Luthra floats
to the surface. You do look handsome today." Ava touched his leg.
"No, I think we'll meet in St. Lucia!"*

"*So, we'll fuck in St. Lucia then." It wasn't really a question
as he sat back up.*

"**Where is your friend,** *Mrs. Courie, your lawyer?" the little
assistant manager asked when they arrived back at the airport.
He looked around nervously.*

"Ah yes, Mr. Chance, he decided to stay a few days, Mr. Grainger."

"That is highly irregular, Mrs. Courie. We have an arrangement with immigration and customs…but…"

"Yes, yes, I understand the difficulties." She handed him an envelope, plain and white and containing cash, which of course he took quickly. Obviously he didn't want to have to share too much of it with his associates in immigration.

Bryce is drinking a gin and tonic, standing on the balcony, *looking out at the pool and deciding that there's no fucking way on earth, wild fucking horses couldn't drag him, that he's going to meet the psycho family Robinson in St. Lucia, Martinique or any place else. But, but,but, the bank manager's desk drawer now, that was another matter all together. He goes back inside and gingerly lifts Karl's glass with a handkerchief and carries it over next to his briefcase!*

The starting of a brand new day.

9

Look, I'm not a completely unworldly idiot! I'm 37. I'm claustrophobic. I've been here, done some of this, but, hey, I'm no Warren Beatty; I've slept with a few women – a small few; I've slept with my soon-to-be ex-wife 100 times at the least. I've shared 2 joints but inhaled them both vigourously. I don't smoke, but I did for about one year when I first went to university… I drink, but only sometimes.

I'm only coming to figure out now that I was always a bit of a nerd…well, I mean, when I came to Toronto and then to New York I didn't fit in at all, so, I didn't bother to try.

I spent much of my time by myself, cause I don't really like crowds. Shrimp gives me hives. I was always reading and watching way too many movies. In my pre college years I was sort of obsessed with them – I knew all the lines to every Monty Python movie ever made and had James Bond themes on CD. I was a walking encyclopaedia of actors and their films; somewhere in college I began to flower, to gain some confidence – some, but not much; I was shy and was awkward with girls. I was good looking enough to attract their attentions, but not confident and smooth enough to take it very far. Getting pass the first date was always an achievement for me.

I have travelled around bits of Europe, North, South and Central America, and been to the Caribbean. But I don't like flying, and consequently I'm not terribly fond of heights. But I do like to travel, in Europe there's the train. I even got laid in Greece... twice (by the same woman). She was French; she thought my awkwardness was cute and due to my being 'American' I guess. And somehow I really consider myself this: American, you know. Perhaps because I was separated from my Grenadian-ness early on — father wanted to forget Grenada.

We didn't search out the community of dispossessed – those who had 'lost a world', who missed their 'home' with its familiar streets, its accustomed fragrances, the peppered flavours of the music and the lyrical tastes of the foods! Those for whom this city, New York, was incongruous with their true Caribbean essence and who wanted to gather home around themselves, like a warm blanket.

Even when I got to University I found myself hiding to be apart from the cool Jamaican 'Yardies', the 'Limin'' Trinis and the cricket crazy Antiguan dreads; I missed out on the 'fetes' and the 'limes', and the bashments [which weren't called that then], the jump ups... I was busy getting in tune with my American-ness; avoiding any of that atavistic roots-ish African-ness, that invades the souls of West Indians, white and black and brown and in between.

But certainly in the back of my mind I must have vaguely missed the life that had been left behind. It seemed so much freer and more full – maybe I missed the limelight that shone on a child of my social position. A lime-light that had disappeared.

I'm a Catholic and a bit of a hypochondriac (as if the two go together – when it should probably be Paranoia and Catholicism and Hypochondria with Judaism). I remember when I was growing up we always added the word Roman to the front; Roman Catholic. It's archaic though isn't it? When was the last time you heard of another type of Catholic? In the 1600's, during the Reformation there were all sorts of Catholics: Eastern Catholics, Greek Catholics blah blah blah. And just so you knew who was who, the 'Roman' Catholics continue their 'Roman' obedience to the Pope in Rome. Anyhow, all the other Catholics have new names now. So, I'm a Catholic and perhaps an agnostic. As in, I go to church but I'm unsure if I believe a God actually exists. I think like most of the people in the pews around me I go to church just to hedge my bets and because I enjoy the company of community; it's like going to the movies (but with less nudity and more violence).

I met Marjorie in my last year of University. I was 25. We had sex, she got pregnant; we got married – like an assembly line process, as if we were making, say, tin cans. Love, infatuation, stupidity – I know I loved her – divorce. I was naïve and soft and sweet and fell in love easily. And she was a Catholic. Why she married me I'm just not sure, because I don't know that she loved me. Perhaps it was panic. Perhaps it was that girl gene, where they long for children and husbands and lives in houses. I don't think that she remained faithful to me for very long. I remained faithful to her though, except in my fantasies of escape.

The body this morning makes my third dead person. I tell myself that I thought that maybe this kind of job would give me good script ideas and stuff and I'd get to practise my camera work. Who knows, it came up, it sounded good, cool good and I took it – I'd worked in some film jobs, gaffer work, 212th in line assistant to the director, kind of work, but I never managed to get in with a group. And if you're not in with a group you don't work consistently. It was never what I'd dreamed it would be in my obsessions with movies.

I wanted to be the producer, the director (the writer/director) – never the star though, never wanted to be the star. My brother's the excel-er in the family, my sister breeds them; somebody had to fill the role of the one who doesn't live up to his potential. I was afraid to excel, I think, to stand out and be noticed; yeah it's the stand out and be noticed bit!

I should have become a waiter or a hairdresser or a fishing guide, like all the other aspiring writers that I went to school with, but I didn't want quite so much company. So, I've been an investigator for four years now, albeit a sort of somewhat insurance investigator – but still, you see things: murder, felony fraud, grand theft, larceny. Well, okay, you hear about murder, felony fraud, grand theft and larceny; mostly you just see misdemeanour fraud and petty larceny.

"We, who am I kidding we? The FBI thinks he was knocking over the First National Bank of Antigua." Back to the conversation with Ed, Detective Ed, while he's searching his drawer for a fresh pack of cigarettes.

"How much?" I wanted to know.

"Nothing! No money! Couldn't break into the safe they said..." and I saw him smile a little. "Freddy you got any smokes man?"

"What then?" Maybe I am naïve for asking.

"Client lists? The rumour is that he robbed the manager's

desk of its personal files. Did you hear about a Mr. Luthra? This guy that went missing in Bahamas and they found the body in Eleuthra? Ha, funny that Mr. Luthra in Eleuthra. Cigarette?"

"No." Shake the head, repeat, "No."

"Well anyhow, yeah, he was the bank's manger in Antigua. He was in Bahamas on "business" Christ this is 6, 8 months ago eh Fred? Our boy Bryce was there at the same time. The manager was last seen in the company of some people calling themselves Ursula and Andreas Ketner, sometimes calling themselves Ava and Karl Courie." He phrased it almost as a question. "You don't remember this?" He has walked away to Fred's desk for a cigarette and is now talking to me from across the room as the cigarette keeps going to his mouth and then retreating.

"It's been a bad year, my mind's been on other things." I wince like I'm feeling pain, like indigestion!

"Ah!"

"And how does Bryce fit in?" I ask.

He sits in his chair. It's one of those grey things that recline at the back and swivel at the bottom and roll around on three casters. The chair groans.

"He was last seen, as Mr. Carroll Chance, in the company of this couple, Ursula and Andreas, who fit the description of Gretchen Moll and her son, Hubert who hail incidentally from Akron Ohio." He lights the cigarette, finally.

"I'm lost." And believe me here, I am.

"This is the big times, boyo." He swivels first one way and then the other. "The major fucking leagues, young Chris." He was smiling that fucking smile again; the 'I know something you don't know' smile.

"Are you up for this, young Chris?" The chair came to a stop; big exhale of smoke.

"I'm in over my head, Ed; I know it, you know it... I only got this job because I was born in Grenada." And I wonder all of a sudden what that means, exactly, to anyone who isn't.

"You were born in Grenada? I been there, loved it, loved it. Grand Anse Beach, the Grand Etang Crater and National Park, Concord Falls, Elfin Woodland."

I look at him as if he's speaking Greek, and frankly other than Grand Anse Beach, he may as well be, 'cause I have no idea what he's talking about.

"What does Grenada have to do with this?" he continued.

"It's an island," I say as I shrug.

"Ah..."

"Fred, I'm gonna go take our young Mr. Sherman here over to his plane now. So, I'm on the radio if you need me."

I think of Marjorie.

Marjorie and I started off okay. Expectant first pregnancy has a habit of making you desperately in love with your partner. So we loved. I was busy wrapping up my degree and working and she was working part time in the home and part time in the outside world. We were supportive and loving and worked together. We did stuff together, we dreamed together, we found time to make love.

I love children. I love Todd, our son. Actually, truth be told, I almost worship the ground that Todd walks on. But children disrupt your life completely, no movies, no music, no peace and quiet, no TV, no enjoying a meal, no sleep, no embrocative bathing in that last orange light of day, no sex, no conversation.

And no end in sight because it is a process that goes on for years (supposing you don't have another). And if your marriage isn't based on strengths, children put an enormous pressure on it. Well I suppose ours wasn't really based on strengths.

And so our greatest joy was probably the start of our marital demise. With Todd also came the joy of financial, as well as interactive pressure, and I think it became quickly evident that I was lacking in potential in this department. And she was lacking in the patience and effort ethic department. We quickly reached what one might call the 'Chandrasekar Limit' of our marriage and from there began to implode, descending into the black hole of desiccation and diffusion that would end finally in a divorce.

I 'kiss' my teeth; it's a West Indian thing that you achieve by sucking air in around clenched teeth, as I think of this. Anyhow, it wasn't all bad, you know, of course not. We had some moments that I remember. There was that week that we left Todd with my parents and went to Fort Lauderdale and stayed at the Pier 66. A friend of Dad's from the old days had brought an 81-foot Swan ocean sailer across the Atlantic for delivery to a customer and we spent the week sporting out on board. There were the early days when we operated as a family – the times that we lay in bed together, the three of us and played and read and slept and loved and cuddled. Before she got bored of being a mother and tired of all the work that I wasn't able to afford to get her out of. How when she was a child in Puerto Rico, her mother had a nanny for her, a cook and two gardeners.

When in Rome…

10

"Look, young Chris, here's my card," Ed had said as I was stepping
*out of the car at Miami airport. "It's a big world out there you
know. So call if you need me,"* he said, looking at me, all father-
figure-like.

I wanted to call him now – five days in the Cayman Islands
getting the slow runaround to nowhere – wonder if he'd know
what to do…

"Ms. Starr, please."

"She don't be in today."

"Oh, ahm, this is Mr. Sherman again, will she be back in office
today?"

"She not on island, Mr. Sherman."

"Oh…yes, ah, but…ahm, she's expecting me, Chris Sherman…
from, from New York."

"Yes, but well, she ain't be here, Mr. Sherman, she gone to
'Liccle' Cayman. Be back in a couple of days."

"Do you have a number where I can reach her?"

"She never leave no number."

"You don't know where she's staying?"

"No."

"Does she call in?"

"Not yet."

"Can I leave another message?"

"If you want."

And here I am quoting verbatim from the transcripts of my life.

"Detective Hannah please."

"He not in today."

"This is Mr. Sherman again, ahm, do you know if he got my last message?"

"He got de message."

"Will he be back today?"

"He don't come in yet today."

"But he got my message?"

"He got it on he desk!"

"But he never got it personally."

"He ain't been here to get no message, sweetie...he off the island!"

"Is everybody off island?"

"You an' me we is here!"

"Ah...when will he be back?"

"He neva say."

"Can I leave another message?"

"If yu want."

You have to understand that I don't get this. There's none of the mañana in me anymore. I'm so un-West Indian laid-back-cool-no-problem-man: I'm New York uptight – I'm not a 220 volt 50 hertz dread, I'm a guy; a 110/60 cycle true-blue, real Yankee dude. And this shit makes me effing impatient.

But sometimes you just have to wait, I guess.

I read Mr. Bryce's file from start to finish three times and here I am looking at it again with Peter Tosh providing the sound track from the local radio station. It's what I'm doing while making my phone calls to find people who should've been expecting me but weren't home.

I think that right now, besides the fact that he's dead, I know Mr. Bryce better than he knew himself. Not that that means anything. For ten years the FBI knew more about him than he knew about himself and they still weren't able to catch him. He had to pretty much drop dead at their feet.

Stewart Bryce, they believe, was born in Iran sometime just after World War II, to an English father, Chance Bryce, who himself had been born in India, and a Canadian mother from Winnipeg, Carroll Parkman. Both parents were killed in Palestine during the troubles there and he was sent to Winnipeg to live with relatives, where he was adopted as Stewart Parkman.

At 16, Stewart Parkman walked out of the house in Winnipeg and out of life. When he reappears he is Stewart Parkman Bryce, about 26 years old and an American citizen and serving in Vietnam in the quartermaster corps. He's already suspected here of being a thief; although nothing shows on his military record, the FBI files show that "things" under his jurisdiction go missing: guns, trucks...a chopper! There was a photo of him with ears pinned back and looking the regular army geek.

During the American pull-out of Vietnam, Bryce disappears, and Carroll Chance first appears shortly thereafter in an Interpol listing as someone spoken to during the investigation of a major robbery of a guest at the Raffles in Singapore...

And so the file goes on and on, with hearsay and supposition and close calls until 1982, when he, as Stewart Bryce, is arrested in France under suspicion of grand theft but actually held on a charge of holding false passports. He escapes custody and is next picked up in Dallas in 1989 holding stolen jewellery from a heist in Chicago. The police car transporting him to court was involved in an accident and Bryce was again able to escape. There's a mug shot here, you know the TV kind with the numbers along the bottom. He looked a little dishevelled as if he might have put up a fight.

They always seemed a step behind him. He was elusive and obviously very skilled.

There's a litany of jobs he may have and some he definitely had been involved in.

And then he was gone – poof! Nothing for a few years and then he supposedly surfaced again for the Hudson house job; that is the job had his hallmarks all over it.

The last page in the file had a notation about Effrain Shapiro.

Effrain Shapiro was the name of the jeweller whose card Mr. Bryce had had in his wallet. Originally from Montreal, Shapiro had a string of jewellery stores, Paradise Jewellers, in Cayman, Bahamas, BVI and St. Martin. He was cruise-ship central for overpriced "duty free" ornamentation.

I had his file too; it was thin. I wondered what my file looked like.

The FBI had questioned Shapiro as part of the investigation, but he had nothing to tell them. He had no criminal record, no history of criminal activity. There was nothing, except the card, to tie him to Mr. Bryce or Mr. Chance. Although he did admit meeting Mr. Chance at a party and having lunch with him once two years previously. The Cayman Islands police who aided in the investigation could find no local link between the two men.

"Nothing between them on the surface," Detective Ed had said and then smiled – *I was beginning to really dislike that smile when he used it without explanation.*

"What do you mean by that?" I had asked.

"Oh, I mean, they're hooked up alright! Why? 'cause it's perfect; you heist some jewels here, you dash off to the islands, some jeweller breaks up the pieces and turns them into something new. None of the stuff ever showed up at fences in here, none of it…that's where it all went."

"How'd Bryce get the stuff out of the country?" I leaned forward, eager to know.

"Ocean freight, air freight couriers, I'm just guessing here, talking without thinking too much. A box of jewels in a consolidated ocean or air container…needle in a haystack, especially outbound."

"How did he get in and out of the States if they were always looking for him?"

"Bahamas, maybe Canada. Right now America may be a lot less porous than it used to be, but in his day he would probably have come in by private plane or boat – they come in all day everyday in Florida from the Bahamas – using false passports and ID at points of entry where the passage control is somewhat more lax than say Miami International. It used to be pretty easy to get in here you know, and it still ain't impossible; Mexicans without much money still do it everyday. In the old days, you know, pre 9/11, if you were to motor in from the Bahamas, dock up at say, hey I don't know, Pier 66 in Fort Lauderdale, you'd radio customs and immigration and tell them you're there and how many and they say well sit tight while we send someone right over…in days gone by it might have been that you didn't want to bother, people used to go out and come back in every day and don't bother. Still happens I expect."

And none of that was any help to me at all as I sat here five days later with my thumb placed firmly up my ass doing little or nothing that I couldn't have done in New York, except worry about the turns my life was taking.

I must have called Mr. Shapiro two hundred and twenty four times in four days – after I couldn't reach anyone else I began to try him – I felt like a debt collector working a dead-beat lead and I was becoming very very tense.

"Relax, Chrisy, nothing you can do till they show back up right buddy?" O'Malley said to me down the telephone line from NYC. "Ain't your fault, right? Is the condo nice?"

It was nicer than nice – six bedrooms on two floors. Eleven feet exactly from some of the whitest, softestes sandy beaches you ever saw, with water so blue and still it looked like a mirage. It was nicely decorated in French West Indian antique mahogany furniture, old enough that the wood had begun to move away from the deep red brown of fresh blood drying on a new carpet, to the deep gloss black of old blood staining an aged floor. I was sitting in this barrel chair that just seemed made for sitting in, looking at a dining table that could have seated the Royal Family.

The place came with a maid and a woman who came in to do my ironing. I'd say, very nice.

"Look, Chrisy, I'll tell the fellas upstairs the story, you order a couple of fucking Pina Coladas and relax."

"Mudslides!"

"What?"

"They drink a thing called mudslides here; a sort of chocolate colada!" I remember the faint nut taste of Mauby, a Grenadian drink made from tree bark which had the same colour as the mudslide.

"Whatever, man; just, Christ, Chrisy, you got the ticket, pal. Hey, if you gotta wait for the cavalry you gotta wait for the fucking cavalry, forget about it." Which ran together as 'Fugeddabuttit'! I could hear him throw that 'Yo whateva' shrug at the phone. "Ain't your fault, right. And this Shapiro no problem."

Ida's the name of the maid. She was black and Honduranian, came from one of the Bay Islands, but must have been born on the mainland.

Ida's tall and big and has a huge high ass that she likes to squeeze into blue jeans, which are three feet across the seat. And she, unlike most Bay Islanders who speak both English and Spanish fluently, she speaks terrible English.

" 'ow you estas dis marnin' mista Cherman? Jew wants me hacer algo lunch-che?" She can't say the word breakfast, so anything to eat is lunch(-che)!

"Eggs," I answer almost like a question. "Ahm, juevos scramble-ado," she understands eggs; seems she understands English far beyond her ability to speak it.

What am I doing here anyhow? I ask myself. I mean I know what I'm doing here – but what am I doing here for them? That's the big question and the one that worries me. What do they know and when did they know it?

I'm supposed to what? To just sort of come here, meet with the police, see Bryce's apartment…where, what again? My trained eye would catch some crucial piece of evidence that everybody missed that would lead straight to the missing jewellery and the Blue India sapphire – I think to myself sarcastically – yeah right.

So what then? I sound terribly redundant to myself, but what exactly is it they have me doing here? I was nervous and so I made the silly call:

"Sir, yes it's me, Chris Sherman. I, I, well, it suddenly dawned on me, sir…"

Even over the phone talking to Franklin big-cheese boss-man made me nervous.

"Ahm, what exactly would you like me to be doing here? Ahm, I'm just finding it all a little unclear you know." Almost as if I'm begging for an answer?

He laughed. "Have you found Ms. Starr yet?" I could almost hear him playing with his tie.

"No sir, nor the lead investigator on the case…I can't even find that Shapiro guy?"

"The FBI?"

"The FBI, sir?"

"The FBI, yes, yes, I spoke to an agent, Agent Froeman." I can hear him looking through notes. "I believe that I briefed you on him being the agent assigned." The crinkle and click of dry fingers on smooth paper, "Do you remember? Agent Froeman is there in Cayman working on the case, he was to get in touch with you, hasn't he?"

"Froeman, yes, I remember, but no, no, not at all."

"Who's Shapiro?" he asks.

"The jeweller, the one they think might've been fencing Bryce's takes. When is agent Froeman to get in touch with me?"

"Ah, yes, well I don't know, but I'm sure he will! Look, Sherman, ahm, Chris, don't worry too much, your job is to represent the company; as an investigator and a guy from the islands, you should fit right in." He's definitely playing with his tie now. "They're all very close to something and I'm sure as soon as Detective Hannah gets back to the Caymans he'll be in touch."

"You knew he wasn't here?"

"I heard, yes. He's gone up to the Bahamas to follow some leads. If you really feel the need, you could go see Minister Jefferies, he's minister for Trade and Industry, he and I have spoken. He's on island!" I write MINISTER JEFFERIES on my pad.

"Sir, perhaps it's a silly question, but couldn't Ms. Starr represent the company?" I've taken the phone and walked out on to the veranda to look at the sea. Nice sea, very nice sea! I try to think of it in 'American' terms, but can only see it as 'icy mint' blue, which is much nicer than the possibility of calling it Tid-E-Bol green.

"She's a woman Chris…" as if I were stupid. "And besides, she's, well, she's not an investigator, is she, Chris?" Duh! "So just relax, man. Is the condo nice?"

Better than nice, but, say hey, why do I feel like I'm getting sidelined on purpose here – huh? Who's playing who here becomes the big question – and I'm just not used to the games.

11

Maybe I ought to relax a little. Maybe I ought to have a hot shower, take my shoes off and go have a look around; enjoy the sea, the beach…enjoy some local lifestyle. And I did just that.

I'd drifted by a series of now mysterious twists and turns right into the very heart of the town. I'd heard the music and seen the signs of things that reminded me of my lost youth and driven in…

There are 4 men at a table playing dominoes, under the tin roof of a rustic bar in the courtyard area of what looks like an inner city Miami motel.

I drift from there and end up at the fish market on the waterfront; a couple of guys with their feet in the surf and often their heads in the clouds of alcohol they've been drinking from 5 a.m. are cutting up fish on a piece of ply board under a make-shift tent. But it is an event, and I sit on the wall along the road side and watch the action.

A long narrow 'Canoe' in blue and white with a large Mercury engine on it comes on shore. When I say long and narrow, I mean like 14 feet long and 4 feet across the beam. That's not very big, is it? I mean I wouldn't go to sea in it, but they do, everyday.

I remember in Grenada as a boy how colourful the boats were – these, 'cause there are two of them close at anchor, are dull in comparison. You'd see them pulled up on Grand Anse Beach in greens and yellows and blues and oranges and a myriad of combinations of the same, with fantastic names like 'What Jah Mek'. The Grenada boats were different in shape too, round-er and wider, not Canoes, but what's sometimes called a Cat Boat or, in Grenada, Work Boat. They had a flat stern and a large tiller. In the old days the 'Work Boat' would have a sail, but by the time I was a boy everybody had small (like 25hp) engines as well as sails, which were mostly left furled. Slow but a damn sight easier than rowing.

And then in my continuing journey to occupy a day... I find peace while dangling my feet off the concrete pier towards the water that seems so calm.

When I return to the apartment, Minister Jefferies, of Trade and Industry fame has returned my call.
"Mr. Sherman I received your message rather tardily, how can I be of service to you?" He has a deep West Indian voice and tries to tinge his Caribbean English with a slight touch of the Queen, while tossing in archaic speech, or grandiloquence in order to sound learned. He does have a doctorate in Philosophy and a degree in Economics, but on first meeting him I took note that they seem to have been wasted, as his intelligence is directed only at the possibility of the next silver lining to his pocket. Yet, ultimately he is uniquely charming where many of his compatriots are egotistical bullies, thugs and imbeciles. Somehow I'm glad that Franklin suggested that I call him. I feel foolishly safer in the glow of his attention.

He arranges to meet me day after tomorrow for a drink. He will call and confirm. At least someone is alive and working on the Island!

The apartment at Beach Bay –
Boredom finally took me there the next morning. I've got nothing to do. I'm facing another day with a whole empty calendar, devoid of appointments until tomorrow's drink with Minister Jefferies.

I can't relax.

It's at the end of a long, empty road. It's on the sea. On your right is a fabulous, huge, Mediterranean-style villa, on your left (a casual toss of an eyebrow) the Beach Bay Condominiums. I come to notice something; that I'd forgotten how bright and vibrant the greens are in the Caribbean, rather than the dull hues of New York.

There's a new phase going up, so says the real estate sign; the sign's old. It's brown and white. There are two buildings separated by unkept grounds and 200 feet of semi-asphalted drive. The first building looks like a house, but isn't. The back building looks like a cheesy condo unit and is.

Mr. Bryce's (or Mr. Chance's if you prefer) place had been in the first building, ground floor, right-hand side of the building, if you're facing the sea.

I set myself up to do some surveillance.

The little townhouse complex looked like a Canadian house and I'm not sure I could describe exactly why if you asked me.

The road made quite a climb to the parking lot, about 4 feet, straight up a hump; the car tilted back at what seemed like a 45 degree angle. There was space for eight cars; but in truth it all looked kind of unlived in. There was a low wall that was a mix of quarried stone and coral rock that was holding back a large, overflowing Bougainvillaea that was orange, pink and white varietals all mixed together in a massive jumble.

I parked the car in front of a piece of tacky pink lattice fence.

The sea was about 100 feet away, as I stepped out of the car I could catch glimpses of it through the scrub bush that had grown up where the new phase, phase II, was going to be. Phase II with its better floor plans and grander views.

Progress? What would Marjorie's phase II progress be? What would my soon-to-be ex-wife's future plan be? Better views and a nicer floor plan? A trade up, to merchant banker, from I man the Rasta dread that never managed to be the island epitome.

I don't remember if that was what she wanted. She was an island girl herself.

I don't even remember what she said she wanted. She came from Puerto Rico; funny, I never think of Puerto Rico as a Caribbean island, sort of South South Miami Beach South, you know.

I don't even remember what I wanted.

I looked in through a window of the villa; but couldn't see anything. I walked around the back, looked in through the glass doors, nothing. The doors were crossed with yellow police crime scene tape.

I was thinking of breaking in, then the sound of tyres on the gravel – A 340 S Mercedes.

"I drive nothing but Mercedes," says Ava Courie to the rental agent at Hertz in Castries, St. Lucia.

"We 'aves a Honda Civic." replies the agent.

"A Honda Civic!" As if it were a question. "Where can I get a Mercedes?"

"I'll ask de manager," uttered a coquettish young black girl, St. Lucia written all over her pouty lips and big round, 'come look at my etchings' eyes.

"My girl, I think you'd better ask the owner, the manager will just be another useless step."

"May I help you, madam?" enquired a tall, slim, black man with a perfect moustache who is affecting an accent that he feels goes both with his position and the tourist across the counter.

"Are you the owner?"

"I'm de manager."

"Hmmm, well then, why don't you call the owner and tell him that you have a customer who wishes to rent a Mercedes and not a, a Honda."

"We…"

"I'm not interested in "you". I am interested in "me" and I'm interested in a Mercedes. Karl, darling, I'm failing here, could you please explain to this young man that I drive nothing but Mercedes."

It was a white 280 with a manual shift and it belonged to the owner's wife.

"Gretchen and Hubert Moll, *now there's a story for you young Chris, you got a year? Pull up a chair and I'll tell you some, Fred, baby, just jump in here anytime you've got some info to add…*

"The first thing that you oughta know is that she likes Mercedes Benzes, young Chris, really likes them. But she just doesn't seem to care whether she can pay for them or not. Hey Fred, what was the name of that movie we saw on the box the other day, the one

where the alien inhabits various bodies and uses them up...and when he wants something he just goes for it by inhabiting different bodies...and he wanted to be president?"

"Christ." Fred: looking older than his 44 years and shaking his head. "Man, I don't even remember who was in that thing, but you always knew it was the alien 'cause he kept flicking his tongue out his fucking mouth..."

"Yeah, shit, this is going to annoy me all day. Anyhow young Chris, it don't really matter, the point is she's like that. At least we should say allegedly she's like that, been arrested five times, only ever got her stuck on one case, she spent a good few years inside. She may have murdered one husband. People just have a bad habit of disappearing around her and her son. He's dangerous, but not without her I don't think. With her he's fucking deadly.

"These people, young Chris, ooooeee! I wish I had a real picture to show you, we've got the mug shots, but they're not, well, they just don't do justice. Anyhow, if they're involved in this you're in for it big time, baby, and maybe, maybe you oughta just jump on the fucking plane back to NYC today."

12

If I'da known it was going to be my lucky day I'da stayed the fuck at home – but some days you just don't see it coming till it's standing on your toes and growling in your face with your nose and lips firmly between its sharp little teeth.

The day had started yesterday just after my trip from the beach, but before my phone call back to the office, with the message from Marjorie and divorce papers…

"Chrisy, are you there Chris?" I wasn't.

"Look, Chris, I, I sent you a FedEx package today…ahm, you should get it tomorrow. Chris, it's the, well, I've signed the, the ahm, the divorce papers came yesterday, Chrisy, I've signed them and I've sent them to you. Would you sign them and send them back. I'll…" That semi-static, badly recorded, answering-machine voice and then the cut-off after "…I'll".

Whatever else she had to say obviously wasn't important because she never bothered to call back.

I'd just stared at the machine a moment. Gee, thanks, sweetie, all that effort just for me.

Hello! Hey! Give a guy a fucking break, for Christ's sake. I'm in the fucking Cayman Islands, not fucking Manhattan, save the papers for two weeks.

All this I screamed at her in my head, but I didn't use the word "fucking" then, I'm using it now for effect, and because this is me now, not me then.

13

"Hello… I'm looking for Pease Bay?" she says; which brings me right back to the house at Beach Bay, Bryce's house and the 340S Mercedes pulling up the drive…

And she's talking to me, with her head just barely stuck out of the car and I'm sort of leaning over and around to see her face underneath the brim of her big black hat.

"Sorry?" I say.

"Pease Bay?"

I step around the fender.

"Pease Bay?" she says more slowly, as an Englishman would to someone he knew only spoke Italian!

"Hmmm, I…I'm just visiting." I'm edging down the fender. "I don't know, I do know that this is Beach Bay." I turn and sort of wave my hand around.

The car door opens and she steps out:

Tall and elegant and I'm sure quite old, but it's hard to tell and then there's the accent, just a slight one, but there none-the-less. She's wearing the big black hat and her Chanel glasses and (over) dressed a lot like that Carrie girl in the movie <u>Four Weddings and a Funeral.</u>

"Beach Bay! Hello, I'm Ava."

Ava reminded me of a Mrs Betrand that I knew, as a boy, in Grenada. I can't put my finger on exactly what it is that made them similar, maybe it was the old girl sensuality, maybe the way they dressed. Mrs Bertrand, like Ava, had this, hmm, sort of wealthy elegance written all over her and seemed intimately comfortable with her whole self.

So, you see, I'm distracted and so this is where I don't put two and two together – I'm not expecting Gretchen Moll or Ursula Ketner; I'm not looking for Ava Courie, I'm not even thinking of Ava Courie. So like the broad side of a barn, I don't see it standing there in front of me. Vroom! I miss it completely.

"Ava, hi! Hi, I'm Chris, Chris Sherman." I find myself staring at her.

'Yu tink itta a go so when I hol' yu tonight, I goin do all di tings which yu like.' And there I am with a General Degree lyric going around in my head; a lyric which had been foreign to me a week ago, but have to admit makes for a great soundtrack for the life that I'd like…

"You're an American." It wasn't really a question.

"Yes, yes, from New York."

"Ah, I have a home in Manhattan." She seemed quite ageless and the Anne Taylor dress showed some tantalizing bits of flesh.

"I live in Queens."

"Yes, I've heard of Queens, I believe I must pass it on the way to the La Guardia airport." She said this without the slightest touch of irony at all.

"Do you stay here?" She indicated Mr. Bryce's place.

"No, no, I just took a turn down a road to explore and this is where I ended up," I say nervously, as if she might know my plan.

"Ah then what a lovely coincidence. Are you here in Cayman long?"

"I'm here on business…my office has sent me here for two weeks to a month to help the local branch with a problem, so here I am. I'm staying on Seven Mile Beach, The Cayman Club.

"Well, we, my son Hans and I, are just up the road from you then and we are here for much the same time, too. Perhaps we will meet again?"

"That would be nice."

"Yes it would, would it not."

And so that was my first meeting with Gretchen aka Ursula aka Ava, Moll aka Ketner aka Courie. And when she left me, there was just the lingering sensation of her perfume and her presence. And in moments all of it was gone as Marjorie came screeching back into my head along with the decision not to try to break into Bryce's apartment today.

The emotional turmoil of the disintegration of marriage is brutal – and then those divorce papers hit your desk and the turmoil turns to a relieved sadness, but a sadness nonetheless: a weighty sadness, with all the bits and pieces of self-doubt, self-blame and self-pity.

And I was running the gamut of all those emotions here and now. I didn't notice the sun was setting or the fact that I'd changed my mind about the breaking and entering.

The furniture in Mr. Bryce's apartment was all well worn and comfortable and cottons and canvases in pastels and stripes with a slightly Southwestern-Caribbean feeling.

I sat in the car and watched the house, walked the grounds and watched the house, stood under the trees and watched the house. Thirty minutes of waiting and watching; it's what I do. Always, always, always, make sure before you act...sort of! The power was off and it was hot and still and dull, even though it's like 5:30 and dusk was almost here. There was a lingering smell of soap and cologne in the air which made me wonder if someone had been here recently, although I saw no sign.

I opened all the blinds, I went and found the fuse panel and flicked the main switch, and the power came back up. The place was clean and fairly tidy, nothing seemed immediately out of place although I knew that the police had searched it during the investigation and there was still yellow crime scene tape outside the doors. It was only like three weeks since Bryce's death and it was still an open case.

I opened the French doors at the back of the apartment and looked out at where the sea ought to be but there was only a small 30 x 20 lawn with three coconut trees and then the bush. Unkept and untidy; the junior variety of secondary-growth forest... I slipped the lock pick back into its case – one of those things you learn.

We actually took a course in breaking and entering, and I got a little diploma for it: *Chris Sherman has completed the advanced locksmithing course.* What they don't teach you is what to look for once you're in the door.

One and a half hours of nothing, most of it spent sitting on Mr. Bryce – Chance's couch staring at the room, wondering what to look for and where to look for it. Actually, most of it spent thinking about life, about Todd and Marjorie. I was weak. Here I am looking for excuses to hang on to the dead, sort of like embalming your long dead mother and sitting her in her favourite chair to keep you company…it works but it's just not very sane. 'This wasn't me', I want to scream. I'm no detective, I'm the picture taker – snap snap, grin grin you're on candid camera. So then a further brilliant idea comes to mind: Shapiro! Shapiro, the jeweller, who won't return my phone calls.

Why am I here? As I drove up along the Seven Mile Beach I was angry-ish; I'd sat in Bryce – Chance's – living room and worked myself into a stew before leaving and heading back to town…'Why am I here' seemed to be the question of my day really, in both the actual and the philosophical sense. But right now it's the question fuelled by fear of some conspiracy at which I am the centre that's bothering me and not the question of some actual reason for my being and the grand plan that some semi-benevolent god was planning for me.

I was headed in the direction of the Cayman Islands Yacht Club, which is a housing development and not a boat yard. At the back of the Yacht Club is another development called Vista Del Mar.

Vista Del Mar is one of the few gated communities on the island. At the gate was a uniformed guard, but if you park just up the road and duck through the hedge you avoid the gate, the guard and the need for an invitation – and that's just what I did. And then I ambled by the guardhouse on the inside and said hello as if I was out for an evening stroll.

" Hello."

"Evenin' sar."

"Evening."

I glanced at my watch: 6:02pm.

The jeweller lives in here: Effrain Shapiro, owner of Paradise Jewellers and supposed non-friend of Mr. Bryce – Mr. Chance.

Shapiro's front door was open. I call out and I walk in. A nice house – Italianate I think they call it or Provencal maybe; a very nice house. The barrel tiles on the roof were old. Not new old, but old, old. They were, I now know, "taken off some dilapidated farmhouse in Tuscany and shipped here to the Cayman Islands (to stick on top of a brand new concrete and Dryvit coated home by the sea) to give it the architectural air of aged authenticity – I don't know what that means, it's just something a man told me.

The door led into the entry, the foyer, which opened onto the great room, which opened onto the pool deck via the patio which all sat beside the sea of Cayman's North Sound. The North Sound is a large 10 square mile body of sea water that separates West Bay and Georgetown from Cayman Kai and Northside. It's horseshoe shaped and the top end is closed from the open sea by a barrier reef that runs from Barkers to Rum Point. Much of the shoreline of the Sound is still covered with mangroves, intruded on occasionally by housing developments.

I called out again but got no answer besides semi silence and a flat, electrical hum.

Walked in.

Walked out.

The pool is greyish, greyish-green, and it's not dirty. The Sound here was a grey-green in colour and Shapiro had had his pool done in a Granite Marcite with Granite coping so that the whole effect mirrored the Sound.

There's a steady breeze that's filled with the odour of the sea. There's the constant soft lapping of water at the shore, more like that of the Hudson against the concrete of a wall rather than that of an ocean against a beach. I stood on the edge of it and looked around and I was impressed, and jealous.

Silence; I almost wanted to stay and just have a drink by myself, read a book and see how the other half lived when we weren't watching.

But instead I turned to go.

A man was sitting, lying really, in one of the lounge chairs by the pool, quite dead. Quite fucking dead! Stone fucking dead!

I stepped back.

14

"I…" **What do you say to a policeman who has found you** standing, wet and holding on to what may be the murder weapon, in front of the body of your purported victim? Fortunately, he wasn't a policeman but a Guardsman, a security officer for the gated community.

Jail's a cold place. And very lonely; very lonely and I hadn't even brought a book with me – I was reading H.M. Stanley's <u>Through the Dark Continent</u> – the 'Dr. Livingston I presume' Stanley.

There's a noisy echo about jail. There's a cold to jail, cold with a smell, an odour really, like a hospital gone off. This is not a place I'd like to spend any length of time. I become afraid, wondering if this was going to be me for the rest of my life. You start to imagine high priced lawyers bored with working O.J. Simpson cases rushing to your rescue.

I missed my son.

Did I mention that I was having a day?

And whom do you call with your one phone call from a place like this where you just don't know anyone to call?

Fortunately that one phone call thing is only for movies – they give you more than one if you need it and it's all quite free to you – but I had no one to call.

So I called the head office.

And then I called Minister Jefferies to cancel our drinks date.

And while I was doing this, a man named Dalbert Hannah, Detective Inspector Hannah, was doing his own thing.

He was, is, a big man, tall and black and bald and very some-what fierce looking with moustache and goatee in a tender warrior of the world kind of way. He stood off to one side of the pool looking at the body as his crime-scene people were putting paper bags around the victim's hands. He was impeccably dressed in plain clothes, short sleeve white cotton shirt and tie, blue trousers and comfortable rubber soled dress shoes. His head seemed to come to a bit of a point at the top.

"Where's the photographer?" he asked a short brown woman in a police cap that fit her almost as badly as her black police skirt – the size of a tent with a wide red stripe running down either side.

"He don't come as yet, baby." she answered.

"Why?"

"He gone fishnin' this mornin', Bo Bo, and he don't come back as yet!" Bo Bo being a local affection-ism given to men.

"Hmmm." He looks at his watch. "Well, it's 8:30 pm. Maybe, an' I jus want to throw dis out there, maybe you betta find me another photographer then nuh, sweets?"

He glances at his watch again.

The dichotomy of this life, an almost First World country with Third World trappings – one of the world's largest financial centres where chickens run wild through downtown bank parking lots.

"Is that the gun?" Detective Hannah asked.

It, the gun, was still on the deck, by the pool, where I'd dropped it earlier.

"Yes, sir." An English police officer, one of the few uniformed constables that were around was recording the scene in writing. Dalbert saw 'Tall' Edwards, from the scientific support branch, talking to Chief Inspector Bodden. A slim black man with a fat moustache, Edwards was in charge of the fingerprint, photographic and scientific forensic evidence that didn't include pathological or medical evidence. That was the territory of Forensic Pathology... which until recently would have been the territory of a visiting specialist. The Chief inspector himself was just a fleeting impression behind the glass of the doors that led into the house. Dalbert glanced at his watch.

"Where's the security guard that found Mr. Sherman and... who's the body, Chief?" He liked to use generalised nicknames for people.

"The body's one Elmo Gaunt, sir," replied the officer. "The guard's on the patio, sir...shall I come with you?"

"No. No thank you, Hugh." Shaking his head almost absently. "Elmo Gaunt? Is there any tea?" he asks. As he's walking away he notices an ashtray on the table with two different cigarette butts, one Benson and Hedges, the other Marlboro, red.

"Mr. Sherman, I presume," uttered Detective Dalbert Hannah as if he'd discovered me after some long journey to the heart of darkness... I set down a magazine I'd borrowed.

"Yes."

"You look sad, Sport." He's standing just back from those bars and scratches the apex of his head with one finger.

I look around. "I wonder why."

"Curiosity killed the cat, you know."

"Idle hands make the devil's work!"

And then Rebecca Starr walked in, in all flowing coloured cotton. It's lovely, a skirt, the flowing cotton and a blouse, simple, loose. The skirt is buttoned down the front. She's wearing sandals and a tan and the whole thing is large and tall and elegant and beautiful...and moving slow.

And...

'Baby are you up for dis.'

A rythmic combination of Tom Waits and Lady Saw...but that's not me thinking then, that's me thinking now.

"Ms. Starr."

She smiles. "Detective Dalbert, how are you?" They kiss cheeks. She seems genuinely happy to see him. "It really is as unpleasant in here as they say." She wrinkles her nose. She's talking about both the smell and the décor of the cell in which I now make my home.

"Mr. Sherman?" She points at me.

"Yes, Mr. Sherman." He points at me. "You two haven't met then I presume?"

I just love it when people talk about me in the presence of me as if it weren't me right here with them.

"No, but he has left a lot of messages for me."

"Me too."

And it seems fairly obvious that I'm just a fly in her ointment. I'm just here to interfere with the gentle passage of her strife-free Caribbean idyll.

"Am I getting out of here anytime soon?" I'm still here sitting on my prison cot.

They both look at me as if suddenly realising that I am there.

15

"A friend of yours gave me a call, Detective Ed Mallory, he said dat you were coming and dat you were sure to get yourself in trouble," says Detective Hannah as he's flicking at a file, mine presumably, and it's already disconcertingly thick. He looks more like a middle-aged West Indian executive than a policeman, maybe in a detective that's half the point.

"Detective Mallory?" I'm feeling a little displaced, I glance around the desk not really seeing much.

"Yes, Detective Mallory." He nods.

"Hmmm!" I'm sitting beside Detective Hannah's desk now and feeling a lot happier than I had in the cell a few moments ago. It's funny how easily one can be pleased. But it's almost as if I'm stoned.

Ms. Starr is off finishing my rescue somewhere.

"And you have. Got yourself in trouble, that is." He flicks his chin at me.

"I haven't done anything." Pretty close to whimpering I think. And think that maybe I ought to add the word 'yet' to that statement.

"Except being incredibly stupid." He's leaning back in his chair flicking his pencil between dark deeply wrinkled fingers, which are not as unattractive as they sound.

"Thanks."

"What are you really here for, Sport?" He uncrosses his legs and leans in awfully close to my own personal space. He's as tall as I am but bigger and definitely a lot badder.

"You tell me, you've been in constant contact with New York, what am I here for?"

"Public relations I suppose. Fall guy maybe?" he sits back. I begin to feel like I'm watching myself in 'Under Suspicion'!

"Fall guy maybe;" I say it out loud and it makes me sad.

"Look, detective, I'm an insurance investigator and I'm here about missing jewels, that's all." I believe that I sound more hopeful than aggressively convincing.

"Your being here is making some serious waves; did you know that, Sport?"

"What?" As if he's speaking another language; which he may be.

"Did you kill the man at Mr. Shapiro's?" he asks, so casually he might have been offering me a breath mint.

What I want is a tall glass of water and about six Aspirins.

"Mr. Shapiro, fuck no!" Fear. "Sorry, sorry." Apologizing for the swear word.

"Not Shapiro, that wasn't Mr. Shapiro…he was a man named Elmo Gaunt." He flipped a photograph at me. "A private investigator from Las Vegas; and you don't know anyt'ing about some missing documents?"

I feel some relief that it's not Shapiro. "Elmo Gaunt? What documents?" I asked confused and definitely not looking at the photograph.

"I'm not quite sure yet what documents…but someone over in the Glass House made a call to me very very late last night wanting to know if you had any documents on you when you were arrested. Did you steal any papers, perhaps from Mr. Shapiro's home?"

"Glass House?"

"The government offices, actually the Governor's office." He stands and walks to a Mr. Coffee machine and uses the hot water to make himself some tea.

"Jesus, I just went to see the man." I shift in my chair.

"Did you break into Mr. Bryce's apartment at Beach Bay?"

"…Yes."

"So you don't answer no to everyt'ing then, Sport?"

"No."

"Sure you don't want some coffee?"

"No, I mean yes, no coffee, thanks."

"Why?"

"I couldn't stand sitting around any longer being effectively ineffectual."

He's playing with the pencil again, but I haven't actually seen him take any notes.

"What?"

"I don't understand why I'm here, why I was sent here. I don't understand why for four days I was sitting here with no one answering my calls. I don't understand what's expected of me. So here I am feeling alone and left out and so I decided to do what it is that I do, investigate… I mean, sort of…" Again, mostly the truth.

"Do you break and enter in New York?"

Now there's another one that you just really don't want to answer. "Yes. You know, and yes to the coffee, please, sorry, I'm just nervous. Ahm, half coffee, half milk and three sugars. I like a little coffee with my additives.

"Yes, my job is investigating insurance fraud and sometimes breaking and entering is part of that, I mean if I need to place a camera or a recording device. My job is getting evidence of fraud, mostly in personal injury and malpractice cases."

"Not theft investigation and jewellery?"

"That's all out of my league, man. I really just take pictures."

"But not out of Elmo Gaunt's league. So, you didn't find anything at Bryce's?" Dalbert sets down the coffee for me and continues to stand over me. "You do realise that Bryce's apartment was a closed police scene? Didn't you see the yellow tape?"

"Yes, yes, I realised, I saw the tape. I just didn't know where to start."

"And at Shapiro's?" He smells his tea first and then takes a sip.

"A dead body. Who the hell is Elmo Gaunt?"

"Right, well we'll get into that later…so grand theft is out of your league. So why are you here then, boss man?"

"Fall guy, isn't that what you said?"

"Why you, though, Sport?"

"You don't believe it?" My emotions are running up and down the roller coaster of debility and strength and I feel a huge empty hole in my chest where my courage should be holding tight onto my heart; my balls have tucked themselves up high and tight and I feel a constant need to urinate just a little.

"We've got some dead bodies here and what was it…130 million in missing jewellery – that's a big deal, eh Mr. Sherman?"

"And don't forget missing documents."

"And the missing documents." A raised eyebrow. "Do you smoke, Sport?" He takes out a box of matches and fits a match in his mouth.

"I'm beginning to think I should start."

"Why did you go to Shapiro's 'ouse and why didn't you stop at de gate?"

"I'd called him several times and like everyone else he wouldn't return my calls, I don't know, I had his address, detective Mallory gave it to me... I thought I'd try and see him."

"He wouldn't return your calls, so you thought you would go and see him...and what? And he'd immediately become intimidated and start to chat at a thousand miles an hour?" He shakes the box of matches. The sound is irritating in my state of agitation and I believe that he knows that.

"I don't know."

"You don't know, Sport?"

"You know I really hate that Sport thing."

He smiles. "Irritating, isn't it?"

"You're trying to irritate me?"

"Yes... Sport."

"**Hello again.**" She's back. Ms. Starr to the rescue.

She's with Chief Inspector Bodden whom I can't see from where I'm sitting. But I can hear him. "How's it going Dalbert?"

"Fine Sir."

"Is he co-operating?"

"Reasonably well."

"Good, good. Nice to see you again Ms. Starr, excuse me, please, I've got a thing, ahm, upstairs."

They watch him go.

"Just in time. I think I was beginning to irritate Mr. Sherman."
He stands.

I'm looking done-in I think. I don't stand (okay, so I'm a bit in awe).

"Is he not cooperating?" She looks directly at me, uninterested, as if not seeing me.

"I'm just having a bit of a hard time believing that he's really as, as, well I don't want to use the word dumb, but…"

"Why are you two talking about me as if I'm not here?" I stand now.

"He is irritated. Dalbert, look, can I take him away for a bit, cool him down, chat to him, and we can arrange another chat tomorrow with you at my flat?"

"Yeah, that's fine, you know…we've got his passport, he's not going anywhere. And I trust you. We'll do it tomorrow afternoon, 5:30?" It came out five tirty.

"Fine."

At the door to the station a tall, slim, brown man in a very expensive shirt and lovely tie, pointed at me. The officer he was talking to nodded and he approached.

"Mr. Sherman, I'm Cadien Jefferies. Minister Jefferies." He was almost as tall as I and had a lightness to his eyes. Then he turned to Rebecca. "Ms. Starr, lovely to see you." Then back at me. "I understand you've been having a trifle bit of difficulties?" He put his fingers into a pyramid, pressing them to his lips before speaking.

"Yes."

"Well, terribly sorry to hear." I felt like I was about to be sold a used car. "Can we reschedule our little drinks meeting, I'd like to hear more about your predicament." Somehow I believed that

he'd always be busy and half expected him to toss in a 'Call me
if you need anything,' and a nice smile to boot.

16

"So, Mr. Sherman…" Rebecca Starr let it trail off.
I sat, bent almost double, in her little Daihatsu car.

I didn't want to talk. I might want to cry. I was having a rough time. Look at it from my point of view: seven days ago I was living my life in the guest bedroom of my own house in Queens; it's not ideal but you know where you stand. Marjorie and I are on the road to divorce, but I don't have the money to move out and she aint going nowhere, for sure! It's her house right? I've been paying the mortgage, but it's her house. But, then I get to see my son, the wife's cordial whenever I do see her, so we're separated and it's very awkward but it's not untenable – or maybe that's just what you tell yourself.

Then here I am a thousand miles away. Divorce papers are on their way and right now some asshole, some fucking asshole named Jack, not content with fucking my soon-to-be ex bitch of a wife, is packing my clothes into boxes. Boxes that'll be waiting for me presumably, when I get back home. Or maybe I should call it the house – when I get back to the house – cause presumably Jack's calling it home now: 'Hey guys going home now to fuck the girlfriend!'

And me, I'm being held for questioning in some foreign land for a murder I didn't commit. A murder… I'm not just being held for littering the street, or jay walking. Murder! And presumably what is it they call it on TV? Murder One, the premeditated kind. I mean I don't even understand the (fucking) laws, and I don't have a lawyer. I don't remember anyone reading me Miranda rights? The question of whether they have the death penalty crosses my mind a time or two also. Even if I did have a lawyer, could I afford one? How much does a lawyer cost here? And do they have any or are they all caught up in the lucrative business of corporate tax avoidance. And if I can't afford a lawyer will they give me one or… I mean this is English law right, I guess, and they're civilized right? But who knows, maybe if I can't afford a lawyer under English law they just take me out back and shoot me! It's scary you know? I'm scared shitless.

"You'll have to talk to me sooner or later," Rebecca says.
"This car's very small" is all I can think of.
"It's a small country."
"Hmmm."

"Where've you been for seven days?" I turn and say after a brief pause to glower out the window.
"Relaxing." She doesn't look at me, she doesn't care about me, she's driving.
"As if life here isn't relaxing enough. Didn't you know that I was coming?" I'm petulant, like a dejected high school lover.
"Yes."
"But you didn't care?" I turn to her again.
"I thought you'd get along without me – obviously I was wrong. This is my apartment." She indicates some pinky-grey

things just off the side of the road and turns in. It seems that Rebecca is used to petulance in men and it slips pass her like a soft breeze along the walls of a building. "How do you know Minister Jefferies?"

"I don't."

"I have a place up the beach," I say.

"Yes, but I need to pack some things if I'm going to stay with you." She's out of the car and leaning back in with a hand on the roof.

"Stay with me?" I try not to look down the front of her shirt, which is gaping – she isn't wearing a bra and her nipples are right there at the end of small round breasts that gravity is tugging at. I not only want to look, but to reach out and cup them, lick the nipples!

"That's one of the reasons they let you out – I get to keep an eye on you, matey." Or maybe Dalbert wants me out where I can cause myself more damage.

"How nice." Forced to live with your torment I think to myself: your indifference and your disdain.

"I could always just take you back to jail," she says as she walks off.

"You're pouting," as she gets back into the car.

"I'm having a very bad day." And I am. "Where's my car?"

"They're still checking it down at the police garage.

"You didn't kill him, did you?" she starts the car.

"No, fucking no, what kind of goddamn question is that?" Everyone thinks I'm guilty already.

"Hey, hey, okay. I don't know you matey. Remember, we've just bloody met. All I'm quite sure of is that New York's sent you here to represent their interests." As she's backing up – it's like here I am having a crisis as my world collapses and hers is just going on as normal and I want to scream at her to stop driving and pay attention to the fact that it's all screwed.

"Yeah right, and why? Why me? Why not you?"

"I don't know a thing about it." Looking both ways to turn. It's as if she just doesn't care.

"Right." I'm angry and so it's sarcastic.

"I don't. Maybe they sent you since I know rather little about breaking and entering."

"Very funny."

"What possessed you?"

"I don't know – illogical-isms." Sure the word's impulse, but it's not what I say. As she shifts gears I look down at, first her hand and then the fact that she's now wearing a dress that buttons all the way up the front. The kind that puckers to expose a little tanned breast and which, unbuttoned to mid-thigh has fallen in such a way to show off a lot of long long leg.

"What?"

"I was fucking frustrated." I'm watching the world blur by outside the window, unfocused.

"Try masturbation." A sense of dry humour!

"Not that kind of frustrated."

"Look, I'd been trying to reach everyone. No one answered a single call even to say hey we're not there, and I was feeling lost. Then I call New York and get the gentle brush off from head office." The view outside my window is rich with colour, but I'm missing it all with my preoccupation.

"I come in to a message from my wife, who ten days ago seemed quite fine with our living in separation in the same house, but who's now busy, in Queens, packing my stuff and fedex-ing divorce papers to be signed ASAP.

"It all became just too damn much, I wanted to get on with something and get home to rescue what was left of my crumbling life."

"Why?" It was a good question; cold, but good.

"Do you mind if I smoke?" she asked.

"I don't know why, and no I don't care."

"Do you? Smoke?" She, after a brief pause.

"Oh no, no. Not since college." Which isn't really all that true – I'd tried to smoke in college 'cause I thought it suited the artistic English lit studying bent.

I held out my hand, which was trembling. "Will it cure this?"

"A drink might." She slows so as not to run over a cat that's crossing the parking lot.

"Then let's do both."

"Look, I'm sorry, I'm very sorry." I'm smoking awkwardly, holding it with two fingers and a thumb, taking little puffs and spitting out the smoke. "And people dig this?" I point with my lips and chin at the cigarette.

"Yes, I dig it. Have your hands stopped shaking?"

"Yes. These mudslides are very good – I'm not much of a drinker you know." We're at the same Sunset House next to the tank farm at which I'd passed the time three days ago now, sitting at a picnic table under a blue umbrella on a patch of grass that seems to be clinging to life.

"Ah. You don't have to apologize at all you know." She focuses a moment on me before looking away at the pool.

"I do, I was gruff and I pouted a lot."

"Yes you did that. You're in a bit of trouble...but just a tad. Dalbert is just trying to get some answers. I'm quite sure that he doesn't think that you had anything to do with the killing. Did he do a trace test for gunpowder residue on your hand?"

"Nope, they said the fact that I'd been in the water and the chlorine from the pool would have affected the test."

"He works on intuition quite a lot, he's a good man... I got the impression that he's not working on the premise that you killed the chap. He might think that you have some information that'll help him though." She's... I get this cool bohemian vibe from her, the 'with it' chick. But then here we are drinking before noon – doesn't she have work to do?

"You know him well then?"

"It's a small island," and she smiles a smile I don't quite understand.

"New York already knows what happened, we'll have to call them shortly." Rebecca tells me around the smoke from another cigarette.

"How nice for me."

I am drunk and smoking and it's barely like 11 am. I feel like a Tom Waits song all smokey and filled with bourbon.

This isn't me, I scream at myself. But I'm not listening.

"I believe that fate's brought us here," she says.

"Us?"

"All of us."

"There're two kinds of people here..." she continues, talking of the Cayman Islands, which by some accounts is the fifth largest financial centre in the world – New York, London, Tokyo,

Frankfurt and then Cayman – a little island paradise in the western reaches of the Caribbean. "There're those that came here for the lifestyle, loved it and never want to leave. And there're those on the fast track, all suited up and making the cash and using the dynamic market scenario to build a resume so that they can move back to the world and the big time."

"And which are you?"

"Well," she said looking down at her own bare feet. "I came here as one and I've become the other…which are you?"

"I'm on vacation."

"Holiday, you'd like to think you are, Sherman."

She'd actually grown up here, in that sort of halfway expat kind of way, – holidays on island, school terms back in the UK as 'they' called it…the United Kingdom, Britain. She went to schools that I'd never heard of, but obviously meant something to the people that mattered. She went to one of the colleges at Cambridge – mentioned the name, but lost me again.

"Would you like some?" As we drive along in the car.

"Ooh, a joint – I don't…is that legal here?"

"Nothing's legal here, do you want some." See there it is, the 'coolness' – fuck the devil and who cares.

Today's a new day.

The first day of the rest of your life Sherman!

"Sure."

I'm fucked up.

And she's naked and riding me like I'm in need of a good fucking.

Her shirt's on but her skirt is off.

And my fingers are being enveloped by the flesh of her full round ass.

This is me evolving baby…no, no the evolution is happening and I am in it.

17

"**Dalbert, can we do this tomorrow?**" **Rebecca says into the** phone on Wednesday morning about 10:22am.

"He's not well! He's vomiting right now," she continues. She lied about the vomiting, but I was not well in my body-my-temple. I think I've been overstimulated and oversexed.

"Nerves I expect," she says. "Its been rather a big few days for him."

Ain't that just the truth.

As she said, it's a small island, so she knows Dalbert socially, she grew up with his '*cousins aunty's brothers sister*', so he knows her – besides, where am I going to go even if I wanted to run etc. etc? It's a different world out here; this insidious, incestuous, intricately intertwined life that is a small island; when you meet someone local around here the first question invariably is '*a who you farr?*' Who're your parents? There's none of the invisibility of New York; the same people revolve closely through your life in different places at different times every day.

People here are free with the sharing of themselves, there's no phoning ahead before dropping by for a visit. So even now when mass immigration has caused a dilution of the propinquity that makes small island life so familial, this sort of Caribbean-ness seems to percolate through society infecting even the most reserved of newcomers.

"Am I going to die?" I ask, feeling a little like death warmed over.

"You might." I notice that this time she hasn't taken off her skirt, but has taken off her blouse. Small breasted but with a full ass and strong thighs. She is tall. I'm wondering if I'm ever going to see her completely naked.

She's scraped out two lines of cocaine on a mirror and snorted one.

"Would you like some?"

"No."

"It'll bring you back up," she said as she climbed back onto the bed, like some flesh leopard creeping up to devour me, leaving her skirt behind.

Unlike all the American girls I've known and that French girl that time (who had hair under her arms but only a narrow patch of pubic hair), Rebecca has a full triangle of bush, fluffly, dark chestnut, but under control.

Two days of sex, Sherman, two days of sex!

I find myself bruised and sore when I next wake up.

It's strange how a little sex can change one's outlook on life. I feel embrocated; I'm searching for a simpler word here when this one comes to mind – let's just say I'm feeling well oiled.

And then she's missing.

And you, or I for that matter, try to get a clear picture of exactly what the hell just happened.

My head hurts.

I think that my heart hurts.

I walk, naked – I limp, naked down to the living room.

Empty! The kitchen, empty!

But there's a note.

'Had to go out.' Was all it said; no 'hey dude that was great.' No 'Chris, thanks that was lovely, just what I needed.' No 'will miss you while I'm gone.'

And it was dated with the time, last night.

Empty.

I have been devoured.

Sucker!

Used!

Fool!

Hey, wait a minute, Sherman you've been used – you've never been used before, Sherman. I've been fucked for fun.

I go back upstairs to the Mahogany framed bed with the posts crafted to look like bamboo poles. I plan to lie down for the duration.

'I believe that fate has brought us here.' Isn't that what she said to me when I wasn't quite so sober and my head hurt far less?

I find myself smoking one of her cigarettes sitting in the shade at the edge of the sand nursing four aspirins and a rather tall glass of bubbly water. I've never seen this particular water before. It's nice, it's English; Hildon, 'Gently Carbonated'. The bottle suffers nicely from an understated English elegance, looking alot like a bottle of Gin. The fridge is full of the stuff.

The cigarettes are Benson and Hedges Gold – I haven't seen these since the days of my boyhood, they're not my Mother's American Benson and Hedges in their tacky gold gilt and bronze-ish box – these are the English version in a loudly subtle all gold box.

I'm taking to cigarette smoking quite well. I notice, for instance, that I'm already holding it lightly between two fingers.

And it brings back memories of summers in Flushing or maybe a weekend at some cottage in Connecticut or Jersey or upstate, sitting out back where Dad would have the barbeque going and there'd be the sounds of rum in glasses and the smell of cigarettes. At that moment, in that place I find a certain warmth and comfort to memories of home.

"Hallo, Chris Sherman." I hear the voice, but I don't immediately recognise who it is. She's wearing the same hat, but much less clothing, much less. Ava. Ava, whom I'd met (was it yesterday?) at Beach Bay.

Despite my sunglasses I have to shade my eyes to see her properly.

"Ava?"

Who am I? I light another cigarette.

"Yes."

She is walking a little Shitzhu dog.

"Is this where you are staying, Chris Sherman?" She looks pass me at the building.

"It is, right there, ground floor."

"Very nice. May I join you?"

"Certainly. Is this your dog?"

"His name is Clive." That doesn't answer the question really, and the dog seems odd to me.

"Hey, Clive, you are an ugly little man." I bend to pat the dog and smile. "Ah! Can I offer you a drink?" I hold up the nearly empty bottle of Hildon from my crouch by the dog. "Bubbly water?"

"I would like this, yes."

"I'll get a glass." It was Miss Ida's morning off, no maid! Having a maid is an odd sensation for me these days. Sounds nice, someone at your beck and call; but at the same time someone's in your virtual space. Someone you're not completely comfortable with or relaxed around. I grew up with maids as a small boy, two maids and a gardener. I'm not sure exactly where I stand on this subject now.

"I'll come. You're limping? " she says.

She takes off the hat when we get inside and the dark glasses. Ava looks 51 or 52, a quite lovely Catherine Deneuve-ish over-50 thingy, though – I mean, she doesn't look the 60 that she is. She's dressed in a black Bikini that is really just strategically placed triangles of nylon and cotton-lycra held together by strings of the same.

She takes the glass and sips.

"Hmmm, very nice, refreshing – thank you. This place is very nice. Is it yours?"

She is walking and looking.

I am watching her ass – where Clive's gotten to I have no idea, and I'm not really sure that I care either.

She comes to a stop where an A/C vent blows cool breeze on her body.

"Oooh lovely, it is awfully hot and I think I am burnt." She eases down the edge of her swimsuit in front to show me a tan line I cannot see. "Do you have any lotion darling?"

"I'll look."

"I'll come."

You know, it's like the Twilight Zone here, I'm walking in the skin of a guy who I don't even begin to know – this Chris

Sherman, this Sherman the stud, is charming and cool, the West Indian male version of me. Not the me me, the him me.

It's as if having (not) killed Elmo Gaunt I'm now a cooler version of the me I used to be – Chris Sherman 'secret agent man'! If only I'd known that she was fucking me and not vice versa.

"After you." I gallantly offer at the bottom of the stairs.

It is a delightful climb.

"Oh this is very nice." She's looking out at the view. The apartment was originally two apartments; the one above the other. The master bedroom had once been the living room of the upstairs unit.

"A shower – it is better to put on moisturizer on wet, cool skin – may I borrow your shower dahling?" as if at this stage in our relationship this is an ordinary question.

Is it the tropics or what? I've been to bed with exactly seven women in my entire life up to now – and in one day I've increased my resume by one third, I wonder how this'll help me when next I go for a job interview!

"Yes, yes, ahm, yes, let me get you a, a towel."

When I come back, the door to the bathroom is open and she is showering. As I hover near the doorway, she opens the curtain and switches off the water. The hair on her vagina is a lovely auburn and dripping with heavy beads of water.

And the radio is playing a song, *'Gimme de lovin' mek me bawl.'* I'm beginning to really like Lady Saw.

It's not until after we've finished fucking that I begin to worry about where Rebecca Starr and Clive the dog have each gotten to. A friend had once said that *'a standing cock has no conscience.'* It actually seems to bleed any rational thought out of one's head until two and three quarter seconds after orgasm when it all comes flooding back. The same friend would be apt to ask me if I weren't more worried about Rebecca than the dog. But at that moment all the blood hadn't flooded back to my brain yet and so I begin to worry that Rebecca will come storming back and that Clive the dog will have run off and been lost in a circus or something!

"You have company?" Ava raises her chin at Rebecca's dress, which is draped, casually, over the chair as if expecting its owner back shortly.

"Yes, sort of... I mean she's...yes, a guest!"

"I must go then before she comes." It doesn't seem to bother her in the least. I'm on another planet, I know it, this is Mars!

She stands by the door to the bathroom. "That was very nice, Chris Sherman – it is not something I do very often."

"What, making love?"

"Making love to Chris Sherman, darling." She smiles and it is a lovely smile. "It must be all the warm sunshine. We'll still make time for that dinner, you can bring your friend, yes?"

"Uhm, I'm still horny, darling." God I love it when a woman says that to me without the slightest hint of criticism in her tone. "I shall have to go home and fuck myself while I think of you, Chris Sherman." Okay, so I'm hooked.

Chris Sherman, you stud!

I follow her outside and we kiss cheeks goodbye. She thanks me again for a lovely hour well spent. And Clive reappears in a fashion that seems to show he's quite used to this sort of thing. More used to it than me, obviously – and how I manage to pull two women in short time I'm not quite sure, not quite sure. I'm not...

Women seem to like me a bit you know, I'm tall, I'm handsome, got a little OLIVE in my skin, speak a little funny even after all this time away from my roots – but I've never been a 'closer'; nervous, self conscious, awkward. And then I got married young, leapt at the first girl who didn't disappear after the second date...

Ava's gone and I sit down in the soft white sand to smoke again, this time with a drink, a gin and tonic. Smoking comes easy to me – like water to a fish! I dig in my toes to where the sand, although dry, is cool.

Today I'm like a dichotomy of myself.

"Hey Marjorie, Chris... Chrisy, look, I just got your message of yesterday. Sorry... Sorry to hear that." I hate talking to answering machines. Everyone I know hates talking to answering machines – so why the fuck did we invent them in the first place?

"The divorce papers are on their way, I got that, as soon as they get here I'll sign them, I'll...

"I don't know when I'll get back, things are a little, a little strange here; it may be a few weeks yet, look if it can wait, if...look I'd really like to just talk a bit about it all before, you know..."

I am sad in that weighty way that people tend to call blue.

I go for a swim in the sea just before sunset and it's lovely.

She's left me for someone else – No, Sherman, she's left you for herself. She wanted something that just wasn't in you to give. The big score?

I don't really want to face the thought of going into my 40's a divorced guy; the single one at a party full of marrieds. *'No, I'm divorced now, my wife doesn't live with me any more, she's living with Jack.'*

'Ah Jack...with the big cock?'

I close my eyes and slip under the water and then back up again pushing my hair back as I surface. The evening air is cool and cleansing. I wipe the saltwater from my eyes.

Perhaps I'll survive.

I've been left before and survived. There was Elizabeth; she found me...what was the word she used...vacuous. And I'm not, but what I wasn't, was a Communist. I might have been vaguely termed a right-wing socialist.

There was Penelope, who dated me for a month but found me timid in bed. I wasn't really timid, just inexperienced, and was frankly surprised when in the middle of fellatio, and without warning (or lubrication) she suddenly inserted her left index finger in my rectum. Me, I squealed like a girl and lost my erection. She, became embarrassed and that was the end of our relationship. Rebecca licked my rectum yesterday and I didn't mind that at all, Penelope!

This isn't really cathartic, though; I mean it might be if Rebecca were still here, but she's not. So I'm only just depressing myself.

18

"Fix this, Mr. Sherman," **said Franklin.** **"We have a corporate**
presence in Cayman that we want to protect. Are we clear on this,
Mr. Sherman? Rebecca Starr knows the island, she's well liked,
follow her lead." He's a bit pissed. Why do I feel like the blame
for everything's coming down squarely on my shoulders?

"I haven't seen Ms. Starr since sometime yesterday," I answer
a bit lamely.

"Sherman, I don't care, listen to me, follow her lead and fix
this, this thing. Fix it or don't come back, Mr. Sherman."

Hey! Who the hell is Elmo Gaunt? Was what I really wanted
to ask him, and fuck you, was what I really wanted to say.

"Hey, good morning, how was your night?" The return of
Ms. Starr!

I almost laughed. I think I guffawed a bit, though, or snorted
really.

I heard this thing once that some cowboy named Clay Hollerman
said – *'no way in the world a man's supposed to ride a bull, but
that's the whole point!'*

"Hi…" I got laid by a lovely woman. "Boring?" I inflect as if it were a question for her to answer and therefore not exactly a lie on my part. "You disappeared off my planet." "I had things to do." And she must have because her hair's been trimmed and it's a different colour altogether! The auburn's gone and replaced by blonde frosted chestnut! I'm having a breakfast of fresh fruit and fresh ground Kenyan coffee that Ida has prepared for me. I'm wearing a sarong and a T-Shirt, feeling the island epitome – not this island's epitome but, you know, the 'Thomas Crown on holiday in Martinique' island epitome.

The only West Indians I ever remember wearing sarongs in the days of my youth were ones who'd lived in East Africa or Indonesia.

"So you didn't get my messages then?"

"The six of them? Yes – look, Sherman, babe." And she smiles here to let me know it's cool, she's just doing it for effect. "Let's get a little something understood here. Yesterday was yesterday. What's that face about, chappy, you got nicely shagged didn't you? Come smile for Becca, come on, we had a good time, didn't we?" She picks a piece of fruit from the table.

"Yeah, yeah, we did – look, I'm, I'm a bit of a fragile sort, girl. This" and I wave my arms "this isn't the 'me'. Just think of me as some schmo from the big city who never lived the fucking big-city life. My wife's leaving me!" Rebecca looked nice in her new hair.

"You said." Yawn. Bored.

"And I've never been fucked by two strange women in one day before," I say opening the newspaper that seems to arrive with my breakfast.

"Two?" Suddenly I have your attention, Ms. Starr.

I'm sitting in the sofa looking out over the paper at the sea and I can now hear her standing behind me.

"Yes – wild days. Do you have a cigarette?"

"You got laid after I left?"

"I must have looked horny." And I started laughing oddly. And shaking my head. "Would you like some breakfast? Sorry, look sorry – yes, I met someone, a woman I'd met before and well she wanted... Not that it matters to you." I continued.

She laughs then.

"Sherman, you absolute stud. I didn't know you had it in you...some of that West Indian flavour coming out in you after all."

"So you and I aren't love at first sight then, huh?"

"Oh, I don't think so, but it's a nice thought, Sherman, a nice thought. Yes I think I'll have some of that breakfast now. I really do want to hear this fucking story, Sherman."

"You've changed your hair," I finally manage to say.

And I want to hear your story, I think to myself.

So, Rebecca's father had been a lawyer – now retired – who had come here in the late 60's, 69 I think she said. And she had grown up here, then a girl of four. She had told me that I couldn't imagine what it had been like here in 1970.

"We actually, and I'm not exaggerating this, used to have to come inside at dusk because the mosquitoes were so terrible. The swarm would last about an hour and then it would be semi-safe, the sprayer trucks would come out and the mosquitoes would go away. There was nothing there, here, on Seven Mile Beach, quite empty.

"The Beach Club was here and the West Indian Club, that's now somebody's house – the Galleon Beach, that burnt down…you could play mini golf across the road from Beach Club and there was a drive in theatre at Bodden Town."

"Bodden Town?"

"It's the first place settled on the island; it's on the South Coast about 20 minutes from town. The first movie I remember seeing there was <u>Von Ryan's Express</u> with Frank Sinatra. Mum loved Frank Sinatra.

"I went to school in Cheltenham, I was a weekly boarder from nine years old." This I could understand, same life, different reality, but I didn't say so, I just wanted to listen.

"Holidays here were fab, premium was the word we used to use…lots of kids coming out from UK and Canada and life was free because it wasn't dangerous and we all mixed together. These days there's a bit of self imposed segregation, you know. There's a huge Caymanian versus Expat issue.

"Never used to be like that at all, and I think with the old crowd, it still isn't really." She said in the wistful way one remembers a myth that one mistook for a memory.

"After Cambridge I stayed and worked in London, in the city, for six years. Then Daddy retired and came back to England. They sold the house in Cayman and bought a flat out here in South Sound that they could use on hols." Using an English-ism for holidays.

She continued. "I hadn't been to Cayman for seven years and came on hols and just couldn't bring myself to leave. Told myself that the job offer I got was a fast track back to London with big money in my pocket and a Cayman bank account. But it never really was you know."

I want to ask where Cheltenham is, was, but I don't have the nerve, she'd tossed out the name as if I was supposed to know it.

Miss Ida came in with fresh cut pineapple.
"Como are you miss Rebecca?" She's wearing a wig I'm sure.
"Fine Ida, fine. How are you?"
"Passing well miss Rebecca." And then she sashayed off swaying her massive 'Bunky' behind her.
"That's a hell of an ass." Rebecca whispered to me.

"You're still pouting, Sherman."
And so what, maybe I was.
"I tell you what, Mr. Man, let's wipe that glum out of your life, why don't I spend the day with you?"
"No work?"
"Work to live, don't live to work, chappy," a winning smile. "I tell you what, let's do the Sand Bar."
"More drinking?"
"No, no, pouty boy, it's a spot in the North Sound where the water's like waist-deep and the bottom's sandy. It's a splendid day out, we'll borrow a boat, Ida can knock together some lunch, we'll have some fun. Maybe go to Rum Point or the Kaibo, get naked and tan our nipples, get all oily and wet." She's teasing me.

It's a hell of a spot on a day like today. The Sound is a mostly enclosed body of water five miles across and about nine miles from the reef at the north end to the mangroves at the south end. The northern one third of it is blue water, the other two thirds, around the edges and the entire south are that greeny-grey of wet soapstone.

The Sand Bar itself is about the area of three tennis courts. At one end there was a tourist boat anchored up with about forty people in the water snorkling and looking at the Stingrays that over-populate this particular spot. About a quarter mile away, near the channel out to open water, is a spot about twelve feet deep that's called Stingray City. There's a Barracuda at Stingray City, but the Stingrays have all moved to Sand Bar, presumably a better neighbourhood.

Besides the tourist boat, the Sound seemed empty. The water was cool and fresh, there was a nice soft breeze, the sun was hot and bright and my shoulders had already taken on that gritty feeling of dried salt on sunburn. The Stingrays were all down by the tourist boat, so, we have the water to ourselves.

"I need a T-shirt." I said.

"I need a fuck," she replied.

The boat Rebecca'd borrowed was a 26-foot Roballo open fisherman, which stood out of the water almost three feet above our heads at the bow and cast a nice cool shadow on the water. We had anchored as far away from the tourist boat as possible for privacy and Rebecca took me into the shade on the far side of the boat.

She really was lovely naked, her back turned to me, her hands above her head holding on to the gunwale of the boat and as if art were imitating life, Erma Franklin's version of 'Piece of My Heart' was playing on the boat's stereo.

There's this stunning moment everytime I enter her; like a shock that runs from the head of my cock to my brain. It's a *'you're in there boy'* moment. I love that moment with Rebecca.

I'm out of my league. Here's a girl who has a passion for giving blow jobs and a driving aggressive want to have as much sex as she can possibly fit into a day. Her wants and her attitudes are like those of a twenty-year-old boy. We all remember that at 23, even I at 23 had those memories. That French girl and I, we had sex all the time; well sex and movies – I saw Grease with her, John Travolta with French subtitles. But I'm average married and 37; sex seems to have drifted away to the realm of convenience and onanistic five fingered fantasy… I'm spent. My penis is sore. And for some indistinct reason I'm sad. I'm sad.

A grey shadow moves along the bottom near me; another passes on some other vector. It's seems like the haphazard regularity of a screen saver as they pass one after the other but not as if on any particular flight plan. The stingrays, bored now with the tourist boat, are coming to examine the 'fuckers' across the 'bar'.

"They're cool," Rebecca says meaning the Stingrays. "Do you want to touch one?" she asks.

But I'm still off in an image of Rachel Ward (and Jeff Bridges) in 'Against all Odds' – it's all the sweat, tans and crystal bright sunshine!

"No." I shake my head stretching out the word and puckering my mouth to show how adamant I am about it.

"They're not slimy or anything! They're soft like suede."

Yeah, suede with teeth! "Still no." Doesn't she know that on the evolutionary chart these things are, in reality, sharks?

"Chicken?"

"Yes!"

"You still look sad, Sherman."

"I still feel sad." I look up and around, the sky is infinite and pale blue. High above are the twin contrails of a jet that's flying from somewhere to someplace else.

There's a faint twinkle of sun on polished aluminium; and I wonder, as I always do where they're going and I wish that wherever it is, that I was there too.

"What do you think, Rebecca?" I ask.

"About what?" she queries as she pops out of the water unto the dive platform that runs along the stern of the boat on either sides of the engine.

"About all this?" still vague.

"All this what?" She's not wearing her bikini bottoms.

"The suspicion of murder, Dalbert, my chances, missing jewels, why I'm here, what the hell I'm gonna do if they actually hold me on charges. I don't even have a lawyer."

"Easy chappy, easy. You didn't kill him, correct?" She reaches over for the cooler and pops out some bottled water.

"Correct. A Pepsi for me."

"Right, and I'm here to look after you." She pops the top on the Pepsi as if to illustrate the point. "I'm to handle things; if a lawyer's needed, we'll hire a lawyer. You're on company business and the company doesn't want to look bad; we haven't brought in the lawyers yet because we don't need the lawyers yet. Besides, if you didn't do it there's no evidence against you."

"Hopefully."

"I know Dalbert, Dalbert and I can deal. He'll talk, we'll listen; if problems arise then we'll have lawyers coming out of the woodwork." Maybe it's just perception, but I think she opens her legs just a little here. "Now Sherman, relax."

Am I supposed to eat that?

19

"**Elmo Gaunt? So you're telling me that the name means** nothing to you at all, Sport?" Detective Hannah's chewing on a matchstick – but I still hadn't seen him smoke. He's been sitting in a comfortable chair in my living room but got up to pace.

"The first time I heard it was when you said it to me – yesterday, I think." I want to punch him, I'm too scared to of course and I'm sure that he'd win the fight but I still want to punch him.

"You think I told you yesterday or you t'ink dat that was the first time you heard the name. This is really nice my friend, the life eh?" He waves the matchstick at the window, out at all that soft white sand and stodgy pink flesh, but presumably he's not talking about the stodgy pink flesh. "Colonial grandeur eh, Sport?

"Would you like something cold to drink? The fridge is full of some really great water. I don't get you at all, Mr. Sherman. What do you know?" He runs a hand back across his bald head and then around and across the beard at his chin as if wiping something off.

"Not too much at all…but I do know that you have a hell of a wardrobe, I wish I could dress as well." I flick at my shirt, which as usual is hanging out of my pants.

"Yes, why don't I have some of that water den." Détente.

"I'll get it." Rebecca Starr to the rescue. "You want ice with that D.?"

"Please, yes. The new hair looks good on you Becca," then back to me. "Elmo Gaunt, 44, a private detective from Las Vegas, Nevada; specializes in insurance cases, well maybe specializes is the wrong word but he likes insurance fraud – so, you're both in the same game...don't ring no bells?" He's come to sit back down and taps the matchstick on the coffee table.

"I've never been to Vegas. What does his office say that he's working on?"

"We've been trying to reach someone since yesterday – no luck."

"What's the FBI say?" Rebecca asks.

"Who, Agent Froeman? He isn't back on island yet. He's still in Nassau I think. What did you find at Bryce's flat Mr. Sherman?" He has a notepad and it's open, pen poised.

"Nothing. No nothing." I stand and walk to look at a painting on the wall. It's in reds and yellows, an oil of schooners at sunset, the clouds streaking across the sky as if a storm's coming in the morning.

Deep breath, deep exhale. "Ahhh boy!" he scratches his cheek. "What am I to do 'ere, Sport? You're the "it" boy you know, my friend."

And I do know, at least I'm getting the impression. And it wasn't how I'd imagined it, my coming here, not what I'd planned. Frankly I hadn't planned at all.

"What possible motive could I have?" begging for an answer that maybe I just don't want to hear.

"One hundred and thirty million in missing jewellery for one t'ing – maybe the two of you were competing on finders fees, ah

Sport? This water's very nice. Well what can I say Mr. Sherman, stay put ah Sport!" He looks for a place to throw his matchstick. "Rebecca is the one keeping you out of jail right now so just be cool ah, you're all we got till somet'ing better comes along."

Karl sat in what was for him just another empty house, watching the television. There was no furniture except for the small Sony TV and some stools in the kitchen – but the view was lovely. Boggy Sand Road…an out of the way little enclave at the very top end of Cayman's 7 mile beach – this is one of the nicest stretches of beach anywhere in the world.

Ava is all dressed up in an exciting Hawaiian print mu mu, as if expecting a luau party to erupt any minute.

"Dahling, how are you?" She walks into the room, the heels of her sandals clicking on the highly varnished blonde oak floors.

"Mother." He smiles but doesn't turn from the TV. "I'm fine." He raises his chin at the TV. "Friends."

"Ah hah. Has Elmo called?" Elmo 'the dead' Mr. Gaunt wasn't likely to be calling, but she didn't know that yet. Ava always used Elmo as her eyes and ears. He was as corrupt as she was. They had first met almost 20 years previously when he was a dirty cop and she was an amoralistic thief. They'd taken to one another instantly, in the cerebral rather than sexual way – birds of a feather.

"No." He still doesn't look up.

"He was supposed to call when he got onto the island, after he'd checked into a hotel. He should have called. If he calls tell him I'll be back later okay darling?"

"Hmm, yes."

"I must go out. Will you be alright dahling?" She has walked to the large picture window, then executes a perfect three point turn.

"Yes." He still doesn't look up.

Karl-Hubert from Las Vegas via Akron, or vice versa, with the Swiss German accent and the Italian flair for dressing in soft leather loafers and Milanese cut clothing.

He misses Europe, he misses Switzerland, he misses being far the fuck away from Mother.

He looks up suddenly in the direction she's gone.

He raises an eyebrow, shakes his head and then turns his attention back to the television. "That's one scary lunatic bitch," he says slowly.

20

Welcome to my party –

Two days later and suddenly Rebecca…but my friends all call me Becca…is already sleeping in the other room, well, in one of the other rooms.

No drugs, no drink, no sex for you, Sherman my lad.

I'm just not sure how I feel about that. Truth be told I'm a little bit stunned and quite a lot sad.

And lonely, and I liked the sex, the two days of sex. I can't recall the last time I had two days of continuous sex.

I'd forgotten that I actually enjoyed sex. It was strange the first time I'd come to the realisation that I hadn't felt horny in months – now I knew that I'd missed being horny.

My new life is bizarre; now I want to use the words 'fucking bizarre' – but then it was just bizarre.

Marjorie called earlier just to give me a headache, which now I can't get rid of. It's this horrible throbbing dullness right behind my left eye that's making me squint. *Angst for the memories!*

Trying to sleep is not succeeding.

At 12:40 I decide to go downstairs and get something cool to drink.

It's very disconcerting to walk, unsuspecting, into your own living room and find some impatient soul flicking your lamp on and off in such a way as to scare the living shit out of you! Then he leaves the lamp on so you can't see his face but the pool of light illuminates half a leg, a quarter of an arm, a whole hand and an entire gun!

"Mr. Sherman?" A soft whisper; with a feminine touch to it, despite its deepness.

"Yes." Not really sure if I want to answer that question. I am very scared.

"I'm Effrain Shapiro."

Eeek!

"Yes." Almost as if my tongue has swollen.

"Who was that dead man in my house?"

"A man named Elmo Gaunt." My mouth is very dry.

"Why was he there?" I find myself focusing on his hand – a chubby, fleshy appendage with long large fingers, the nails of which are perfectly manicured.

"I don't really know."

"What do you know, Mr. Sherman?"

"That's a popular question. I really…would it hurt me to say that I really don't know much at all?"

"It might."

"Mr. Shapiro…"

He leans forward, half into the light:

And is bald.

"Mr. Shapiro, I really don't know anything. I was sent here, at least I think I was sent here, because I work for a particular insurance company and I'm from Grenada. I mean I was born in Grenada."

"And?" I notice that there's a lace handkerchief, the edge of which is just protruding from his shirt sleeve.

"Just that. Can I sit down?"

"No. Grenada?" He has the lips of a silent movie lover; the kind that if painted, women would pay for.

"Yes, they wanted to send someone from the islands.

"Typical... What do I have to do with all this?"

"The supposition is that, well," I swallow heavily and my throat hurts; "that you were the fence for a man named Bryce."

"Chance." He faded back into the shadows, taking a sudden wry smile with him.

"Mr. Chance, yes. Did you kill him, Elmo Gaunt, I mean?"

"No. Is there someone else in the house with you?"

"Yes."

He noticed the smile that I just couldn't help. "Ah, a woman!" He let the word 'woman' run freely, naked like a nymph, around on his tongue!

"Yes."

"No. No, I didn't kill Elmo Gaunt – perhaps Elmo's dead because someone thought that he was me."

"You didn't know him?"

"No. Your friend is awake – I suggest that you consider that this visit never happened, Mr. Sherman." He turned off the light and I heard him standing. "We'll talk more; I think you'll find that we'll both be needing a friend here shortly, Mr. Sherman.

"We might help each other."

And then he was gone.

And then a brief flash of light: where, on the beach, he stopped to light a cigar.

'What the hell just happened here' is the question that runs through my head as I sit, stunned, on the sofa, staring out the door through which Shapiro had just left; my heart's still beating very fast. Have you ever jumped off a boat into deep, deep water? There's this sinking feeling you get, like your head's going to be dragged down and out through your rectum, like gravity is sucking at you, focused intently and incredibly at your anus. I get that feeling right now.

21

"I want you to see this Mr. Sherman." Detective Hannah says to me in the car. I now feel like everybody's best friend – like the most popular girl at prom time: the visitation from Shapiro last night and then this morning a "date" with detective Hannah.

The hospital is new, fresh and clean and almost cozy, with its polished linoleum tile floors in grey and off white and Vinyl walls in a spotty peachy brown. We'd parked in front of a set of double doors on which a plain piece of white paper said: *Morgue Access, No Parking*. Obviously this didn't mean us. The door through which we entered into this little building, off the main body of the hospital, said Forensic Reception. There was no one to receive us. We just went straight through another door at the back of the small reception room that said Forensic Science.

Elmo Gaunt was on a stainless steel table that had an indent in its centre, so that the body lay in a hollow and its fluids could be channelled to the end between the legs. His feet are turned in, I guess that alive he'd have pidgeon toes. He was in a bit of disrepair and undoing, sort of like coming into the mechanic shop to see your car half pulled down – fluids and bits and pieces all sort of scattered around along with the dirty tools that did the job. And he hadn't been particularly fucking attractive to start with – way too much body hair!

Elmo had been shot just above and behind the ear on the right side of his head. The pathologist had a piece of stainless steel rod sticking in the entry wound and the body was propped slightly on its side, turning the head and the entry wound slightly up. The top of the skull had been removed and the brain was lying in a steel dish on the scale. Another rod seemed to be tracking the path of the bullet through the brain tissue.

The exit wound was on the left cheek and had removed part of the palate and several top and bottom teeth.

"Eloise, how are you?" She was about 5'2" and square-ish.

"Detective, ay, I'm well." She was making notes on a diagram of a skull. The indication on the sheet was that of about a 20 degree angle of penetration through the occipital lobe of the brain, the sinuses, and the palate.

"And this is Mr. Sherman." He seemed to be watching me.

I was trying not to look at the body… I'm trying to make a habit of this, not looking at bodies.

"Mr. Sherman." She was a Yorkshire lass with blonde hair and an odour of Ylang Ylang – a sort of almost sickly sweet yet tantalising aroma that belongs to a particular tree with drooping, yellow, cream flowers and bright, green leaves.

She had come to Cayman ten years previously. She was the only local pathologist, not because she was qualified, but because no one else wanted the job, as such she'd been doing post mortems for sometime. Recently though she had been back to Scotland Yard's Scientific Support College and studied forensic pathology. It had been Elosie's dream to be a Police criminalist of sorts.

"Yes. Nice to meet you." Her hands were bloody, so she didn't offer one. And I wanted to leave the room. It didn't smell at all like I'd expected, frankly it didn't smell of anything but the Ylang Ylang and me.

"Well I actually haven't gone that far yet as you can see – the entry and exit wound, the path through the brain, ay. Fragments of the bullet – those will have to go to the States for confirmation, but it all seems to be damage that would be fairly consistent with the point three eight calibre gun that you found on the scene.

"We've got the algor and rigor mortis and have pinpointed the time of death to somewhere around 3:30 pm. It was a cool day so the sun wasn't really a factor. He wasn't moved as his blood had all pooled in his buttocks and lower back, ay. I'm still working on an approximate height for the person shooting the gun – I'm trying to get an answer from FBI's VICAP folks in the States as to what the powder burn spread on this particular three eight might be, ay." She got close to the body and turned on a blue light so that it shone on the back of the skull. "As you can see the powder burns and residue marks cover an area of, oooh, about 2 ½ inches in diameter. From that they should be able to tell us how far back our chap was standing and then I can tell from the angle of penetration from what height he was shooting and how tall he might be."

I was duly impressed.

And then she added. "Of course, I've never actually put this to practice outside the classroom…not at least in a murder investigation, ay!"

"You look a bit off Mr. Sherman?" Dalbert rattling my cage, wondering what nice feathers might come loose in the shakeup.

"Not my idea of a swell date detective."

" 'ave you not seen an autopsy before Sport?" he's looking at me over the roof of his car; the same kind of Chevy Cavalier cops in the States might drive if they were looking to be really inconspicuous.

"No." I'd been in the autopsy room in Miami, but that's not seeing an autopsy.

"I wanted to see your reaction... I don't t'ink you had anything to do with all this, you know, but I wanted to see your, your reaction." He did a thing that was like a slight twist of the neck, as if his neck was stiff and he wanted to stretch it and then changed his mind.

"Ah. Do you have a cigarette?" I'm lounging on the roof arms out, absorbing its warmth after the cold of the morgue.

"I thought you didn't smoke?" he looks at me strangely.

"I just started – hey, that's right, that's right you asked me in your office if I smoked. Why?"

"Just a question – so you've just started." The last being a little louder as he ducked into the car and then leaned over to open my door...

"Rebecca," I say, as if that is the meaning of everything, of life even.

"Ah."

"No, not ah...look, I'm... I'm going through a divorce." As if this is some kind of explanation for all that ails me; it's like it's my fucking crutch.

"I'm lost out here in, in this third world; I'm in the middle of something I, I don't want to be in the middle of. I'm scared and way the fuck out of my depth, excuse the language – so, if you don't think that I have anything to do with this am I free?"

"I '*don't think*' doesn't mean that I do know, Sport – as of today you're still the 'it' boy, Sport."

"Fuck! Stop and let's buy some cigarettes."

Six hours later I'm sitting and staring out at the sea – and smoking. It's one of those the-views-are-all-cruise-ship days. There are three that I can see and the yellow funnels of one that I can't. I know one of them's the Carnival Sensation.

And at about the same time, Detective Hannah is going through the things in the dead Mr. Elmo Gaunt's hotel room and comes across four items – a piece of paper with my name on it, a photo of the Blue India sapphire with my number on the back, a deposit slip for a bank account in the Bahamas, which would strangely end up being tied to a company that was owned by me, and a really tasteless pair of Wallaby suede shoes.

Alone, I decide to walk across the street to Café Mediterraneo for some food and a drink, maybe two drinks.

"Well, Mr. Sherman." I find Minister Jefferies standing at the door talking to Bruno Deluche (partner/manager of Guy Harvey's Island Grill his business card says). There is a tall, lovely young blonde lurking close by, patiently.

"Surprise!"

"I'm living across the road."

"Very nice. Mr. Sherman, this is Bruno. He used to manage this place, now he's one of the owners of Guy Harvey Grill. He's French, from France you see and has great taste in shirts!" Jefferies has a $70,000 a year job as Minister and $1,000 pair of shoes on his feet so as not to frighten the leather in the $70,000 BMW 7 series he drives.

"Bruno, enchante – c'est un beau restaurant ici!"

"Ah, vous parlez francais?"

"No, no Bruno I don't really, I studied in school, and I've been to France, but it's bad French, bad."

"Ah, Minister Jefferies speaks fluent French." Bruno adds.

I'm duly impressed; I'm in exalted company.

"Will you join me for a drink Mr. Sherman?"

"What about your date?" I indicate the blonde.

"Oh she'll wait at the bar." He says in a dismissive offhand way – not that I believe that he's only a chauvinist, just that he's used to people doing whatever he says and whatever he wants. Minister Jefferies is an important man.

"So, Mr. Sherman, your difficulties?" The waitress approaches, we're in a booth on the right of the room that's called Capri.

"What would you like to drink?"

"I'll have a vodka orange juice." I don't really drink, but a vodka orange is easy to handle.

"Two please. Your difficulties?"

"Do you really want to know?" I look around the room.

"Probably not, but then one never knows how one might, ahm, profit from information." He smiles. And I like him, this, this…amiable 'ginal' (to use a West Indian word meaning scoundrel – but one with connotations that underline that adjective amiable).

22

"**What a lovely morning!**" **Rebecca's in that sleep dishevelled** state that can just make a woman look so much more attractive sometimes. She's wrapped in a blanket. "Cold?" A palliative interrupting my moment of self torture…

"You're smoking?" And the sun is rising somewhere behind us so our horizon has shed its grey for pink, but closer to hand the sea still reflects the last of shadows. Yet at the very shoreline in front of us, as if it has carried the blush of morning from its distant edges, the sea shows its lovely face in the soft light of dawn and is easily recognizable for just what it is! Normally one would be drawn to make comparisons between this and Grand Anse beach in Grenada. But, I just don't remember it in this sort of context. Certainly the surroundings were more lush and off to the right, I'd have seen the face of the hillside above Belmont and a little further the grey walls of Fort George and probably the tower spire of Scots Kirk, the Catholic Church along the Esplanade. But at a mile away it would have all been a little indistinct. Up close it was much the same. White, white sand and blue, blue sea.

And I'm wearing shorts and realise that my legs are really pale.

"The new me," I say, not quite as coolly as it sounds.

"The new you, Sherman…he still seems awfully sad," she says sitting beside me on the sand and relieving me of my cigarette. "It's so beautiful here."

And the tinted sea is lapping against this improbably lovely piece of beach. And her new hair really suits the colour of her eyes or something.

"Do I really, I mean…you know, still seem sad?"

"Yes." She contemplated the cigarette a bit, took another drag and looked out to sea. "Would you like to fuck me again, Sherman?"

'ebry hoe 'ave im 'tick a bush.' More of those West Indian proverbialisms, meaning; 'There's someone for everyone'.

"For some odd reason I've been thinking about you…" I can't believe she's still talking. "Who knows, maybe it's all this bloody proximity; you're so close at hand. You're not my type at all, you know." She finally closed the whole thought process off with that perfunctory bit of information.

"I sort of wish you'd look at me when you say things like that," I said, not looking at her. "And I don't mean the not your type thing. What is your type?"

"I don't know exactly."

"But not my type?"

"Exactly."

"So… Why then?"

"I don't know. Do I really have to look at you?" She looks at me.

"No."

"I don't know Sherman, I really don't know. You're nice and kind and sweet and funny and sad and tall, you're tall Sherman."

"You could call me Chris."

"I don't want to call you Chris, Sherman."

"Yes, yes – I'd like to fuck you again," as if saying the word fuck was uncomfortable. "Fucking you would make me feel a lot better," and I smile at her.

"I'm no good at this, you know, Rebecca."

She shifted closer in the sand. "So, we'll learn."

"Marjorie it's me, Chris... Chrisy, look I just called to speak to Todd, our son...ahm, how's he doing? God I really hate talking to this answering machine day after fucking day...could you guys at least try and call me back so I can speak to him."

Becca is somewhere upstairs powdering her Pumpum – West Indian vernacular for vagina.

I walk out onto the sand as if not knowing what else to do.

There's the smell of coconut oil mingling with expensive perfume – the constant human traffic; the back and forth. I look right and see the ordered chaos at the Beach Club; it's as if that distant crowd is pulsing; it's a moving mass of living tanning flesh.

"A yu dat, White Guy?" He was a black man with his hair worn in dreadlocks. He had a goatee and eyes whose whites were actually red.

"What?" I'm nervous and I'm unsure.

He held up a photograph and then looked at me – obviously making a comparison.

"Easy nuh dread, a yu dat." He smiled nicely. He was tall and not dressed at all for the beach.

"I..."

"Is awright pussyclate – I jus' mi wan' fi see de man me fi kill." And then, all of a sudden as if he'd been born in New York...sort of... "The man's sent me to kill you, zeeeen!"

"What?"

"Wha'?" He mimicked me. "What, is it jus' me, dread? or don't you fuckin' speak English? Somebody wants you dead friend an' I'm the hand of God."

"Holy fuck!"

"Yeah, Kinda! But...is your lucky day, dread...somebody else paid me more not to do it."

"So, see me here my frien', my job now to make sure that nothin' happens to you."

"Your job's to make sure nothing happens to me."

"Ites, yes, you 'ave a gun?"

"A gun?"

"G – U – N?" he said slowly.

To which I nodded slowly and said "No."

He shrugged. "Is alright I 'ave a few."

"Give I man one of your cigarette, nuh." We're sitting on a tree stump looking out at sea. There's a small wooden sign in front of us that I can't read now, cause the words are on the other side, but I know it says: *'facilities for the use of owners and guests only'.*

There are two worlds existing side by side here on this little island and he and I are like the bright shining Bennetton billboard example of that. And I'm not talking the black and white of it really – I'm talking the million dollar condo living expatriate versus the unsung unseen local (ish) working man and community that lives in this sort of out of sight, out of mind, and off the beaten tourist track. – Okay, I'm stretching the point of example a little bit 'cause sure, I'm only pretending to live in a million dollar condo and being hired as a (fucking) killer doesn't really qualify you for blue collar status.

"Cigarette?"

"Where yu from, White Guy?"

"Grenada."

"You got Yankee man written all over you, bwoy."

"What?"

"You've got American written all over you!"

"I grew up in the States."

"Yu don't got none of the islands left in you, man – you like Reggae music? Dancehall?" When he spoke to me he flipped back and forth between his version of American and the Jamaican with which he was naturally more comfortable, as if he suffered from an incurable speech impediment.

"Ahm… I."

"Fuck!"

"Who paid you?"

"To kiss you or to kill you?" He smokes the cigarette like it's a joint.

"To kiss me."

"Dunno."

"To kill me?"

"Dunno."

"Fuck!"

"So it go, my friend – *'swap black dog for monkey.'*" He has no physical smile, just a sense of humour around the eyes.

"Huh?"

"Six a one 'alf dozen of the other."

"Oh." I now comprehend it stated in plain American. "Not really in this case though."

"For me it is." He's very casual and seemingly unconcerned about – everything.

"What?"

"I get paid either way, my dread."

"Yeah. Look...damn! This is... Look."

"My name is Desmond."

"Desmond? Desmond. Desmond – so what do we do here Desmond?"

"I brought my bag, is in the car." He called it a 'ki-yar'

"You're going to live with me?" A bit of incredulity in my voice, I suspect.

My life was spinning way out of my own control.

"One big 'appy family."

"Lovely, join the crowd, it's beginning to be strange to be me."

"So how does a thing like this work then, Desmond?" Rebecca wanted to know from our new-found friend.

And none of us knew the answer to that one, or why it was really happening; it just was.

And who was I going to check up on Desmond with... And how was I going to refuse. Desmond was to be my guardian angel. And someone obviously felt that I needed a guardian angel. I sort of felt that I needed a guardian angel. Rebecca and I talked about it and thought that it mightn't be such a bad idea. I sorta thought it was she who arranged it, but didn't want to say anything to hurt my ego.

Anyhow, it, Desmond, just sort of came to be one of the facts of my new life, like the occasional use of that big blue rubber dildo during sex – different, not unpleasant, but different.

23

In the morning Detective Hannah was standing outside the door looking in from the beach front. He wore cool, heavy plastic framed, dark glasses with pink lenses and a sad expression.

"Detective," I said tentatively.

"Sport…can we take a walk?" he looked sad.

I looked at Desmond first and then at Becca. They both shrugged.

"Yes."

"Alone…" He dusted something off a sort of powder blue bowling shirt which he wore with Khaki trousers and another particularly nice pair of sensible shoes.

They both shrugged again.

I scratched my head and scrunched up my face. "Yes."

"Good." He scratched the apex of his bald head.

I lit a cigarette as we walked.

"What cigarettes are you smoking now? Enjoying it?" I almost expect him to make a note in his book.

"Ahm, Benson and Hedges and enjoying it – can you tell me something – I mean, like the guy back there that you didn't meet, Desmond... Desmond's real name is Ishmael Greene, but they call him Desmond. They do this all over the Caribbean – I've got these friends, family friends from Antigua – Edward, Dennis and Carol, but everyone calls them Hank, Carl and Peter. Why?"

"Where's this going, Sport?" He stops, looks out to sea, then back at me.

"Chit chat detective."

"Hmmm!" he obviously didn't want to chit chat. "I found this in Elmo Gaunt's things." He handed me a piece of paper with my name on it and stopped. I took three steps before I realised that he was no longer with me. I stopped, and turned back, he met me halfway.

Then he handed me a photo of the Blue India with my number on it. It's a fantastic stone, Franklin had shown me photos of it from the files in our offices. It had been on TV too a couple of times, I think on the Discovery channel or something, along with that diamond that Richard Burton had given Elizabeth Taylor.

And then the deposit slip.

"Is there something I should know, Sport?"

I paused and then sat down on the sand. I looked up and then at the pieces of paper again, individually.

"No...no nothing."

"I found these among Elmo Gaunt's things."

"You said."

"And there's nothing you 'ave to tell me?"

"No. And I wish there were." I stared out into the middle distance and just shook my head.

"Does this mean you're beginning to think I'm lying, Detective?" I add.

"I'm beginning to think that the evidence is pointing in that direction, dat's what I'm beginning to think." He didn't sit with me but stood uncomfortably as if the beach was a foreign land to him.

"But you don't believe it?" Rebecca wanted to know from Dalbert when we explained the new events to her.

"Who's this?" Dalbert asked, turning to Desmond.

"Desmond." I offered.

"Ishmael Greene?" he countered.

"Yes, Desmond."

"And what is a Desmond when he's at home?"

"What?" I'd never heard it put that way before.

"Desmond?" Hannah looked straight at him, there was a little challenge going on between them – eye wrestling.

"I'm…let's say I'm a friend," and that smile around the eyes that his mouth doesn't seem to share.

"No, let's not, Desmond. Let's say exactly what you are, nuh! Tell me, I'm a big bwoy, don't it, dread?" He changed his vernacular to fit the scenario. And he became a 'badder' man than I'd ever realised he was. Detective Hannah lost the fatherliness and became all warrior. "Eh Desmond, talk to mi, my dread. Yu got fucking East Kingston written all ova yu dread – you a bad man Desmond? You a bad man dread?"

"Jus' a man detective, jus' a man." Desmond seems unworried.

"Oh you is cool, like Johnny fucking Ringo baby." He almost laughed.

"Who hired the muscle?" Detective Inspector Hannah asked me, suddenly changing tone and tack.

"We don't know."

"True?" he looked from one to the other of us.

"True!"

"Friends and enemies...interesting," he said to all of us, and then switching his personality for the other with which he seemed equally comfortable, he turned back to Desmond. "Don't fuck and joke dread, bad man or no bad man yu tek it easy yuh hear! Dis da no East Kingston baby, dis da Cayman Islands – no fucking place to hide from me 'ere an' my bwoys dem been to de real wars, seen? When my liccle hot rass English tactical bwoys 'ave to come fi yu, yu'll be one dead bad fuckin' black man, seen?"

Desmond smiled a little for a reply, at least the closest I'd seen him come to a smile, and leaned his head first to one side then the other and then smiled for true.

But when Hannah had left, Desmond let out a little extra bit of air.

It's then that I find I want to know more about detective Hannah: the man, the myth, the mystery.

And here's the story I get.

He was born in 1950 in Yallahs, Jamaica: a small town East of Kingston in the parish of St. Thomas on the South coast. It was a one road town with a north-south main street that pointed its way at the Blue Mountains in the background. Farming and fishing was the main source of livelihood. The Yallahs river was a dry bed of rock and sand most of the time except in the rains and then the fording was mostly impassable.

' *'im black like 5 pas' midnight.'* A poor black man born to poor black parents.

The middle years were spent growing up in the ways that all country boys grow up, filled with work and work.

In 1963, he moved with his parents to England.

In 1968, he joined the London constabulary.

In 1975, he moved back to Jamaica with a position in the Kingston police as a training officer. Later he became a special constable and then a detective in the Kingston CIB during the "bad times".

And then, in 1988, he'd taken a detective position with CID in the Cayman Islands, a quiet position after the rigors of Jamaica in the height of the 'Posse' days.

That's really the brief of it, the Cliff notes.

"You ever meet him before Desmond?" I ask after Detective Hannah is gone.

"No." He shook his head and stuck out his lips.

"He make you nervous?"

A real smile all of a sudden that took me by surprise. "De Babylon always make me uncomfortable, seen," and he nods, a slow, cool nod.

"Babylon?" I ask.

"Police man." He pronounced it 'puh lease maaan' drawing out his syllables.

"Babylon, police man?"

"Yes! You 'ave a cigarette for me, White Guy." It wasn't really a question since he was already helping himself. "Where I come from police men don't rule, but them rule, seen!"

"And where's that, Desmond?"

Rebecca comes in and drops into the couch. She looks tired. She pulls her feet up.

"Don't mind me fellas." She leans forward for the cigarettes. We'll all smoke and die together, taking as many second hand smokers with us as we can when we go.

"Desmond was just telling me about where he comes from."

"Where?" she asks.

"You know, I nevva really say," and he smiled with his eyes.

"But you were going to."

"Was I?"

"Yes, come on do, too much fucking mystery Desmond darling, live a little, talk to us eh!" responded Rebecca, putting up her feet as if ready to watch a good movie on the TV.

"New York lately, Kingston before dat, Linstead before that." He looked at his palms, which had that burnt pinkness of black people. I looked at mine, which were damp, soft and toned like strawberry mousse.

"Linstead?"

"A town in St. Catherine, just northwest of Kingston; you been to Jamaica?"

"I've been at least 10 times," says Rebecca.

"Where?" He's animated by the talk of home.

"Ooh, Kingston, Mo Bay, Negril, Ochy, Porty," her accent taking on a lilt to it that isn't British.

"You talk it like a Jamaican girl."

"I beens 'ere so long I's Caymanian yu know."

They laugh at their lingos and I don't get it.

"Sherman doesn't get it, Desmond, there's no West Indian left in him, that bwoy's a true Yankee now, pure fucking white man." For Desmond, white man is not a colour but a citizenship; white man is American or European…even if he's black American, he's the white man – might be the white man pickney, but still!

"That true, White Guy?"

"True…true, I don't even like Bob Marley," and of course I smile. I know I don't like 'I shot the Sheriff.'

"Are you a bad man Desmond?" I ask suddenly from behind a cushion I've taken out of the chair I'm sitting in.

"I'm a bad man, White Guy." He does that humour with his eyes thing again. He's taken to calling me White Guy quite happily. "I kill people, that's what people pay me to do, seen?"

"Seen."

And then Ida enters with lunch on a tray.

"We'll eat on the patio," says Rebecca, but I know that it's really a veranda if not technically what we Americans call a Florida room, and Ida heads for the door. I see Desmond eyeing that superhuman backside as she passes, in the way that I might admire a similar view of Elle Mcpherson. It's a West Indian thing that's been left out of my upbringing. Desmond doesn't join us for lunch but follows Ida into the kitchen. Besides the lure of sex I think he's more at home with her than with us.

"Is it time for lawyers yet?" I ask Rebecca.

"No, no. Let's wait a little. Lawyers make you look guilty."

The top's down on the company car, which the police have given me back. It's a Chrysler Sebring convertible. Rebecca's driving, Desmond's in the back sitting sideways, his shirt is blowing, and I notice there's a gun in the waistband of his trousers. He's relaxed behind a cool pair of Maui Jim sunglasses.

There's a guy in the car with me carrying a gun and we're going along like that's the most natural thing in the world. We're going shopping. Desmond's gonna be walking in and out of Kirk Supermarket carrying at least one large 9mm. This is like a posse fantasy film, 'Sherman's Crew'. I want to carry a 9mm too but I'm afraid to ask Desmond if I can have one.

The car is cool; the stereo's playing loudly, the wind, the sun, the stylish clothes, the dark glasses, the guns...it's all like an episode of Miami Vice.

24

I wonder what's becoming of me as I smoke looking out at the moonlit beach and the starlit sea while she sleeps naked in the cool of this night on a dishevelled bed behind me. Desmond is watching TV downstairs; I can hear it dimly through the closed doors and the limpid cacaphony of night by the seaside.

"And you know there's something very important we need to do as soon as possible."

"What's that?"

"Fuck!"

I walk back into the bedroom, pause a moment to look at her – she's occupying most of the bed all sprawled out and clutching what had been my pillow – and I walk downstairs.

I like sex.

And I get it now, why people set free by divorce or death or separation run wild with their freedom. I'm running wild. I used to feel so lonely in my relationship, my marriage. An empty house full of the ghosts of people!

The TV's actually watching Desmond, who's fast asleep on the couch.

I'm pouring myself a juice – I wanted to be in the movies, how did I end up here?

'Laziness' someone answers from the recesses of my head, and mentally I try to kick the mouthy little bastard but miss and bang myself in the shin.

Meanwhile –

"What's this?" Detective Hannah leaning close to the body of Elmo Gaunt in the morgue, his face craning around to let the light shine just so on Mr. Gaunt's neck. The same light is creating an elliptical play of illumination and shadow across his bald head; doesn't he ever sleep.

"It's a handprint, I believe – I would hazard the guess that someone tested the body for a pulse sometime after the blood stopped flowing, ay." Eloise said without actually looking up from her microscope.

"Can we get an image of dat?" Dalbert touches it, just slightly, with a gloved finger.

"It's almost impossible to get a print off of flesh, Dalbert, and…" a little shrug. "And, well, we don't have the necessary ahm, what is it… Kromekote cards or the, the laser illumination equipment, ay. If we had the equipment we could turn off the lights, and using some sort of broad band oscillating laser beam in the green range, I think it is, the green range that is, we'd really see that print stand up on the skin… Maybe we could dust it and try and bring it up under blue light? I don't mean to sound vague, Dalbert, but I've never done that and in the 10 years I've been on island I've hardly had any call for that sort of thing, ay."

"Hmmm – well we've got ourselves a new fingerprint expert, can we call him over, can we try? What's this playing?" He jerks his head at the speaker in the corner of the room. Eloise likes to work to music.

"New U2, you like? I can, ahm, you know I'll try it with blue light and with infra red film and take a photograph of the image and see what we get."

"Yes, yes that would be nice." Hopeful. "This it?" Dalbert picks up the CD case for the U2 album.

"We'll have to reverse the image in a mirror, ay." She's thinking as she speaks, you can hear the cogs turning from lack of use in this kind of situation.

"Okay. Thanks baby, new territory for all of us, eh?"

"Surely not for an old Kingston boy like yourself Dalbert."

In reality Dalbert had seen it all, done it all, trained for it all.

"Long time dead Eloise... Like you said this island's been the quiet home for the last 10 years, nuh." It is obvious that the excitement of this all is something Dalbert has missed in his quiet Cayman(-ian) life and that he's thoroughly enjoying himself.

"Two to six, come in Dalbert."

Dalbert looked up at Eloise to excuse himself and picked up the radio.

"Go ahead Trey?" He set down the CD case as he walked out the door.

"Che ah," he makes a unique Cayman sound – 'Che', like a mimic of the sound of air brakes releasing, followed by an 'Ah' from the back of the throat. "I find you. Look go to Cellular nuh, D."

"7227?"

"Yeah."

"I'm going to borrow your phone, sweetie," Dalbert said to Elosie coming back inside and indicating her office.

"Dat Effrain Shapiro just done show back up ah!" he heard Trey down the phone line. "He say he been on one boat round bout Cuba for bout two weeks now or 10 days the like."

"Ah! Where are you now?" Fiddling with some papers on the desk but not really reading them.

"Round he house."

"He alone?"

"Che Ah, no way man, he goh 'bout six of them hottest gal you ever done seen with om. Nice boat too, ah."

"Nice of you." He glanced at his watch, a Rolex, but then everyone here seems to wear a Rolex – *duty free you know*! "I'll be there in about 20 minutes."

He thought about calling his wife, Grace – but why bother – if she wasn't at church she'd be with one of her "bretherin or sisterin" talking church, talking God! He laughed a little in a sad sort of snort snarfle gurgle! He didn't do church, didn't talk God – he'd seen too much badness to believe that any god actually existed. He wasn't sure he even believed that his Grace actually existed; at least in the realm of him and her and the true essence of what one might term marriage.

Effrain Shapiro and a gaggle of beautiful people were sitting on the bridge of the 121' Fead Ship called Jewel, around what would normally be a chart table. The table was at the rear of the bridge fashioned like a booth seat in a restaurant. It had a couch in a semi circle at the back against the bulkhead and the table curved in the same way. And, seated, the crowd at the table faced out onto the ship's wheel, the captain's chair, the navigational instruments dashboard and through the large glass windows on to the bow of the ship and beyond at the quay and to the left the lawns of Mr. Shapiro's house. At the front edge the table was flat.

A large 25" TV was on a stanchion from the ceiling – they are all watching 'Eyes Wide Shut'.

"They're all on the boat, Bro." Trey is a man whose complexion is what they term in the islands as "red" – neither black man nor white man but generations of mixing back and forth between the two so that the end result was a mixture of both; pale skin with slightly kinky hair. He is thin and tall and red and has a moustache.

Dalbert glances at his watch. "Are they expecting me?"

"I tol' Mr. Shapiro someone'd be 'long, you know."

"Alright, well wait here then." He bent briefly to smooth the cat's soft fur.

"Mr. Shapiro." Almost a question as Dalbert paused at the entrance to the bridge holding open the sliding, and highly varnished to a protectively coated sheen, Mahogany door.

"Detective Hannah," definitely not a question. He ran a hand back over his bald head.

"Do you know me, Chief?"

"Yes! Everybody this is Detective Hannah, Detective, everybody." Beautiful smiles and exposed cleavage all around – Oooh baby!

He was sitting in the middle of his crowd, tucked in the centre of the booth – he pushed what looked like a file casually away from him.

"Excuse me everybody, but I think business calls. Ladies, enjoy the movie." He eased himself round the table, his guests, both those now standing and those sitting simply looked at Detective Hannah as if he were…an inconvenience. "Detective shall we…ahm, the salon?"

He paused just before walking out of the room. "And if anyone gets the urge to fuck don't start without me."

"Detective." He touched Detective Hannah on the back, ushering him into the salon. "May I fix you a drink?" as they passed the bar, which occupied one corner.

A chuckle and a smile. "Yes, yes a drink would be nice, Mr. Shapiro."

"I thought policemen didn't drink on duty." His accent is indistinct American, stateless, nasal, but he is from Israel originally.

"Scotch'll do jus' fine. On the rocks please, Mr. Shapiro." Dalbert's eyes take in the room, slowly, barely moving his head as he does.

"Have you ever seen the movie <u>Eyes Wide Shut</u> Detective?" There's a mocking intensity to Effrain's eyes, which are green and full of the knowledge of sex in all the greasy little ways you could ever dream of.

"No, no I really don't get out dat much, boss man." He smiles at this little condescension. "This's a very nice boat."

"Yacht."

"Yacht. So, you've been in Cuba then Mr. Shapiro?" trying hard to avoid using the word 'Sport'.

"Around and about there Detective."

"Detective Inspector really, that's my official title you know," deciding to play the naming game as well. "I've been to Cuba a few times. Did some training there in the 70's."

"I like it – the women are…lovely." He almost licked the word as he said it and took the handkerchief from his sleeve and smelt it, pretended to wipe his mouth and put it back in his sleeve.

"Do you know, excuse me, did you know Elmo Gaunt, Mr. Shapiro?" Dalbert's eyes are scanning the room.

"Is that the man who was dead on my patio?" He seems rather bored with it all.

"Yes." Dalbert sits back, relaxed, in an armchair.

"No." Never looking up from the drink that he is mixing with his finger.

"But you do know that he was found dead on your patio, Squire? I mean even though you've been in Cuba, yes?"

"My lawyer called me on the satellite phone." He opens a humidifier that's on the table in front of him and selects a stubby Upmann. "Cigar, Detective?"

Chuckle, little shake of the head. "You're spoiling me, thank you. But you didn't rush back?"

"I'm here, aren't I, Detective?" Holding the cigar in one hand and the already lit match in the other.

"This is a nice Scotch, Chief."

"Yes it is, isn't it, goes beautifully with the cigar. What do you want to know, Detective?"

"Nothing really – I jus' wanted to see your boa…sorry your yacht, drink some of your scotch, smoke your cigars and introduce myself." He smiled and then glanced at his watch, paused to light the cigar. "It's getting late Mr. Shapiro, I'll call you in the morning and set up a better time fi talk, to talk."

He set the empty glass on the piano that was near him as he walked to the door. "It was a pleasure ahm, meeting you, Mr. Shapiro.

"Oh…" pause and turn. "No idea how Mr. Gaunt happened to find his way onto your patio?"

"No."

"No."

"No."

"Okay…thank you, and thank you for the cigar, very nice. Goodnight."

25

"We're going to a party." Rebecca tells me.

"A party?" I'm standing at the door to her room. She maintains her own room – sometimes we have sex and she sleeps over, sometimes we don't have sex and she sleeps over. Sometimes she sleeps in her own room. We've not had sex in her room; actually having sex seems like the light version of what we do. We fuck! Yes, to date we fuck! We don't however fuck in her room.

"A party." She nods. She's got a TV in her bedroom and the movie 'Beautiful Girls' is playing on HBO or something.

"I'm not much of a party guy," I say lighting a cigarette. I hand it to Rebecca and light another for myself, cough throatily; I've already got the smoker's hack.

"Oh well you will be tonight, Sherman." She smiles and drops the towel.

She pulls on a dress without the benefit of underwear.

"What should I wear?

"It's casual, wear what you want Sherman – obviously underwear's optional." I hate that smile. It makes me horny.

What's happening here between Rebecca and me is nice. I've never been with the kind of girl that could be with anyone she chose, never been with a beautiful electric sex kitten with a penchant for rough drugs and hard sex. It's a boost to the ego, to the self esteem – this girl likes me and so I must be something, someone. And she makes me happy in a time when I am really, truly, deeply, sad.

"I'm going to have a little drink. Would you like one?"

"Probably."

And as she walks off down the stairs I call out –

"So the underwear's optional then!"

"Hello Desmond are you wearing underwear?" I ask. We're getting comfortable with each other; it's been about a week now.

"You getting crazy, White Guy." He takes the Red Stripe Beer that I hand him. Desmond is dressed to the nines in his party clothes, looking a lot like 'Beenie Man' in a nice wild blue suit and a bad attitude. Actually it's the kind of colour that only a man with attitude could wear – bad or otherwise. He just looks like a bad man, it's written in his eyes. "You must not say 'ello to the man." He says, "That is to try an' send him to hell, seen? You must say 'greetings' or 'hail to the man'." He tapped his right hand to his chest, thumb in. "From the heart, my brother, from the heart," or, in his vernacular 'Fram di 'art mi bredda'. And he smiled a wonderful smile that surprised me because I didn't believe he had it in him.

Desmond didn't waste his smiles, as if he felt he only had so many, a set number of smiles in life; he'd usually show joy only by a softening of his eyes. Maybe this was a bad man thing – I don't know, never met too many bad men.

"I usually just try 'Yaow'," says Becca-Rebecca coming in from the kitchen smiling.

"Rasta can live with 'Yaow'," he says.

I can't see where he's carrying his guns, but I'm sure he's wearing at least two.

I've had a few drinks, a few drinks too many. Just to sort of get me in the mood for whatever, you know. Rebecca lights a joint and she smokes it and she smiles at me and I smoke it.

And so, now I'm tuned, and nicely.

I pass it to Desmond in the back seat, who smokes it as if he was born to it.

This is a party!

People everywhere. A writhing tide of undulating, gesticulating, suntanned, fresh faced flesh.

"Wow!"

It's all that I can manage. Desmond rests his hand on my back gently, nods and slips away.

I guess he's giving me some space, or himself some space. Whatever! But, I see him from time to time, watching me from a distance.

Rebecca takes my hand and leads me in. Somehow, perhaps it's all the practice, she seems to be able to function normally under this level of damage – I on the other hand am just sort of ticking over.

She stops suddenly and I pile up against her.

"Ooops, sorry!" I giggle.

"You are so stoned!"

I giggle.

"Yes you are, you are like so bloody stoned."

I giggle again.

"Wasted…you little girl's blouse you…come, look take one of these, they'll bring you up a bit." All said with a smile that you couldn't help but trust and a little white pill that had my name written all the fuck over it.

Detective Hannah is back at his desk. I'm partying, and he's staring at the phone still trying to decide whether to call her, his wife, or not. He sips his coffee and looks at his watch. 'SINNER!' she would be screaming at him in her head. Twenty-five years – it hadn't always been like this; before God, before she couldn't have any children, before she'd gotten the cancer and couldn't have any children he had already been retreating to the verges of the bed, working nights to hide from the possibility of having to be alone in the same space as her – it was probably why she had taken up with another man, with God. It was uncharacteristic of Jamaican men of his generation to forgive her her infidelities but if God kept her off his backside that at least made him happy. At least this is what he tells himself. After the sickness, she had been a mess and he had cared for her, he recalls the day when he realised both with relief and sadness that she wasn't going to die, that he was going to be saddled with her for a little longer still.

"Dalbert. This just came in on the fax." Eduoardo Tut, who was from Belize originally but had been on the Cayman police force for 12 years, came in.

"What?" He looked away from the phone.

"It's the serial number trace on the Elmo Gaunt gun, Brali. She was shipped a one dealer in New York City, in 1981, Brali."

Detective Hannah swivelled his chair around to face the desk and held the piece of paper.

"Well, at least it don't have Chris Sherman written all over it." He said quietly to himself, then set it aside.

"What?" asked Tut with his hand on the doorknob about to leave.

"Nothing…nothing," shaking his head.

Alone again he sat back, then sat forward again.

He opened the bottom drawer of his desk. There was a bottle of twenty-five year old Appleton rum inside and two crystal tumblers.

"Drink up my friend." Setting one of the tumblers on his desk, he poured himself a short one. Then he sat back, leaned back.

Smelt it.

Rolled it around the glass.

Smelt it again.

Filled his mouth and let it sit a moment on his tongue and rested the side of the glass against his forehead, then on the top of his head. You could have heard him swallow from across the room.

'Come mek we play some ketchy shubey.' Peter Tosh, but it's got a slow rhythm and I don't. I'm dancing to my own beat baby. I am the party, man.

"Faaaack!" a slow slurring drawl despite the fact that the rest of me is moving at knots. Waver, twirl, stagger, strut, stumble…

"Chris Sherman, darling."

"Ava… Ava. Wow! Wow! You look, you look, man am I happy to see you." Talking fast, talking smooth.

"You're high?"

"Ava darling I think that I am, yes, yes, yes! Oooh, he's handsome who's he?" Vroom!

Karl was standing beside her, her arm through his.

"Ah, this is Hans." She touched his cheek with the back of a hand, lovingly. "My son. He is lovely, isn't he? Hans darling, this is Mr. Sherman."

He disengaged himself from his mother and took my hand in a firm shake while he plumbed the depths of my soul with those lovely eyes.

"Pleased to meet you, Mr. Sherman." And then he smiled at me. "Yes, you are stoned, aren't you, Mr. Sherman?"

Still holding his hand, I patted the back of it with my other hand and grinned like a happy child and giggled.

"Yes, yes, Hans, I am..." Giggle again. "Yes, yes, I am.

"You know, that's a lovely accent, Hans, lovely, where does that accent come from?"

And he did a strangely tender thing. He took my elbow and held me steady a moment. "Oh it's a long story Mr. Sherman, a long long story – I shall tell you one day when you are in a better state, yes."

"Yes, yes." Giggle. "That, that, Hans my friend, would be better."

"Mother?" Karl looked at Ava.

"Yes love, you run along. I will take care of Chris Sherman."

Ava has me back against a wall, pants around my ankles making me feel things I don't ever remember feeling. But that's probably the drugs talking to my cock. I'm stoned. I think, I hope that I tried to stop her. I mean, Rebecca right. But I'm stoned, not that that's a valid excuse, just an extenuating circumstance. I'm very stoned. The world pulsating as if it were made up of liquid instead of gas kinda stoned. And frankly, I'm pretty fucking euphoric. So maybe I'm wanting to say 'no no please please stop

stop don't don't' but I think I'm having a good time and whatever you know, Rebecca's a player, right.

At least that's what my vague memory leads me to believe happened. It's the last thing that I remember till just now – and this I don't want to remember. Ouch! My head hurts…no, no, my head really really hurts and my mouth is like the Gobi desert!

And where am I… I don't know, I don't know.

And where are my clothes?

Fuck!

And why the hell isn't there any furniture in the house.

And;

Wait,

Who is that dead body in the middle of the floor?

Aaaaaaaaaaaaaaaah!

26

"He's our friendly neighbourhood FBI agent; Agent Froeman."
Detective Hannah leaned around the body's head so that he could
see part of the face without moving anything.

"What de rass am I supposed to do here, Sport? Ah?" He
looked over his shoulder at me as he unfolded his handkerchief.

And here I am, naked still.

"Look, look, I called you… I picked up the fucking phone
and I called you." I'm scared and my head really hurts. Hard to
think, hard to think.

"And so fucking what dread? So fucking what? He's dead
Sport and dere's only you and me and 'im in the fuckin' 'ouse! An'
I didn't get here till after 'e was dead." Using the handkerchief he
lifted the head a little. "Yep, it's him. Did you touch anything?"
He's a little angry, but still in that fatherly warrior way.

"No…nothing but the cellular phone that was right there." I
pointed at the spot on the floor near the body's outstretched hand
where the phone had been. "I didn't kill him man. Isn't he supposed
to still be in the Bahamas?" I want to cry right now.

"You just said that you don't remember a t'ing. Rass!" Dalbert's
cell phone rings, vibrates really, we both hear it, he ignores it.

"Yes, yes, Agent Froeman's still supposed to be in the Bahamas. Well at least he never told anyone he'd come back that I know of." He stood up, poked the body with a foot. "I guess this is why. Where's Rebecca, Sport? Where's Desmond?" He glances at his watch, I look up at the clock. It's 6:51 a.m.

"I don't know."

"Whose house is dis?" He looks around the room, leans himself suddenly to the side to look at the stairway to upstairs that he can just barely see.

"I don't know. I mean, the last thing I remember was…well, was Ava sucking my, my…"

"Sucking your what Sport?"

"Ahm, my, my penis."

"Your cock? What's upstairs?"

"Empty."

"Who's Ava?" He calls from the top of the stairs, a sound which comes to me indirectly, like a banked pool shot.

"A woman I met a few days ago, yes, yes, my cock!"

I'm staring at the body lying there, its blood, a semi dried now purple-brown; the colour of star apple where once it had been a rich red, the colour of mace.

"Sport?" He stepped back into the room and then he stopped a moment and just looked at me. "Is there something I'm missing 'ere my friend? You're sleeping with Rebecca, true?" He looked around the room as he spoke to me, his head moving up and down and around slowly, like a mime doing a robot impression with just his head. He was I presume, looking for clues.

"Well, ahm, yeah."

"And Ava, correct?"

"Correct." And a dumb nod.

"An' you met the both of them in the last two weeks, right?" Sometimes, when he got excited Detective Hannah's accent would become more deeply Jamaican than usual.

"Yeah, well, ahm two weeks, yes, almost, ahm, more or less. Yes. It, it must be the weather or something. Christ my head hurts."

"What's Ava's last name?"

"I have no idea. We didn't get that far. But with my luck it's probably fucking Gretchen Moll," I add.

"What?"

"Nothing."

"You're naked!" He says as if he's just noticed, but is making a mental note and then goes back to looking around the room. Then stops and throws me his keys. "There's a dirty shirt on the back seat of my car...not very dirty."

"Sherman sport, sit your ass down for a moment and let me think."

The body was just sort of there, right of centre, in this big empty room with its varnished blonde oak floors. It was face down, one arm underneath the body, one arm thrown out and up. There was a large dried blood spot on the back of the head, the hair was hardened and the head, in that spot, looked flat.

And I think to myself I could use a cigarette, no, no I think to myself I really need a cigarette.

"Is this the party house?"

"I, I don't think so?"

"I'm going to call Rebecca, see if she can come and bring some clothes. Is this Ava's house?"

"I don't think so. Man it doesn't have any fucking furniture in it, how the fuck could it be somebody's fucking house…Jesus Christ." I put my head in my hands.

"If you get Rebecca could you ask her to bring some aspirin, a lot of aspirin."

"So tell me again Sport – there's the body, where are you?"

"Ahm…"

And the door opens and it's Rebecca. And we both look at her. She pauses at the edge of the empty living room.

"Hey," she looks at me in a way that I think is a little sad.

"Hey." She looks at Dalbert with a semi smile.

He nods. She hasn't seen the body yet.

She looks back at me. "How are you?" I'm not sure whether she's sad or pissed, sad I think. "You really are naked. I brought you some clothes." She's fidgeting at the step down into the living room.

"Thanks." I'm sheepish now cause I feel like I've done something wrong. Bullshit! I know I've done something wrong.

I'm falling in love with her I realise, weirdly, at a time like this.

"And some aspirin." She takes a really large bottle of Tylenol out of her small purse.

She starts to step down into the living room and notices that Dalbert and I keep looking from her to something on the floor.

"Fuck!" Rebecca stops, in mid step, and backs up to the top step and beyond almost tripping as she goes. "Fuck! Jesus! Bloody hell! Is… Is that what I think it is?" She looks again and looks away.

"What do you think it is?" I cross the room to take the clothes and the aspirin.

"Well it looks like a fucking dead body Sherman."

"Well then, there you have it. It is a dead body."

"Bloody hell, Sherman. Dalbert is he dead?"

"Yes."

She looks again even though she obviously doesn't want to. "God." She swallows hard. "I think I might be sick."

I've walked into the kitchen, the water's on and I wash down the aspirin and pull on the trousers.

"I've never seen a dead person." She turns around to watch me dress. "I've never seen a dead person. Who is he?"

Dalbert moves around the room to stand between Becca and the body.

"Don't worry about that jus' yet Rebecca. Sport, I'm going to run out of time here shortly and I'm going to have to call the station – look, why don't you go with Rebecca now, seen? She don't need to be here an' maybe you shouldn't be here either."

"Why?"

"Because if you stay here, I'm going to 'ave to arres' you and I don't think you did dis. Jesus Christ!" He shakes his head. "I could be way off and then what? I'll be screwed, to rass. But, I don't think you did this Sport, but somebody's leaving your name all over the place.

"Where's the cell phone?" he asked, after a moments pause.

"Ahm, in the kitchen." I look toward the kitchen, feet firmly planted.

"Bring it; bring it come." He's looking around the floor as if searching for something. I realise that he's scanning the room while he thinks, making sure he's not forgetting something.

I brought the phone.

Dalbert took it, put it in the right hand of the body, and closed the fingers.

"Who is he?" Rebecca asks again.

Dalbert took the phone back out of the dead fingers and dialled his office. He paused and covered the mouthpiece. "See you later. Go on. But, hey, don't fucking go too far," he said.

"By the way where's Desmond?" he suddenly asks.

"Desmond?" She looks at me, I look at her.

"Your shadow, where's Desmond?"

And we hadn't missed him until then.

As we got near the door Rebecca looked back.

"Who is he?"

But I don't care – I just don't fucking care. I'm thinking about myself here and about Marjorie and about Todd. Jesus Christ, I've got a son that I miss and I love and here I am in…and does it really matter where I am?

27

"I got a tip." Dalbert smiled and fitted a matchstick into his mouth.

"And of course you don't know who called it in?" Detective Superintendent Macmillan down the phone line sounds dubious. The room was already filling up with people. Eloise was there but standing aside, as two photographers mapped the scene…one working with a 35 millimetre, the other with a Polaroid. She had already stuck a digital 'core' thermometer into the chest cavity of the victim – it looked like a cross between an amp-meter and a meat thermometer. She inserted it on his left side above the third rib.

"No, just a voice on the phone and I came out to investigate." He lies through his teeth.

A pair of officers, one English, the other a Caymanian, were dusting for prints on the front door and the three sets of doors leading to outside.

As the photographers backed out of the room, two more guys started to lay down a grid pattern on the floor with string and Eloise moved back in, next to the body, with Dalbert.

Dalbert saw Chief Inspector Bodden passing, one hand on his chin, the other under his armpit.

She handed him a pair of latex examination gloves.

"You examined the body already, ay?" she asked.

"Yep." There was a slap like a Sea Lion applauding as the glove snapped around his wrist. She'd brought a portable CD player with her.

"Anything?"

"Nothing that jumped out;" just a little white lie.

"Okay dokay," she said and turned on the music. "Helps me think, ay."

Eloise lifted the head gently. "Notice these rings in the blood around his nose?" She pointed with a retractable pointer that looked like a car aerial. "He was unconscious but alive when he hit the floor." She took out a mini tape recorder and tested it.

"His nose is bruised which means he never tried to break his fall – but the rings are the remnants of air bubbles, so he was still breathing." The idea is to do as much work as possible at the crime scene with the body still 'in situ'.

And she began to run it all down, section of the body by section of the body. Touching, poking, prodding, feeling, looking. It all seems a lot like witchcraft, like some sort of haruspication, you know the divining of the future using the entrails of some sacrificial lamb!

"The blow to his skull was made with a very heavy object, flat, large and circular. The blow was made to the apex of the skull and down the left dorsal – a left handed strike; you can tell, because the blow is downward, a right handed person would have struck upward from this angle," she said while turning sideways and making the motion. "Or back handed which would have impacted more to the side of the skull here." This time she used the pointer.

"The rear of the skull is severely crushed" She was pulling hair out of the way with a pair of tweezers. "And there seems to be a trough in one spot on the left side of the skull, here. It goes on pass the main wound, like where a sharp edge may have cut in, ay!" She stopped a moment, setting down the tweezers and moved some of the hair with delicate fingers. "A lot of blood. He was alive for five or six minutes."

"Bled to death?" asks Dalbert.

"Naw, brain damage probably. This's very severe trauma here. I think that he was struck with something like, like…"

"Like maybe a cast iron skillet. You know they have that raised ring around the bottom?" Chief Inspector Bodden stopped in his rounds.

They both looked up; she's still holding the pale dead hand under whose fingernails she had been checking and Dalbert crouching beside her.

The two finger printers walk pass trying not to be noticed. "Oy, boys, can you come and fingerprint the body please?" Eloise calls.

They each look at the other, neither wanting to volunteer. Finally the Caymanian stepped forward.

"I hates this, Miss Eloise, I hates it."

Dalbert stands and looks around at all the activity that's going on. Eloise stands after handing the hand to the finger printers. Chief Inspector Bodden is already standing. The three of them stand together and look at one another.

Someone finally says "Hmmm."

And they go off in their own separate directions.

Dalbert walks toward the back door. He pats his pockets as if looking for a cigarette; he feels Agent Froeman's cellular telephone in one pocket, matches in another.

He stops a passing constable, "Eddy, cigarette?"

"Sure Dalbert."

Inhale, exhale. "Aaah!" His watch reads 8:03am.

"Eddy." As if an after thought.

"Yes Dalbert?"

"Get some divers up here, nuh. We want to search the water for a cast iron skillet?"

"A frying pan, Bro?"

"Uh huh."

Rebecca and I went to breakfast and didn't talk, like that silence after you decide to divorce. We didn't eat either. We sat and listened to the sea and noisily drank our Pepsis.

"Who was he Sherman?" She asked me when we got back in the car, smoking and driving, both intently.

"The missing FBI agent, a guy named Froeman."

"Did you kill him?"

"No." I said flatly.

"I've never seen a body before, not in real life, you know. It's quite a crap thing. I feel absolutely fucking sad right now and, and I never even bloody knew him." She was looking out the window of the car and I'm driving. "There're a lot of people dying around you, Sherman. Have you noticed?" She put another cigarette into her mouth, took it back out again, stuck it back in and finally lit it.

"Yes. Yes, I've noticed… I just hope that one of them doesn't become me. Can I borrow your car?"

"Where are you going?"

"Something my father used to say – I'm going to see a man about a horse. I want to go see someone after I drop you off." I've had two hours to think about where I'm at right now and still have no answers and I wouldn't mind getting one or two.

As I drive away I begin to wonder where Desmond has got to, and I stop.

"Hey, if Desmond calls in let me know. Okay?"

"Where'll you be?"

"With Effrain Shapiro."

I walk in through these large stained walnut doors into an office lobby at 11:11 and boldly approach the receptionist's desk.

"Hi! My name is Chris Sherman. I'm looking for Mr. Shapiro."

"Is he expecting you?"

"No," and I smile in this sad hopeful kind of way. "But I'm quite sure he'll see me."

"He's in a meeting."

"Yes." I nod as if I know. "If you just let him know I'm here."

"I'll call through."

"Thanks." And I smile again.

"Chris Sherman." Effrain Shapiro smiled. "Now, see, you I'd categorise on that list of the last people I expected to see." He's smiling as I walk into the office. "Come, come, sit down, have a seat." He switches off the TV he was watching in a cabinet next to his desk and closes the doors.

"I wasn't sure where else to turn." I started to sit down, but now I stood back up and paced to the bookcase that lined one wall.

"I expect not. It getting hot out there?"

I was sweating, but that wasn't what he was talking about.

"Yeah well it must be 90 degrees outside."

"That wasn't what I was talking about." There's a certain Truman Capote quality to him, which enforces the Brando-ness because there's a certain Truman Capote quality to Brando as well. "Oh, I see Mr. Shapiro, yeah, yeah hot." I look around the office, which is even more expensive than its lobby.

"You can call me Effy, everyone does. So?"

"It's all being blamed on me." I pull out a book, smell it, open the cover, run fingers over it. "Have you read this?" It was a tenebrous novel of pained love and despair and death; real light reading! But without waiting for an answer I continued. "And then, today, another body pops up this morning...at my feet so to speak."

"Ah!" He spun his chair around and came back to face me. "And Detective Hannah?"

"He seems to think I'm not really involved." I've walked down the indent to the window seat and look out at the court-house building. The wall of Cayman history...

"It's all so bare down there now," Shapiro says; there used to be a big Guinep tree there and a little shed where 'the lady under the tree' served lunch...the island's changing. He's using you as bait." Shapiro opens a fridge beside his desk and pours himself a mineral water. He holds up the bottle in my direction to indicate the question – 'do you want some?'

I've stopped in my journey towards a painting by Porges.

"Bait?" And I nod my head in the direction of the water to indicate my consent.

He pours out a glass for me. "That's what I'd do. He probably doesn't have much to go on but the hunch that you're not his man – either way..." He leaned forward and put his elbows on the desk. "The longer you're out there the more likely someone will make a mistake. So, bait." He said it again and I just didn't like the sound, feel, smell, ring of it at all, as it conjured up images of trolling on the end of a hook for the snacking enjoyment of beasty beasts with sharp teeth, rough skin, and cold uncaring fucking eyes.

"Tell me all about it," Effy says leaning back and taking out the handkerchief, which he smells and then tucks away.

I hold my hands out in front of me a moment, look at them, rub them together – I'm thinking...

Just after 2 p.m. Dalbert walked into the Cable and Wireless Earth station in town; right under the dish, at the corner of Shedden Road and Eastern Avenue in Georgetown, there's a room full of racks of the bits and pieces that make a cell system tick. Earl had a desk right next to them. "Earl... I want the phone bill for this cell phone." Detective Hannah pushed the FBI agent's phone across the desk toward the man in the blue and white button collar shirt with the Cable and Wireless Logo on the breast pocket. "I want to know what numbers it called and who called it." The phone is left on the desk like an invitation.

"Dalbert... I... You know the rules man, no way, no how, without a warrant." Earl was dark tan in colour, almost East Indian, with sharp features, and a moustache; his hair was coarse and wiry though. He touched the phone, pulled his fingers away, touched it again.

"Or a bribe, come now Earl baby," Dalbert leaned across the desk and almost whispered the next bit.

"I can't D." He said it as 'cyant'.

"Earl, pussyclate!" A favourite Jamaican expletive. "The man that had this phone is dead, stone cold mother-fucking dead, to rass! Had the back of his fucking skull crushed, you see my friend. It was nice. Nice; you should have seen it. Want to look at the pictures?"

"No way, no thanks man. Look, I, is it this phone right here?" He picks up the Nokia cell phone, then sets it back down, perhaps feeling the vibes of death and destruction through the instrument. "Yes."

Earl looks around suspiciously. "You, ahm, you got 20 minutes?"

"No, but I'll come back, seen."

"Eloise, baby, what you got for me?" One hour later Detective Hannah walks into the forensics pathology office. "Where the rass's my body?" He says in shocked surprise as he stands at the large window looking into the empty morgue lab.

"I tried to call you, ay." She is sitting behind her desk, reading a People magazine that she doesn't bother to look up from. "The FBI showed up with a letter from the Governor." She loudly flicks a page with a finger she has just licked. "The Chief Secretary, The Commissioner and Mr. Macmillan were with them."

By this he's standing on the other side of the window in the body-less lab. "The Commissioner?" he says, but the words are dulled and muted by the glass and concrete and distance.

"Yep, and they decided to relieve us of the body, ay. Where were you?"

"Christ, when did all this happen? I've only had the fuckin' body for 10 hours, it's only been in the morgue for eight, Jesus Christ man!"

"About a half hour ago."

And he comes back into the room and walks again to the window as if to check, just in case he'd been mistaken.

"My phone was dead an' I went over by Cable and Wireless. A few little errands. Shit! Where'd they go?" He set his styrofoam coffee cup down on the desk. "I can't fucking believe this rass."

"They had a plane waiting; did you know that Warren Beatty and Shirley MacLaine are brother and sister, ay?" She holds up the People magazine as evidence.

"Shit! Can I borrow your phone? Who the rass is Shirley MacLaine?"

"Never mind, you know where the phone is."

"Shit! They've probably taken his files too. Shit shit shit, rass!"

"They took Elmo Gaunt as well," she adds as he's reaching for the phone, not looking up from her magazine.

"What!" It was almost a scream.

Dalbert's second call found Rebecca. "Where's Sherman?"

"Hello to you too. He said he wanted to go see someone."

"Sorry, bad bad afternoon. Who?"

"Effrain Shapiro."

"Sorry, 'ow are yu feeling? Are yu okay?"

"No. No, I feel fucking awful, Dalbert. I've…"

"It's okay baby girl, it's okay, jus' take it easy ah! – Look, sorry to come back to this, but do you know who Sherman was with last night at the party?"

"A woman named Ingrid," with a certain sadness to her, she fumbled for a cigarette. "I'm really not sure what her last name is. Was that her house this morning?" Definitely sadness as she fitted the cigarette into her mouth but didn't light it. She stood instead and walked to the window.

"No. No I don't think so. It belonged to a company that's registered at CNB, Griffin and Dunne Ltd. The company is owned by a trust etc. etc. etc. and I can't get any fucking information. Are you sure that her name's Ingrid? Sherman seems to think her name's Ava, seems to think he was with an Ava."

"I've seen her around a lot lately; she wasn't introduced to me as Ava; it was Ingrid and her son Hans, a very handsome, elegant fellow. He doesn't say much but when he does he rather oozes the charm you know. I'm sure it was Ingrid and Hans."

"Who would know them?"

"Michael Zitsky, the lawyer, he knows her. The first time I met her was at one of his parties…they seemed quite friendly."

"See now, what exactly does that mean huh? Were they fucking?"

"Not in front of me…but they were, well they just looked rather intimate what."

"Zitsky the lawyer, eh? Thanks, go get some rest ah girl."

"Did they at least leave your files?" he says to Eloise.

"Uh huh." She smiles, "But only cause I made a copy for you while it was all going on."

"See there, I knew yu was a class A woman." He sat down heavily as if weary.

"Love me dontcha?"

"Today more than ever baby, more than ever." And he rested his palms flat on his thighs just above the knees.

Dalbert was sitting by the pool when Karl finally came walking up from the beach, his trousers rolled up to show off tanned ankles. It was 4:00 p.m. Karl wore a black short sleeved shirt of some sort of Viscose, which was immaculately pressed, and a pair of Khaki trousers. Clive, the dog, came bouncing along on little legs.

"Hello!" He smiled broadly, standing. "Hans, I presume?" He walked from the chair he'd been sitting in to the edge of the pool deck. "Hans Dahlem?"

"Yes." Karl had stopped a moment, and then came forward. He was really strikingly handsome. Clive climbed the steps to give Dalbert a good sniffing.

"Is your mother around?" Dalbert continued talking to Karl as they each walked along the edge of the patio, Karl one level down in the sand, Dalbert above on the edge of the patio like a sentry walking the wall.

"She's gone shopping." He paused at the bottom of the steps that climbed, four of them, up to the patio. "Phew, I'm hot! Are you hot? We can go inside ah? And you are?" He offered his hand as he reached the top of the steps.

"Detective Inspector Hannah, Cayman Islands CID." Everybody always left off the Inspector when they spoke to him.

"Police?" He pushed his dark glasses back on top of his head.

"Police."

"Ah…badge? ID?" The dog had wandered off to smell some bush and then pee on it.

"Yes, yes." Dalbert patted his pockets. "Nice house, is it yours, Chief?"

"No, no we rent ah! I really like that shirt, very nice, did you get it 'ere?"

"No, no, Miami. My ID?"

Karl barely glanced at it as he reached the back door of the house, which was under the shade of a vast Sea Grape tree, and then passed it behind him back to Dalbert.

From the outside, there was nothing spectacular about this house, except its location, unlike the showy extravagance of the house on Boggy Sand Road that they'd recently vacated. This South Sound house was subtle. Probably built in the 70's; this was a plain concrete block house in an "L" shape with an old fashioned corrugated zinc roof. But the touches were, subtle yes but expensive; the screen door, fitted into a Spanish arch which was Mahogany and the screen itself real gut so that it didn't deteriorate in the harsh seaside environment. The furnishings all colonial antiques, even on the patio, which, except for the screens, was almost completely open to the elements.

Dalbert stood at one of the screened arches on the patio looking out.

"I like South Sound myself. Much nicer; well much more Caribbean than Seven Mile Beach anyway, eh?"

"That's why we like it down here. Excuse me a moment please ah, I must wash my hands." Karl stepped up two steps into the kitchen.

Dalbert continued to look out to sea. "Have you ever been on Boggy Sand Road, Squire?" slipping the inquisition back into conversation. "…That used to be like this! It was the best part of Seven Mile Beach not so long ago; now they've spoiled it."

"You almost sound angry. Boggy Sand road…near West Bay? Yes, yes, we used to rent there when we come here. No more, this is nicer. Much nicer ah? Mother prefers this."

"Yes. Whose house is this?" He turned back as Karl stepped back down onto the veranda.

"This, I don't know, you'll have to ask my mother. Something to drink Detective… ?

"Hannah."

"Base to 6 come in Dalbert," his radio squawked at him.

"Excuse me," Dalbert said to Karl, who was now just inside the main living room, back up two other steps from the veranda, fixing two Pepsis.

Dalbert stepped outside and Clive passed him on fast moving little feet to go inside. "Go ahead this is Dalbert." He could hear the clink of ice on crystal behind him.

"Dalbert, can you switch to cellular?" The voice was male and English.

"Is it urgent?" he looked back over his shoulder at the house. "Ah hah."

"It's in the car, the phone…give me two minutes."

"Mr. Dahlem, ahm! I've, look I'll be right back, excuse me." He was speaking through the screen from the patio. Karl answered with a facial expression and a slight shrug as he set down Dalbert's Pepsi on a small glass table.

"Okay see me here, Sport." Dalbert into the cellular phone from the car.

"It's a busy week, Dalbert, we've got another one."

"Another what?"

"Body, D; we've got another damn body."

"Let me guess; Ishmael Greene AKA Desmond Greene?"

"Yes! How did you know boss?"

"Intuition Grenfell… Intuition. Where?"

"He floated onto the beach in front of the Beach Club about an hour ago."

"Look, Sport, I'm in the middle of a liccle something here…put up a tent over the body, get everyone else in there, make sure Eloise is there ah and I'll wrap this up and be there in 'alf an hour."

"I'll tell the powers that be boss man. Where are you?"

"Investigatin' a lead Grenfell, I'll be 'alf an hour okay."

"Okay."

"Mr. Dahlem, any idea when your mother will be back?" he glanced at his watch again. Clive was lying on the couch next to Karl sleeping while Karl was idly petting him.

"No, she comes, she goes detective, I am not keeping up with her ah." He shrugs and sits to light a cigarette. "You would like one?" Karl's eyes are cold, his face expressionless except for the occasional little arch of an eyebrow and a touch of a smile at the corners of his mouth. There's a challenging air about him.

"No...thanks no. Your accent, where are you from Mr. Dahlem?" He really did prefer the word Sport.

"I was born in California [a lie] but I spent a lot of time at school in Switzerland [the truth], so the accent, yah." He makes smoking look both elegant and enticing.

"Does your mother have a phone?"

"A cell phone? No. Do you need to rush off?"

"Yes. Actually I t'ink I will take one of your cigarettes. I've been tryin' to give it up, seen."

"What?"

"Sorry, Chief, it's a Jamaican thing, like sayin' right, right."

"I see." And he has such a nice smile.

"You were at a party last night – at Ricardo Henzel's house?"

"Ricardo Henzel? Perhaps." Shrug. "Parties are mother's specialty detective, she is very social; we were at a party, whose party I wouldn't know. I'm her escort, it saves the embarrassment of dates and of interference where she is not wanted ah!" So proper, so educated – refined. "I am not sure I know Ricardo Henzel."

"But you were at a party, ah Sport?" The 'Sport' came slipping back there, it was always a little more aggressive than 'Chief', 'Squire' or 'Boss Man', it always seemed to have this edge of disdain to it when he added it to a sentence.

"But, yes, we were at a party. Another Pepsi, Detective." He stood.

"No, no thank you. Did your mother leave with anyone?"

"Me." He smiled down from the ice bucket in the living room. Dalbert had to turn in his seat to see Karl.

"Other than you. Did your mother leave the party with anyone other than you? Did she meet anyone else at the party, another man?"

Smile. He stepped down one step onto the patio. He gestured wide with his arms. "My mother loves men – it is her way to compensate for growing old."

"Oh! How old is your mother, Chief?"

"Now Detective that, that is a woman's secret. Hans darling." She smiled, standing suddenly in the archway from the living room looking young…well younger, and in control! But perhaps her makeup was just a little bit askew. Clive opened one eye but didn't bother to get up to say hello.

Dalbert stands.

"Sit sit please." She comes and kisses Karl's cheek. "Darling. But I'm 62 if you must know."

It comes as a small shock.

"Where the fuck is Sherman?" Dalbert says aloud to himself at his car.

28

I'm still in Effy Shapiro's office. We've made an afternoon of it.

"I'm going to give you something and I don't want you to panic." See now when someone says something like that to you, you just fucking know it's time to panic don't you? And I want to say that to Effy Shapiro but he's already gotten up and walked away. When he comes back he's unfolding an oil cloth to expose a blue steel Taurus .380mm.

"Gun," he says.

"Gun," I answer.

".380, 14 shots."

I repeat ".380, 14 shots," like I'm a mimic or something.

He hands me the weapon, holding it on the oil cloth like he was presenting hors d'ouvres on a tray.

"For me?"

"For you."

"Gee thanks!" I haven't actually touched it yet.

He sort of thrusts it forward. "It won't bite."

"I fucking think that it just might, Mr. Shapiro."

"Effy, please." He almost laughs and I realise that I really like this large, jovial, cocksure of himself, effulgent, baldheaded, look-like-Marlon-Brando-in-<u>Apocalypse Now</u>-man, man.

"I think Sherman that you'll soon find a need for this."

"I'd hate to think so." And I touch it. It's cold and heavy – not that I've never held or shot a gun before, I'm just not used to it you know.

Minister Jefferies is sitting in his BMW talking on the cell phone as I walk up the street after leaving Shapiro's office.

"Sherman," he calls out, covering the mouthpiece of his phone, and leans around so he can see me through the window. "How are you? Is everything sorting itself out?" The windows are up, but the sunroof is open.

"I've just been given a gun; it should get much better from here on out," I say talking down into the sunroof, then bending to look at him through the window.

"Ahh," he says, thinking I'm joking. "Well good for you, kill a few for me as well, will you. Listen, call me at my office ah, tomorrow maybe." And he smiles so congenially I begin to feel like his best buddy; but that's part of that politcian's charm, the ability to make people feel that you're their best friend.

Like a cat on a sunny windowsill, Rebecca's lounging, in bed, enjoying the warmth of her own fur.

"That you Sherman?" She doesn't roll over. As I walk up the stairs, I can see her through the open bedroom door. I look at my hand, touch the fingers, rub the two hands together, look at the hand again (perhaps to see if it's changed).

"Yes. Am I in trouble?" I stop and sit on the second to top step.

She rolls over, so that she can look at me, all sort of curled and tucked into the white cotton sheets.

She almost laughs but it's really a sort of sad snicker. "Why should it bother me Sherman? But it does…but it does. I don't know, maybe it's the body, maybe I'm getting soft in my old age. Death's so final Sherman." She sits up, leaves the covers behind, shakes her head. "Sad bloody state of affairs." She looks down, seems to dust something off the bed. "I mean we never promised anything right – I had sex with you mercilessly didn't I? As if it didn't matter right? Look, maybe this isn't love Sherman, but it is jealousy. 'Cause it's nice and I'd like some nice, you know matey? Life's too short, I want to give a flying fuck about someone or something." And who was I to argue, so I just shut up.

"We've known each other, what? Almost 3 weeks?" she looks up as if to get my consent. "But yes, it bugs the bloody fucking hell out of me Sherman. But, it's about wanting something, not you, but the something, the nice-ness that's you." She swings her legs off the bed. "Shit! It's such a crap thing! I'm getting old! I'm getting lonely. I thought you liked me Sherman."

"Oh shit…this, this…I like you very much Rebecca. Fuck! I thought, I don't know what I thought. This, this just isn't my life." Snicker, snort. "This isn't la vie de Chris Sherman. You know I'm a handsome enough guy, or at least I think I am you know.

"But chicks just don't drop over themselves wanting to fuck me, if you know what I mean eh? And I, I…and stoned and drunk. Who the hell is this guy I'm becoming? The me I've always wanted to be maybe, shit! I'm sorry, Rebecca. I'm sorry! I, I didn't want to hurt your feelings. I just didn't know you'd care, you know. I, I thought this sort of thing was your bag, baby."

"That's just it, it is my bag Sherman. It's exactly my fucking bag. Right up my bloody street. I've shared enough men, shared a few women; so why should you be any different?" She's standing by the window looking out and not at me, as if it's a soliloquy with only herself as audience. "But you are. Today, Sherman, you are! Who knows what the fuck tomorrow will hold." And now she turns around. "Jesus why are you sitting over there, come give me a fucking kiss Sherman!"

'Ex fumo dare lucem' it's latin and it translates like a Rastafarian-ism – we smoke, we smoke to live, we live smoking; sitting side by side and naked in the doorway onto the balcony.

"What am I going to do with you Sherman?"

"Effy, Effrain Shapiro gave me a gun this morning."

"A gun!"

"A gun." I'm doing it again.

"Why?"

"I'm not sure. Would you like to see it?"

"OhgodfuckmeSherman!" she said and then slowed to a "Oh yes, Chris, yes."

She called me Chris.

And we were down on the floor, down and dirty! Down in the gutter fucking like the sweaty animals that we wanted to be: grunting, groaning, pushing, pinching, scratching, biting, licking – "F u u u ck mm me Chris, fuckme, yes, yes yes!"

"I wanna fuck your sweet ass!" I say just flying along with that whole sex sweet Rolling Stones kinda vein as I lay my sweat slick skin all over her!

And I'm good. I'm good!

Today we're having sex. Today we're not just fucking, we're having sex. Today I'm a good lay.

I've been a lay before, maybe even an okay lay...but today I'm a good lay – Madonna would like to fuck me today. Sherman you're a stud!

"Someone's trying to pin this all on me." I'm lying on my back staring at the ceiling, my hands, intertwined at the fingers, behind my back.

"Pin what on you Sherman?" She comes up on her elbows to look into my face.

29

"How dead is he?" Dalbert says, pulling a beach chair into the shade of the tent that the Police had set up over the body. They'd also set tarpaulins into the surf below the body to redirect the waves around it. It's now 5:00pm. Toots and the Maytals are playing on the portable CD. He suddenly feels that postpardial call to afternoon nap that West Indians like to refer to as 'Nageritis'.

"Very." Eloise stood from crouching (and still didn't end up much taller) and sat back into a chair that was behind her. "Oowf! We're not going to find very much here Dalbert, he'd been in the water oooh at least 14 hours…lots of sand in his mouth and nose, would seem to indicate that he died right here in the surf. We're having quite a week." She peeled off the gloves and reached for a thermos of tea that was in the sand beside the chair. "Tea?"

"No thank you, love. Well we lost two and now we've got ourselves another one. We're havin' a regular fucking festival here, it's getting like a habit with us, feel like I'm back in Kingston. What did 'e die of?"

"Well…he'd have died from the knife in the spine if he hadn't drowned first."

"Knife in the spine?" He takes out a pack of cigarettes, having gone now fully back to smoking. It had taken only two weeks.

"Quite a thing really." She stood and went to the body. "Come look."

Dalbert followed.

"Here," she eased the hair and collar away to show a neat small incision at the base of the back of the neck.

"Is that as tricky as it looks?" It's hot inside the marquis tent despite the fact that it's late afternoon and someone's had the foresight to set up a fan.

"It would take a bloody fucking artist to perform that little trick ay, Dalbert."

"Oh and he was carrying these, both still in their holsters." She indicates two guns that are sitting on a two-tiered stainless steel cart with the rest of her stuff. "Two 9mm Sig Europeans, nice arsenal, how do you suppose he got those into Cayman?" she smiled knowingly.

"Dalbert." A deep voice booming and with a tinge of the Scottish brogue.

"Shit!" Then, "Sir." Dalbert stood and looked for Detective Superintendent Macmillan.

"Ah, there you are, my boy," as Superintendent Macmillan entered the tent, a bit of cool breeze rushed passed him along with the hum of the people still flocking behind the yellow tape 30 feet away. "How are you?"

D.S. Macmillan was tall, slim, erect and dressed in khaki shirt and shorts looking rather like a member of the 7th corps, the Desert Rats. He had one of those faces that Tony Scott would love – just made for the Ray Ban sunglasses he was wearing. He wasn't normally in his Khakis so he must have been out on official business.

"As you see, Sir." Dalbert indicated the body.

"Yes I've seen it. Can we talk?"

"Walk?"

"Walk."

"You have a suspect?" He took off his dark glasses and slowly folding them put them in his top pocket.

It would have looked like a scene from some David Lean movie, two erect, stiff-upper-lipped men, of varying shades of colour, strolling along the sand side by side, Macmillan with his hands at ease behind his back.

"Do I? Where are the bodies I used to have in the morgue?" retorted Dalbert, looking around as he tapped a cigarette almost absently on the cigarette box.

"Dalbert." A tad firm. "Someone you should have arrested?"

"I wouldn't really call 'im a suspect sir." He exhaled and bent and picked up a stone.

"Then what might you call him Dalbert?"

"A Pigeon?" He threw the stone, but it failed to skip even once and dug right into a small wave. "And you haven't answered me about the bodies?"

"I don't quite follow Dalbert? Correct me if I'm wrong, but the rumour is that he was there in the house with the FBI agent? He was definitely there with Elmo Gaunt, yes? This, this, well we've got this body which belongs to an associate of his? Tell me my man, at exactly what stage do you propose that our Mr. Spencer becomes a suspect?"

"Yes, well all the little fingers do seem to point in his direction Sir, but I don't believe that he has anyt'ing to do with it all. But maybe if I'd been allowed to finish my autopsies?"

"The Americans brought an awful lot of pressure to bear in a short time." He's not wearing dark glasses and is squinting in the softening sun.

"Ten hours… How'd they find out, boss man? I can understan' Froeman, but Elmo Gaunt too, ah?" He looked at the cigarette he was smoking as if it was suddenly awful, threw it down and crushed at it with his foot. It sunk into the sand, so using his toe he flicked some sand back over it.

"He seemed to be an afterthought," MacMillan added, obviously angry at the whole situation. "Look, Whitehall called the Governor, the Governor called me and they were there waiting… the FBI that is."

They both smile at a pair of women passing in bright bikinis – Dalbert fights the urge to turn and watch them. He focuses instead out to sea where a pair of Jet Skis are tearing along on the calm sea and moored boats dot the still surface of the water.

"This Spencer, the supposed insurance investigator?"

"Sherman, Sir, his name is Sherman."

"Sherman," with a dismissive wave of the hand as if names were unimportant. "Arrest him Dalbert, do us all a favour and arrest him. This place sees 3 murders a year on a bad year Dalbert, we've had three in the same amount of days. They're going crazy out there, they're screaming all the way from the bloody Queen on down to the Legislative Assembly's backbenchers. My life's a nightmare. Bring him down to Central and lock him down, Dalbert. Put him behind bars, make everyone rest a little easier, and then we shall worry about it ah, then we'll deal with hunches and the missing bodies and the unfinished autopsies later; okay old man?"

"I don't really want to do dat, Sir."

"Why not Dalbert?"

"He's the only bait I have, Sir."

"If he's not the killer you mean, old man." A widen-the-eyes look with a dip of the chin attached; all that was missing was the knowing wink.

"He's not the killer, Sir."

"Dalbert." D.S. Macmillan stopped. They turned to face one another. "I want you to arrest him and bring him in. You can make sure to let him loose afterwards, I'll force bail with the judge, but there are lots of people talking on the telephone about this one."

"I've heard." Dalbert turning again to look out to sea, not facing the Chief Inspector.

"Right then, so you know the story my boy. Let's do this by the book Dalbert ah?"

"Sir." This time Dalbert does let his eyes follow a nice looking woman.

"Eloise, are you ready to move him down to the lab?" Dalbert asks, coming back under the tent.

"The photographs aren't quite done yet, about quarter an hour." She's sitting back in her lounge chair drinking her tea. "Sure you don't want some tea? It's Earl Grey."

"No, no thanks girl. Can I borrow your phone?"

"Certainly, it's in my satchel."

"Thanks."

"Sherman, you're alive." Dalbert walked away down the beach, paused and turned to face inland holding the cell phone to his ear. "Listen my friend and don't speak." He took the phone away from his ear a moment to look at it, then put it back. "I'm going to have to arrest you – we've found Desmond an' he's dead. Wait wait wait, listen. I'm going to be 'bout 15 more minutes here, then I've got one other stop to make. I want the two of you gone by the time I get to you, seen! You don't 'ave to go far, just go…somewhere. And call me later."

Dalbert walked back into the shade of the tent. "I love this song." It was Toots' 'Sweet and Dandy.'

"Can I have that tea now, sweet girl?"

"Sugar?"

"Two. Want to join me in a smoke?"

"Boys we have an arrest to make." Dalbert spoke to four uniformed patrol officers about 25 minutes later.

"Will we need the USG sir, the tactical squad?" asked one of the English officers.

"I don't think so Henry, we're not after Al Capone 'ere." He crushed his empty box of cigarettes. "Anybody got one cigarette?"

The regular police officer didn't carry weapons. Dalbert didn't carry a weapon. The tactical squad or the always mobile Flying Squad members were the only ones with weapons at hand, all other weapons were locked down except under special release, and even the tactical squads had to have express call to release their own weapons from lock down within their vehicles.

"I've got to stop home and change my clothes and a quick shower ah – I'm smelling a bit rank. Then we'll go make the arrest, by that time the warrant should have been written up. So, why don't you guys go pick up the warrant and meet me at the Cayman Club in half an hour, seen?"

"And Henry, don't bother to try the arrest widout me, okay?" he added, patting his pocket for a lighter.

30

I am scared, and not just a little. I sit on the bed with the phone still in my hand. Rebecca's in the shower; I almost just get up and run away – almost pull on my jeans and a T-shirt and just leave, I come close. I don't know what the fuck to do.

So I say it, out loud, to myself. "I don't know what the fuck to do."

And I can't get my eyes to focus on anything.

"Fuck!" and I shake my head and fall backward on to the bed.

"Fuck!"

And I think of a poem I read recently:

The reason you so often in literature have a naked woman walk out of her house that way, usually older, in her front garden or on the sidewalk, oblivious, is because of exactly how I feel right now.

*****

Still, if you want instead, for once, to hear about how the person came to be standing there, naked, outside, you should talk to me right now, quickly, before I forget the details of this way that I feel...

And I know how they, how Ms. Hecht (who wrote it) and the old lady in her front garden feel, right now I know, so you could ask me, I could tell you.

I want to call my son. I want to speak to my son. I want to go back home and sit on the couch with my son and play *Karmageddon* – Aaaaaaaaaaaaaaaaaaaaaaaah! – I love my son. Right now I wish I was my son.

I hear the shower turn off and I realise that if I want to run I'd better run now before she comes out. And I've got to breathe slowly and deeply and sort of hold myself to the bed or I'll just freak out and dash for the door.

'If I had it my way I would fly away with you.' Sings Hi Tide, a local band, on the radio and it's a great song and fits the moment just about perfectly. And I let the phone slide away from my fingers and its curly cord contracts and sort of sucks it slowly off the bed and it bangs against the bedside table and clunks on the floor.

II

31

Dalbert was sitting at his desk looking at a photo of Ava and
Karl Courie and a photo of Ingrid and Hans Dahlem and a file
labelled Gretchen and Hubert Moll that had all come in over the
Fax machine in the last hour. Neighbours of the empty house where
Froeman had been killed had reported seeing a couple fitting the
description of the Dahlems at or around the house in the days
before the killing. Dalbert thought he'd keep this little bit of
information to himself for a little bit.

He lit himself a cigar, seemed to take slow, extreme pleasure
in smoking it!

He blew out the smoke slowly.

"Bingo!"

He set the cigar down, smiled and clapped his hands together.

Ava and Karl Courie are Gretchen and Hubert Moll are Ingrid
and Hans Dahlem, last seen in the company of Mr. Bryce, master
jewel thief, who was last seen breaking into the Bank of Antigua,
where Mr. Luthra, last seen in the company of Gretchen and Hubert,
was manager.

Detective Superintendent Macmillan is suddenly standing inside the door.

"You find him yet Dalbert?" It's only a rumour, but Dalbert can never look at Superintendent Macmillan, without wondering if he's really wearing women's underwear under his clothes. Supposedly, and this is always how these things get started, someone saw him in the men's room in a pair of black lace and silk women's panties.

"No sir, no, but I'm still 'ere." He shuffles the papers on the Couries aside, calmly puts something on top of them, as if pushing dirt under a carpet when no one else was watching. "Still here. I've got men and informants all over the street looking out for dat boy." He starts to wave the cigar smoke away.

"It's been two days Dalbert. Is that a Cuban?"

"No, it's a Jamaican ahm, Macanudo." There's a snow globe thing on his desk from Moose Jaw, Saskatewhan, Canada that someone had given him. It has a scene of a moose, oddly coloured, with bad antlers standing amongst tacky, too green, pine trees. Of course, when you shook it, snow fell around the moose. Dalbert picked it up and turned it upside down with a snap of the wrist before setting it back down on the desk to watch the snow filter down from the polyethelene sky.

"Do you have another?" asked Macmillan while touching the corner of Dalbert's desk as if looking for dust.

"Sure, here. I know it's been two days, I've been sitting here for two days, right here, my feet up on this desk…for two days."

Macmillan lights up and sits in a creaking chair on casters.

"Hmmm nice. This is all making your bloody day, isn't it, Dalbert?" He watches the smoke float up toward the roof. The two men seem to like one another.

"He's not guilty sir."

"Yes he is, old man, we just don't have all the proof yet. I mean man look at it, Dalbert, who the hell else could it be! Where's the girl?"

Superintendent Macmillan was still so British, strange how a man could be away from the influence of home for six years and never assimilate…but in Cayman, Macmillan could have all the comforts of home. He could have his pub, with a copy of the Times and the ale and bitters on tap to wash down the Fish and Chips with a side of mushy peas *'joost like mum used ta maake'*, in the company of lots of lads of the same ilk. Warmer than London with a clear crystal blue sea for a view – but you needn't adapt, you didn't need to learn the language – the place had adapted to you, you no longer had to adapt to it. Cayman's what one might call 'Third World Lite'.

"Where's Stella Starr?"

"Rebecca Starr sir."

"Ah quite right, Rebecca?" He rubs his eye.

"She must be with him as well!"

"Come on, man, where could they hide, can't be that bloody hard to find them?" He flicked through a copy of the Caymanian Compass, which was sitting on the desk.

"This isn't East Kingston, sir, two white people don't exactly stand out like a sore thumb!"

Cayman's demographic 60-40, white to black!

"Hmmm. Still. Hungry?"

They both thought of food then, Dalbert of Welly's, Country and Western or Macdonalds soul food, Macmillan of Casanova's, The Triple Crown or Brasserie! Their menus might occasionally meet over The Lobster Pot, but Dalbert never went there anymore.

Sure Dalbert liked the fine things in life, but there was a certain comfort level; he'd been to 'Babylon'; lived in London, but he was still really the cop from Kingston. He preferred fry fish with Breadfruit and stiff cornmeal dumplin to Shrimp Dianne in a delicate garlic sauce. Besides who would he go with? The 'church sister' – Grace – she'd only look at him with dismay, hiss her teeth and shake her head with disapproval. Sinner!

Had his indifference turned his wife this way, had the cancer he wondered; or had she followed the path of Jamaican evolution? Like the Hispanic female predilection for going from size 4 at 17 to size 12 at 25, West Indian women seemed to go from being 'bashment skettels', sluts, at 17, to Jesus loving God fearing Baptist zealots by age 40!

"Why'd they come take those two bodies sir?"
"I really don't know Dalbert." But not looking at him.
"Who doesn't want what found out?"
"Isn't that what you're supposed to find out? You're the detective; bring him in Dalbert; there's no conspiracy here, just a thief and a murderer, bring him in. I'm going to get some supper."

Dalbert decided to drive to the Breadfruit Tree Garden Café.
Eastern Avenue is like night and day compared to North Church Street. It is Cayman's Kingston compared to its Miami Beach. The Corner and Blue Marlin, Crew Sports Bar, the air pump at Eastern Avenue, Texaco where mostly Jamaicans mixed with a few Honduranians and Cubans and Costa Ricans waited in turn for a chance to use the pay phones. Pay phones in this country were like social magnets, like the 7 Eleven's or Circle K's of American suburban youth.

Even the Circle K in a place like Vaughn New Mexico, population 300, on any given evening had three people lounging in the parking lot, that's one percent of the population drawn to just hang. Maybe it was the bright lights. Well one percent of Cayman's population stands in front of pay phones on any given night...that's 500 people.

Dalbert drove slowly down Shedden Road in his Chevy Cavalier, the one with the rental car license plates and the tinted rear windows, turned on Eastern Avenue and parked on the roadside. Two men nodded to him as they passed him standing by the car.

"Respect," said one in the deep timbre of Jamaican bass.

"Supa," said the other one – which was a respectful term meaning Superintendent.

Dalbert nodded and crossed the street.

He ate alone; there was the possibility of other women that he never took. Jamaican men are notorious for being great and prolific lovers, 'keepin' a few t'ings pan de side!' But Grace had driven the taste for women out of his system almost completely. Not that he didn't look and imagine – *'no matter how good she looks to you right now, some guy, somewhere, thinks she's a complete fucking lunatic!'* Dalbert did his work and went quietly home, keeping his dreams and himself to himself. He had acquaintances but no friends. Slightly untrue...he had friends back in Jamaica.

"More limeade, Supa?" asked a big ass black woman with two gold teeth, straightened hair, and a cool pair of Air Jordan's.

"Latanya, baby no t'anks...food was well an' good as usual." He pushes away the plate that had been Oxtail and rice with spinners and green banana. But his mind is back to the Moll-Courie-Dahlems and his fingers drum the table and he fits a toothpick into the corner of his mouth.

He notices Minister Jefferies walk in with not one but two young and nubile blondes on his arm. Some guys have all the luck!

Just down the road and round the corner there's a series of 'Do-it-Yourself' warehouses. Dalbert eases to a stop in front of one and gets out of the car. Tapping his fingers on the roof of the Cavalier he looks around, slowly. Then opens the warehouse door onto a deeper darkness, with only a slice taken out of the corner of it by the dim illumination from a security lamp on a post nearby. He pulls down the door behind himself. There's a moment of complete darkness made even more disorienting by the all-encompassing hum of an air conditioning unit. And then he switches on the lights.

In the centre of the warehouse a 'cherry' 1979 Aston Martin V8 Osca India in Chichester Blue, with the Magnolia hide interior and a 5 speed manual transmission.

The car gleamed and glistened and sparkled and shone – the light flittered and capered and gambolled and danced around the surface as if it were too slippery to grab a hold…shimmering like a bright winter sun off of an icy pond. Dalbert bent and blew a spot of dust away.

It was up on two mechanics floor jacks, it's wheels hovering as if by the same miracle of its paint, just so off the ground for fear of damaging them. If the hood were open you would have seen the engine without the grease and oil of daily use.

Dalbert eased himself into the car like a new convert into a church pew. He dreamed of driving this car, windows down and music playing loudly.

Stepping out of the car now he left it idling behind him and went to the workbench. He opened the Jo box with a key. In the bottom drawer he pulled out a soft chamois rag and unrolled it. In the rag was a Ruger Blackhawk .357 magnum, looking like one of those colts from a Western movie, and like everything else in the room, in the same meticulous condition as the car.

Ava Courie is crying into the cotton of a plain blue Mu Mu. She's sitting out on the veranda where earlier Dalbert had sat, and she's sobbing. She feels weakness creeping in where strength powered by psychosis used to lurk.

"Mumsy, you're crying?" Karl comes to the door of the house, which seems lit in a dull yellow, like the dim flavescense of candlelight and he pauses.

"I'm frightened darling, I'm very frightened." Her breathing is heavy as she tries to regain control of herself.

"Frightened?" He lights a cigarette, exhales slowly. He stands back a moment, withholding affection at a time when it's needed, calculating his game.

"Somebody here knows more than we do." She wipes her own tears away, trying hard now to gain composure. "Do you have a cigarette, sweetie?

"Somebody has killed Elmo, somebody has killed that FBI agent, somebody killed him in a house we were using and left that boy there."

"You're the one that left that boy there." He hands her an already lit cigarette and sits down next to her. He touches her hand with a certain indifference.

"Yes, yes but I left no body, Karl. I left no fucking body! Not the fucking body...somebody knows something, Karl!" She's making fists, she stands, turns and walks a few paces. "Jesus Christ!" Sniffle. "I do not like this. I felt this way just before I went to jail. I don't like jail, darling."

"Who could be doing this?"

"I don't fucking know who, Karl. This is what is scary, somebody eiz playin' viz us."

Karl looks up at the stars, the sky is full of them. He realises that he hasn't stopped to look up in a long time – you don't see the stars in Las Vegas or Miami or New York – you see stars but you don't see all the stars. You don't realise how vast and beautiful the night sky is. He smokes slowly for a moment.

"Are you sure it's not your friend Sherman?" he says finally. Karl is enjoying her fear and discomfort. He can see her losing her edge. The game is turning in his favour.

God, how I hate her, he thinks to himself sometimes, God how I love her! He is caught in an Oedipal cycle in which power is the ultimate goal: who holds power over the other. Who controls the fear, the passion…like boxing where points are scored on a vague impression of a thing called 'ring generalship.'

As she grows older, he is strengthened because she grows more fragile, begins to fear death and loneliness, no longer possesses the power of beautiful youth over men. No longer holds court over her own fear. Age is her Kryptonite and like Lex Luther, Karl uses it to gain strength over his nemesis.

He comes to her now where she stands and rests a hand on her shoulder.

"My sweet boy. You love your mummy don't you? You are my comfort." She leans back against him and he strokes her hair. She is vulnerable. He could quite simply just snap her neck.

"Yes, Mother. Look at the stars, look." He points up. "Do you remember that night we drove from Las Vegas to Albuquerque? Just before you got arrested? Before I went to Switzerland?"

"Yes, we had a convertible Mercedes sports car." She smiles weakly.

"That you hadn't paid for."

"That I hadn't paid for."

"I remember the stars that night and the cold." He kisses her on her neck.

"Hello! Excuse me for intruding." Dalbert appears around the corner of the house. Karl and Ava separate, like teenagers caught half-naked in a basement! "I knocked but nobody answered." He continues. "Sorry to disturb you." But he wasn't really, he'd intended to disturb them, wanted to disturb them. "I'm, I'm really looking for your friend Chris Sherman, he's dropped out of sight." And he's doing nothing of the kind. He's playing the game and fucking with their heads because he wants to see which way they'll jump and what'll happen exactly when they do. "Have you heard from him? Has he called?" There's a lot at stake here for the winners and the losers!

Dalbert is still standing in half shadows at the corner of the house. There is a light behind him, which silhouettes him but makes it almost impossible to see his face.

"No, no," says Ava. "No. Why, what's going on? Won't you come in, Detective? Is he a suspect in those killings you spoke to us about?" She drifts slowly from Karl.

"There's been another killing, an associate of Sherman's. A man named Desmond Greene. I can't come in right now, Mrs Dahlem, thank you. A lot on my plate as you can imagine." He looks around before saying, "We've had more murders here in four weeks than we usually get in a year. I just wanted to stop by and say that if you hear from him you must let me know ah." Dalbert's accent, his bearing, his persona changes; he's the London cop, not the Jamaican one; and it's because of the company…

"Certainly, Detective." Karl taps on a cigarette.

"Inspector," Dalbert corrects him, because he wants to.

"Sorry, Inspector Hannah." He almost spits out the word inspector. "If we hear from him I'm sure that mother will let you know."

"Thank you. Sorry again to bother you."

"Inspector," Ava calls after him as he starts away. "So you have no idea where he is?"

No he doesn't, but I'm lurking in the corner of Shapiro's garage. Not the one at Vista Del Mar, but the one at The Sovereign where he owns an apartment. The Sovereign has a series of garages, as does the complex where I'm living, at the front of the property. In it is a 1991 Range Rover – white, with all the safari body kits all over it: cages for the lights, steel running boards, front bull bar with Cibie spot lamps, safari roof rack with rear facing flood lamps (you know for those times of dangerous reversing in the wilds of suburbia) – and me.

"Dalbert, we have the female suspect," he heard over his radio, as he played with the Ruger in the dim light of the dome lamp in the Cavalier.

"What female suspect?" He was unloading the three of the hollow point slugs, the gun in his lap, so he spoke into the radio and then set it down.

"Rebecca Starr, Dalbert."

"Have you apprehended her yet?" He held up a Glazier round – this is a blue- tipped, lead surrounded shot – a shotgun-shell-like packaging for a handgun. On impact the blue tip of the Glazier round gave way and little pellets exploded into the body.

"No, she's entering her home now."

"Stand by… I'm on my way, Star. Don't do anything, please. And if the fuckin' USG guys and their guns show up, muzzle dem please. An' Andy, if she leaves, call me, but don't try to arrest her, copy?" He set down the radio and slipped the three Glazier rounds into the empty chambers so that the gun was loaded: hollow point, glazier, hollow point, glazier.

"Copy."

"She alone?" he picked back up the radio.

"Yes." Any shooting that he did with this load would be shooting to kill. He slipped the gun into a holster and put it in the glove compartment.

"Okay.

"Dalbert out."

Effy Shapiro had told me to stay put till he called. He told me where to go and where to find the key. In moments I've become a fugitive from justice.

Earlier I hadn't run. I'd wanted to run, but I hadn't. Calmly we, Rebecca and I, had talked about it. We would leave together right then we decided; with Rebecca going one way and me another. She would drive straight to a friend's house and stay for a day and then go back home. Divide and conquer. Besides, they didn't want her, they wanted me.

I'd walked out of the apartment with a small bag with a change of clothes and I crossed the street to the pay phone at the Esso gas station.

I was standing there calling Effy Shapiro when Rebecca turned one way up the road and the cops pulled in to the driveway in three Chevy Suburbans like the urban assault team they were. It was minutes later that Dalbert showed up with his team.

By then the door'd been busted off the hinges and guys with loaded MP-5's and plain blue overalls had crawled all over the empty apartment.

Shapiro said I was to cross the street to the Sovereign, apartment six. There was a spare key in the clay pot by the door. I was to spend the night there. The next night I was to go down to the garage and turn on the phone in the Range Rover and he would call me. That would give him time to work things out. And so here I was, waiting – and I didn't know what for.

I'm an accused murderer.

The dome lights in the car illuminate its insides, but out here, except for a pool of light right beneath the door from a hidden bulb, it's dark. I'm feeling claustrophobic.

Shapiro had laughed when I called him earlier.

"Oh boy, sorry I'm laughing but this is funny when you look at it from way out here."

"Glad you think so. A lot of bodies Mr. Shapiro." I'd opened the phone booth's doors and shuffled to the other side so I could look out at the street, but had my back against the back wall of the booth – this was when I saw the cops raid the apartment.

"Effy. Yes."

"What about you?"

"I'm untouchable Sherman, don't worry about me, I'm not the kind of people they kill."

"So you don't think they mistook Elmo for you anymore then?" Cradling the phone in the crook of my shoulder, I lit a cigarette.

"No, no they mistook Elmo for Elmo, alright. Now, what he was doing at my house is another matter. Perhaps a warning..."

"Elmo's an associate of some people named Ava and Karl Courie, who were associates of Bryce's, so I can only suppose they were looking for missing the Blue India," I say.

"Or missing documents."

"What?"

"Right, right, Bryce stole some documents in Antigua for Ava and Karl Courie." This is when the shoe should drop, this is when the tree should fall in the forest, this is when the lights should come on and somebody should come home and I should cry out 'Hey, I fucked Ava Courie!' But I'm still lost in the Ava and Hans scenario and missing the obvious completely.

"What?" Shapiro missing something.

"Dalbert, Detective Hannah asked me about documents; seems that Bryce stole documents from the bank manager's desk in St. John's; from some guy named Luthra. Luthra who happens to be dead, washed up on some Bahamian island with a bag over his head and his hands tied behind his back."

"Nice; but you don't know what kind of documents...forget it a minute, look let's get you in and out of sight and we'll talk more on this later."

So here I am waiting in the semi-darkness, huddled like the first ancestors in the safety of a new found cave, out of the elements but still full of trepidation about the night. I wanted to call Marjorie. I wanted to speak to Todd. I wanted to lie on a bed with Rebecca naked beside me.

"You didn't kill them all did you Sherman?" was the last thing Rebecca asked me.

'You sheltered me from harm, kept me warm, kept me warm.' and now you ask me a question like that.

And then the fear began to set in, clawing its way up my leg like a spider. What was I waiting here for? What if Shapiro was part of the whole thing? What if I was just sitting here waiting to be killed? And I began to sweat: not a cold sweat, but one that stayed strictly in my armpits, dissolving my resolve as it did my deodorant. And literally I began to smell my own fear.

Dalbert parked the car in front of Rebecca's apartment. Two of the USG boys materialised out of the dark in their blue combat outfits and baseball caps, each carrying an AP 5 at the end of loosely hanging arms.

"Who called you bwoys?" Dalbert with one hand still on the car door.

"Ernie," said one, a Canadian boy, named Eric. And he wondered who'd called them earlier to raid Sherman's apartment but didn't ask.

"Is alright...she's an accountant, I don't think you'll be needin' those, Sport." Dalbert pointing at their weapons; he was both pissed and dubious after the action earlier. "Anybody have a cigarette?"

Three puffs to get it going, a deep inhale, slow exhale. "Mmm, that's better. Look, bwoys she's not on the warrant and I don't really want to scare the fuck out of 'er." He paused for reflection. "So why you don't all go take a sat and go lock the big fuckin' guns back up in the back of your pretty silver Suburban." Dalbert adjusted his trousers and stubbed out the cigarette and walked off, leaving them looking at his back.

"Are there men with guns still out there?" Rebecca asked as Dalbert sat relaxed on the bottom of her stairs and she, tense and clutching her knees, sat at the top of them. The stairs were tiled in an earth tone, with a sort of Morroccan inlay between them. The whole apartment had an air of 'India' about it actually.

"Yeah, fuckin' idiots." He chuckled. "I asked them if they were scared of a little accountant." He looked up at the corners of the room that faced him, then back down to the floor, back and forth as if looking for something on the wall.

"I'm scared, Dalbert. Well actually, I'm scared and, and I'm fucking pissed."

"Hmmm – don't be."

"They came to the door you know. I'm sure they did it just to show me the guns." Then she added, "Do you think he killed them?"

"Who, Sherman? I don't t'ink so puss, but you never know these things you know!" He looked out across the room, then back up to her. He eased back against the wall, relaxed. "So you don't have any idea where he is?"

"No. And that's gospel D. We split up on purpose, he went his way and I went mine;" and she smiled a little then at the thought of me, the Sherman me!

"Alright, alright." Dalbert leaned forward resting his hands on his knees as if getting ready to get up. "You going to be okay here by yourself?"

"I guess so Dally." It was another nickname she had for him. "I'm sad, very sad. And yeah a bit scared. Are they going to hurt me D? Are they going to hurt Sherman? I'm, I've fallen in 'like' with him, Dally! Like in an odd sort of way, you know? Not love, what the fuck is that anyway?" But Dalbert didn't know the answer to that question, wishes he did. "Another word for comfort?" But Dalbert knew no comfort in his love. Becca made a funny, scrunched-up face, almost like a wince. "He's not like the boys that usually blow up my skirt and I think that's it." *I want a shy guy!* She scratched her head. "He walked through the door at the right time," and she looked a bit sad. "Do you like him D?"

"Yeah," he stood up. "Yeah I do. It's a sad t'ing, no matter how you feel it – love, like, lust or just a little temporary lubrication. Look, sweets, those guys outside, with the guns, aren't after you. So don't worry, but call me if you need me nuh."

"Alright, let's go home." The USG boys and Ernie were all outside in the parking lot.

"What?"

"She don't know nothing."

He looks around himself. He's suddenly reminded of something he read, and he smiles. It was an old Zairois proverb: *'He who wishes to herd elephant must first know in which direction the elephant is already heading!'*

So, you wait, given enough rope, somebody, somewhere was bound to hang themselves.

32

Rebecca sat at the top of the stairs long after Dalbert had left; *'no one has described fully the horror of this illness called anxiety'.* Like waking breathless and without a voice from a nightmare to find a cold and empty bed; there was no one to turn to her and say, 'it's just a dream'.

Fear and a clawing asphyxiation of the spirit gnawed at her. She stripped off her clothes because they were irritating her skin and stood for a moment there in the passageway at the top of the stairs, not knowing which way to turn. Nakedly un-sexual, her shoulders drooping, her breasts lifeless, the bushy fuzz of her pubis, dark and lacking the electric indication of possible joy. She had shed her sensuality like a cloak and was listless.

She went to the shower and stood under the stream of warm water, motionless, without the dissolute passion with which one normally attacks a hot shower; she was more like a passenger awaiting a late bus in the unending cold London rain. No licentious goose bumps ran up her flesh at the first hot caress of the water – 'you've changed, you used to be so much fun'.

Rebecca poured herself a glass of wine, sat down on the sofa and ran fingers vigorously through her wet hair. She was in a pair of loose drawstring pants and a baggy T-shirt.

'I promised myself I'd never feel like this again,' she said to her head.

'Smoke a joint' the head said back to her. 'Drink your wine and let's go to bed. Fuck this feeling, it's just not you babe! You've got shit to do, life to live, you don't need to fall in "like" with some nice young chappy!'

She looked at her fingernails, thought they needed filing. Pulled feet up and examined her toes, her arms round each side of her left leg, her head and chest through the middle. She heard it start to rain. Seeing the remote for the stereo in front of her she picked it up and turned on the stereo.

'I never had to knock on wood, but I know someone who has.'

She remembered a time when, in a house not far from here, her father put Mercurochrome on her scraped knees and blew on it to make it dry. It was bright red. She missed that little safe comfort. Looking at her watch she realised that it's four a.m. in England and she can't call him to beg him, 'Daddy, Daddy, please come blow on my knee.'

Dalbert is still sitting outside of her apartment, his car against the sparse Oleander hedge. Why he's still there he's just not sure. But he is. His window is barely open as the rain is beating down. He's smoking and listening to the radio.

"Dalbert, it's Eloise."

"Dalbert here." The radio.

"Come see me ay! I've got something for you."

The moon is a small and dull crescent almost completely obscured by clouds and rain.

"What?"

"Just come in and I'll tell you."

'**Quiet as a tomb' is an apt expression;** the morgue is so quiet that it seems to be absorbing noise, like a black hole. His feet make no sound as he walks to the door through which he can see Eloise's broad back and square head.

"That you Dalbert?"

"Yes."

She swivels around in her chair. "I was just looking at his blood." She's sitting in front of a microscope that can fit two samples side by side for comparison. "He had the AIDS virus, ay! You should have a look, the slide of the left is an untainted blood sample, the one on the right's his sample."

"Is dat what yu wanted to tell me?"

The rain has gotten very heavy, you could hear it beating on the building above the sound of the air conditioning.

"No. You going have a look then? Is that rain?"

"What am I looking for?" He bent over the microscope, lifted his head and looked for the focus knobs, bent again.

"Nothing, one looks just like the other. That's the thing; you can't test for Aids with a microscope, you have to run a specific test, an Elisa test, ay."

"Ah…and?" She's playing with him, teasing him, drawing him along.

She smiles. "I ran a CCA, he tested positive for Cannabanoid, about 200 points over the mean."

"Weed?"

"Yep, weed, and quite a lot of it, his blood's saturated with THC, ay."

"Ital weed Eloise. Jamaican bad man, THC in his blood's no news, I coulda guessed that. But, that's not what you have for me?"

"No." She opens the file. "You really want to know?"

"See now you're just fuckin' with me aren't you?"

"Yes. Okay, here it is, I had thought, for a moment anyway, that Desmond and Agent Froeman might have been killed by the same person. But I'm almost sure that Elmo Gaunt was shot by someone left handed, ay."

"The other two were killed by someone left handed?"

"Right handed, at least it looks that way, ay."

Now, see these are the sorts of things that you don't normally notice about people right away. In casual contact, unless you're looking for it, it doesn't immediately dawn on you what hand a watch is worn on! You never recognise the habit that left handed people have of cutting their food, as if unused to utensils and then, in the American way, laying their knife aside and eating with just their forks. You never notice a lefty until he signs a document or writes in front of you in that oddly twisted overhand style as if he's writing backward in a mirror image of someone who writes right handed.

"Wait a secon' you said, you just said you 'thought for a moment anyway' – what's up?"

"They were killed within two hours of one another, ay. Desmond at around 12:30 and Froeman around 2:30 am. Very hard to tell with Desmond since he was in the water…might be less time, ay. I don't think there was enough time for the same person to do both."

"So we're talking three killings here? Right and left handed. Chris Sherman's left handed," he says very softly to himself almost as if distracted.

"What?" Eloise

"No, no nothing. Any cigarettes in 'ere?"

"Earl, sorry to trouble you – I need another favour." Dalbert spoke to Earl, the Cable and Wireless man to whom he'd taken agent Froeman's cell phone. "I need a wire tap an' a recording device on one phone an' I don't want to go t'rough channels."

"Who?"

"76 hundred, Rebecca Starr, yu'll get it done?"

"Yeah, yeah."

" 'ow long?"

"Soon!" A typical West Indian answer. "By the way, friend, I have that phone call list for your Mr. Froeman."

"Agent Froeman...great, I'll come get it."

It's late. Dalbert looks at his watch, realising that he's now simply avoiding going home; the house would be dark and lonely and that odd picture of Jesus, looking like Rasputin, would be watching him, as he walked through the living room, with reproachful eyes. He wondered if Grace had put it there specially to haunt his evenings.

33

Maybe it was Elmo Gaunt's death that really started to change me. Maybe, it was getting vigorously laid by scads of hot babes; well okay, only two to you, but scads to me. Maybe it's the drugs or the drink, or the cigarettes. Maybe it's being on the run from the law. But let me tell you what, I'm the start of a different fucking dude from the broke-up, beaten-down boy that first got off that plane at Owen Roberts International nearly five weeks ago now.

I think to myself just how I've changed; I mean today for instance, looking out onto the beach I found myself wondering what it would be like to fuck every woman I saw. I saw them all grunting and naked and flecked with sweat, their heads thrown back, bodies arched as I pumped them full of cock from behind, my fingers making imprints in the flesh of their shoulders, their hips; pulling at suspended breasts, grabbing handfuls of glossy hair. I think of sex all the time now – even the thought of Marjorie doesn't turn me off. I find myself itching to masturbate in those moments in between partnered sex.

I look in Bryce's mirror as I enter the apartment's bathroom; my hair's grown out badly, looking unreal as if I were wearing a bad toupee, my eyes are red from the joint I've just smoked and I'm smoking a cigarette carelessly as if I were born to it. I undo my trousers and sit down to use the bathroom; I haven't relaxed in the bathroom for three weeks. The beginning of relationships when you want to make that great impression; that time when you hide to use the bathroom, pretending that bodily function doesn't exist for you. Those halcyon days of frequent uncomplicated sex and care and attention and affection, days when you always bathe before going to bed, when you never fart or belch or smell your underarms. Days of the pretence of infallibility; days when you blindly believe that you're your own 'love pontiff;' that you hold lordship over this particular love.

A time of patulous consent to question and answer; this particularly short lived openness, which is always a first casualty in the contest of relationship. Because that is what a relationship is, a contest; it is first a contest of conquest, then of orgasm, then of territory, then of role and position, then property.

I try to recall what it was like in the beginning with Marjorie and come quickly to realize that I was never comfortable with her.

Here's a litmus test for you that I've recently derived – I mean this is the 'new me' litmus test not the 'old me' litmus test; I could never conceive of masturbating either in front of Marjorie or out of her sight when she knew I would be. If a guy can't masturbate when he feels like it he's in the wrong relationship.

…I like to masturbate now like I did when I was 16 – I like to pull out my cock near orgasm and jerk off till I cum on Rebecca's chest between her lovely, lovely tits! I like the look on her face as she watches me do it; this is the Sherman now.

I wish I had something to read; I've almost given up on my H.M. Stanley's <u>Into the Dark Continent</u>. It started off beautifully, but there are large stretches of dry, dry prose…yawn.

I look around, but the bathroom's empty. There's no trace here that this was part of anyone's home, no sign of any personality. No shaving foam can with the rusting rim leaving Bauxite coloured circles on the Linoleum. No old toothbrush, its bristles bent and scattered from use. No half-used soap in the shower, cracking like an empty lake bed in a drought. The room didn't smell of anyone but me.

Finished, I walked back into the bedroom. The bed was stripped. The light from the bathroom made a wedge of progress into the dimness.

Where to start?

I'm the guy who hides the cameras, the bugs, the recorders – I'm not an investigator.

And then it dawned on me just so…why not start as if 'I' were hiding something, where would I put the camera? Where would I hide the bug?

The police station smelled aseptic, like that space just outside a well cleaned public bathroom. Dalbert stopped by the desk of Constable Tut.

"You finish getting the names from the call list for Froeman's phone, compadre? I need to know who he called and who call him ah!" He had earlier given the phone number list, that he'd received from Earl, to Tut.

Earl could provide Dalbert with the phone numbers called, but would have needed a supervisor to provide him with the names and addresses attached to the phone numbers. Dalbert didn't want too many outside eyes in the loop. It was Tut's job to put names to the numbers.

"Nearly done with she, Brali; I'm about halfway now, alright?"

"Please please please, pretty please before you go home ah, Tut?" Dalbert, putting his hands together like he was praying.

"Yah man, Brali – I promise, I'll leave she on your desk when I done."

"Thanks."

34

I liked Bryce's sofa, it was stylish, it was comfortable and now it was the only empty spot in the entire apartment. I was sweating. Somewhere along the line I'd gone from method to madness, from calm to outright fucking panic. I looked around at the destruction I'd caused like I was some act of God. Cushions, books, papers, magazines, clothes – every drawer I'd looked in turned upside down – all scattered around, some less their contents, which I'd added to the general disarray. Pillows I'd dis-embowelled just the way they do it in bad mob movies, took the stuffing out of cushions, turned mattresses over.

My pulse was racing, my breathing shallow. I was on the verge of tears, and so did the only thing I could think of.

I took a hot shower!

It was a shower without a tub attached, small mosaic tiles on the floor, 6" tiles for the sill, the 'gunwale', and the walls…it seemed very old fashioned. I set the gun on the windowsill.

And then I did cry. I sat on the floor, the warm water beating down on me like jungle rain and I wept, sobbed, bawled.

It's a bit of a sad damper on the day when you come to realise that someone (someone a lot badder than you) is going to try and kill you. I wanted my maman, my mummy… I could see her, as I often did, lowering me through the window at the farm, into the midst of the bigger children playing games, from which I was excluded for being small and annoying. No matter how she has aged and evolved this is how I particularly remember my mother.

"Where are you, Marjorie? It's Chrisy, Chris, Marjorie, please."

I just wanted to speak to Todd, to tell him that I loved him and here I was communicating with her fucking machine.

"Marjorie, fuck man, I just want to speak to Todd for Christ's sake, I just want to speak to my fucking son. God how I fucking hate you right now!" I was standing at the window looking out at the rain and the dark.

And then I hung up the phone hard.

I remember she'd said the same thing to me on the day she said she wanted a divorce.

I wanted to call Rebecca.

'They'll have the line tapped' my head whispered to my intellect. Which answered, 'This's the third world man, they won't have got it done yet.' I'm having a moment of that American/European prejudice that anything outside of 'our' world is just tribal back-water.

I light a cigarette.

How good it felt, all that soothing smoke coursing through my lungs, shifting its nicotine to my bloodstream and depositing it along the nerve pathways.

"He's on a cell phone." Earl says down the phone line to Dalbert. "I'm tryin' to do a couple of things here for you, Dally;

I'm tryin' to triangulate, to find the signal and then the computer might can tell me whose signal this is. Boom!" And Dalbert heard him clap his hands down the other end of the phone line. "D, Dalbert, this phone belong to Paradise Jewellers."

"Shapiro!"

"What?"

"Nothin'."

"An', wait, wait, de phone's somewhere out in Newlands, Savannah, Lower Valley; he's between the cell site at Tall Tree and the Bodden Town site. So Savannah or Lower Valley." He pronounced it 'Lowa Walley' in the Caymanian fashion.

"He's at Bryce's house, Beach Bay."

"I'm, I'm…well, I better not tell you where I'm at in case they're listening, but…well I just wanted to let you know that I was safe, safe, and that, well, I'm safe."

It can't really be love, I think to myself, because love hasn't had time to germinate yet – it might be lust or maybe it's all just about safe anchorage in stormy seas. Gee that's romantic isn't it, Sherman, safe ports in a storm. But then that's the reality of it all isn't it – I dig the chick, but what is it that I dig exactly? I don't know her well enough to love anything besides her sense of humour, the colour of her eyes and the quality of her pussy. Jesus, does this even sound like me? When did I get so cynical and so, so (fucking) cool?

But at the moment I call her I feel what I think is love, I feel that fuzzy feeling in the pit of my stomach and the twitch at the base of my spine. I feel that low pressure centre in the middle of my chest that seems to want to suck tears from inside my soul and spurt them through the corners of my eyes.

So you tell me what is it? If it ain't love, what exactly am I suffering here? And suffering it is, cause the joy is painful, like an alligator clip to a stimulated clitoris! "I'm scared Sherman," she says. "Dalbert was here earlier, lots of policemen with guns. This isn't New York, they don't carry guns all that often." Hearing her I picked up a photograph that was overturned at my feet. Bryce and somebody, a woman that I didn't recognise. I tossed it back into the rubble. There was another that I had to stretch for. "Yes. Thanks for the pep talk; see, I was just feeling sad before, now, now I'm scared shitless. Look, I better go." I swallowed hard.

"Why don't you let me come be with you, Chris?" She used my name again. I smiled to myself, sadly; and there was that tingle again.

This picture was of an older woman who didn't look unlike Bryce himself; his mother? You disconnect yourself from these things sometimes, stop realising that these people have lives that go deeper than the shit that you're trying to pin on them. Bryce was just a dead thing to me, not some guy with a mother, a mother who might actually be missing him.

"I can't think of a good reason…but give me a moment and I'll try."

But my mind was running after my own parents, my own life. I had a good life. What kind of life was Todd going to have?

And was it me, was it my own inability to achieve that would affect him?

I remember boat trips to Petit Martinque. I don't even have the chance of owning a boat. My hazy days of laziness have gotten me here. By the time I was Todd's age I'd caught my first Dorado Dolphin just off Raimier Island, where the old whaling station used to be and the ruin still stands. I'd seen my first Marlin caught; they look so magnificent alive, the way the light plays off of the blues and greens and greys of their bodies. I'd been to Barbados, to St. Vincent, to St. Lucia, to Trinidad, to Canada and to England. I'd actually sailed to Barbados. Christ, I've never even taken Todd to Connecticut. "I want to be with you Sherman," she says.

She, Rebecca was sitting on the toilet talking to me and contemplating some crystal meth in a little itty bitty ziplock bag. And she was battling in her head between the forces of wild sex and drug addled parties past and the stoic possible future one might expect of beautiful warm everlasting love and complacent couch sitting in moments between screeching beautiful children. Perhaps she was even half lying to herself about the prospects of a balance between the two.

"Tell me something Sherman."

"Tell you what?"

"Anything!"

"I'm scared," I answered.

I decided just to keep going, in for a penny in for a pound. "I'm scared of all this shit going on, I'm scared of what's happening to my life with my wife and son, I'm scared of you... I'm very scared of you! You're like an itch under my skin. I've never had sex like the sex I've had with you." Chuckle. "Never been drunk and stoned and laid all at the same time. I've never been so fucking loose, you know and had so much fun. That scares the hell out of me." There are other things that scare the hell out of me right now, but, I don't tell her about them.

"I want to stand here and pretend I don't give a damn, but, like right now, right now while I'm talking to you, inside I'm doing a Carlos Santana guitar solo. It's crazy, crazy..."

"Come home and fuck me Sherman, come home and fuck me in all the ways that you ever dreamed of...you can do anything to me Sherman, I like it all." There were catches in her throat, tears fighting with reason.

"I want someone to fulfil me Sherman. Would you like to try?" And even now I suppose that she really did.

"Yes, yes I think I'd like to try that Rebecca." And I would, I would – whether I can or not... Fuck!

That's when the power went out; there was a flash of lightning, a bang of thunder and the lights all went out!

"Shit. I'll call you back."

I walked to the sliding door and opened it.

When I came to I was bleeding and hurt. What was the warning he had given me?

'Go home white man, them no want you 'ere.' It was a poor example of a West Indian accent. Punctuated with another kick; then a punch, then throw me across the room through some furniture: the lights come back up, flickering. I stand and say something like; *'fuck you!'* And I'm a blue belt in a form of karate called Mu Du Kai; which of course I've never used as self-defence, just as something to get me out of the house on Tuesdays and Thursdays. But I raise my hands like I'm going to fight and throw a punch, a nukimiwaza I think it's called; maybe that's a kick? It might have been a tatizuki, anyhow; I should have known better. It's deflected with a cross block that numbs my lower arm and I take a blow to the gut and another to the jaw. I stagger back, this guy looks and fights like Wesley Snipes.

I step into a cat stance, shake my head. I want to do the Bruce Lee thing and signal for him to 'bring it on' with my hand; look I'm in shape, I jog (don't all nerds?) and I do karate...

The lights go back out to the clap of thunder. Lightning flickers across the sky illuminating us in strobic oddity.

I step in and throw the roundhouse kick. He blocks it easily; shuffling in to take my thigh on his shoulder before there's any power to my kick and I get three quick shots to my stomach in return. And then one more to the head and a spinning back kick (that I have time to think is beautifully executed); which sends me flying. *'You in the wrong fuckin' place, white man.'*

The lights come back on. I take a nasty blow to my ear that hurts like hell; then some serious beating and throwing and kicking. At some stage I realize that I have no desire or strength to try and fight. I'm outclassed. Wesley Snipes is beating the shit out of me, and then with a groan I pass out.

But it comes like a moment of clarity as I open one eye. I know where to look! I know where Bryce has hidden stuff. It's dark inside, no power again. I try to move and it hurts. I'm lying among what used to be a table before it broke my fall – a straight kick to the chest, he got great hip extension; and I picked up and flew backward like I'd been punched by Mike Tyson.

"Uuuurgh!" I raise my head and look around, but there's no one there.

"You still here?" And I beg, pray, hope that there's no answer.

No answer! I look at my watch, I've only been out about six minutes. My head hurts. I remember the gun in the shower.

"Look," swallow hard. "Whatever you want, whatever, you, you just show me a way to get out of here without getting arrested and I'll go. I'll go." I'm pleading.

But no one gives a shit, so I roll over and push myself up. Ouch; serious ouch! And I cough something wet and spit. The lights flicker and then come back on.

"Fuck!"

Pain is sometimes exhilarating. And I feel that now. Weee!

I straighten up and there isn't a part of me that doesn't hurt, but I'm happy. I know something that they don't, so screw them.

A roll of documents, three rolls of money, a painting and some precious stones; a mix of diamonds, rubies, and emeralds and one big blue blue sapphire (the Blue India ya think?) were in the bars on which his clothes had hung in the closet.

It was a fact that I'd remembered from his file. On losing Bryce from custody many years ago the FBI had gone back to his premises and found the wooden closet rails on the floor and noticed that they were hollowed out; just a small note in an investigation file from 20 years ago; but I remembered it.

It took only about five seconds after my discovery for the panic to begin to set in – I didn't take the time to read what I had or count the money. It looked like a lot. I looked around furtively and then limped out of the house, into the rain and to the car.

I'd taken five steps before I realised that it was raining. Even in the dark everything looked so green, and full. The leaves on the plants seemed to have plumped like a pregnant woman retaining water. It was then that I noticed I wasn't wearing my shoes and that I'd left the gun on the windowsill. I got to the car. In a bit of a fluster I opened the right side rear door and rushing, reached up under the passenger seat and stuffed the goods into the seat between the cushion and the springs. I then dashed back inside to find my shoes and the gun. Walking, I remembered that I'd not called Rebecca back.

"You've made a bit of a mess, Sport." Dalbert was standing in the doorway to outside, spots on his jacket and beads of water on his bald-head. "What happened to your face?"

"Hi!" and I stepped back against the wall, wanting to run.

"Hello. Your face?" he pointed his chin at me.

"A little warning."

"From who?"

"I don't know, Wesley Snipes I think!"

"What?"

"You have a gun in there?" He had his hand inside his jacket.

"No. What's that about Wesley Snipes?" He was leaning casually in the doorway as if I'd invited him over for drinks.

"A guy that looked an awful lot like Wesley Snipes told me to go home, that I wasn't wanted. He punctuated his sentences by beating the shit out of me!" Unconsciously I touched my battered face.

"Ah! You find anything?" He waved his hand at the disarray!

I chuckled and even that hurt. "No." And I looked sad and battered enough to cover the quick lie. "You going to arrest me?"

"I have to."

"You don't seem terribly interested in Wesley Snipes."

"Oh I am. You going to come or do I have to come get you?" He moved his hand and in it was a gun. He smiled then and said, "I lied! But it's not a real gun." It was one of those things that fires two electrodes at you and gives you a nasty little electric shock, leaving you paralytic and twitching on the floor.

"We'll have to leave your car, Sport," he said loading me into the back seat of his car, doing that thing where they hold your head down for you. The rain was coming down light but steady, and I couldn't see outside because the dome light was in my eyes. I had to lean forward to avoid the handcuffs digging into my wrists and my back.

"How'd you find me?" I asked as he slipped into the front seat.

"Cell phone."

"You seem angry."

"You're fucking up my life, Sport." He turns around from the front seat.

"These handcuffs are uncomfortable."

"They're meant to be. Your face looks rough." My right eye is puffy and my cheek cut and my ear is swollen and red. He shook his head. "What is it you expect me to do exactly, Sport?"

I thought of telling him about the stuff that I'd found. But then a little devil that liked the thought of money and jewels kept me quiet for a moment. And then there are the documents that I hadn't read – I wouldn't want to be presenting him with incriminating evidence against myself, with so called Bellerpontic letters. At least this is what I tell myself, but I think, in reality it was that little touch of greed and ego fulfilment that was clouding my judgement.

"Come on Dalbert, Detective Hannah, the cuffs hurt, what am I, Al fucking Capone?"

"Look who's done become the big man now? Swearin' and smokin' and fuckin' pussy like it's going out of style." He shook his head and turned back to face front.

Then suddenly he banged on the wheel twice. "Jesus Christ! Alright, alright, turn your back let me take off the cuffs. Shit, I can't reach from here. I, let me get out and come round." He got out of the car and opened my door.

"By the way, a friend of yours showed up here today… Franklin Carpenter, your boss I believe," he continued.

I hit him pretty hard in the side of the head with the .380 and he staggered back and slowly sank to his knees. I didn't mean to hit him so hard but I panicked. I meant to stun him, you know, to rattle him a little bit just to give myself the upper hand but I panicked.

I stepped out of the car holding the gun awkwardly in my hand. The night was lit oddly from the dome light in the car and a security lamp at the edge of the complex. We were both getting wet; the knees of his trousers were already soaked. I could hear the constant static of the surf crashing just 100 yards away. Sheet lightning lit up the sky, static energy passing from cloud to cloud.

"Ouch!" was all he said! When he pulled his hand away from the side of his head it was covered in blood.

"I'm, I'm sorry Dalbert, sorry."

"Where'd the gun come from?" He seemed stunned, dazed, like a man in shock.

"A friend." Water dripped off the end of my nose. The blood from the side of his head ran down diluted to spread a stain across his collar.

"That hurt. I don't think I like the friends you're keeping these days, Sherman"

"Just, just please keep your hands where I can see them, I'm really nervous, I'm really scared and I've just had my ass kicked by Wesley Snipes and I'm just not very fucking happy Dalbert, not very fucking happy at all. Do you mind lying down?" I could tell he didn't like the idea at all of getting his clothes soaking wet and dirty, Dalbert was fastidious that way. "I'm going to cuff you… Okay?"

When I loaded Dalbert, cuffed, into his own back seat he said in a very strangely calm kind of way, "I'm goin' to be very angry in a little while." And it made me nervous.

"I'll call someone." I took his cell phone. "In a little while I'll call someone and tell them where you are."

"Don't call the station."

"What?"

"Imagine how embarrassing this would be." He sort of indicated the hands behind his back with a little twist of the waist and shove of his elbow. "Look, type in this number, it's a friend named Earl. Call him, he'll come get me…quietly, you know."

"Okay."

Then I saw his eyes look beyond me at something and his mouth begin to form words that I never heard him say and I started to turn.

BANG!

And it sort of did that in my head and I saw stars and went down and mostly out – it was turning out to be a rough night for me getting beatings.

In an 'in-and-out-of-focus' haze I saw Dalbert scrambling back against the far door in the back seat of the car; I bounced free of the ground like a flat ball, like one of those medicine balls, that doesn't really have any spring to it. The air all rushed from my lungs. The person, I couldn't tell if it was man or woman, was hooded. Dressed like some SWAT team member. I came back to rest belly down, my cheek against the pavement of the parking lot; the rain was washing the blood across my face. The hooded figure reached down and picked up my gun – it's okay when you see a scene like this in the movies, some guy wearing latex gloves picking up a gun with your fingerprints all over it, but in real life…

I want to scream 'don't', but I can't think enough to form the words. And I see the muzzle-flashes; I don't hear the gunfire, 12 in all, fire darting out of the end of the barrel like the flames of hell reaching out for Dalbert. The hooded person drops my gun on the pavement, I see it bounce and wobble and then settle through the haze of splattering raindrops, but still my world is soundless.

35

Rebecca believes that *'the wrong fragrance on a woman can be as shocking as bright red lipstick on a nun.'* And she's stoned! *'Yes, yes yes, now this, this is me,'* she thinks, as she looks at herself in the mirror, naked, wearing only her ameliorated mood and applying bright red lipstick to pouting lips.

And then, suddenly, in the angle of the mirror she sees that Dalbert is standing in the doorway to her bedroom, leaning against the jamb.

"Bugger, bugger! Fuck!" Flinching, she jumps back and turns; she really is beautiful naked (but then aren't all women that you love? Something about that affection that turns flesh into divine interpretation of sexual attraction).

"You scared the fucking dickens out of me D. Bloody hell!" She is completely unconcerned by her lack of clothes; as if her nakedness in front of Dalbert was a natural course of life. "Jesus, Dalbert what, what happened to you? You look like bloody crap, matey." She's half laughing.

"You should see the other guy." His clothes are a mess, the knees of his trousers stained and dirty, there are powder burns on the front of his white shirt and a red spot in the middle of his forehead. The sleeves of the shirt are surprisingly white and clean where the jacket used to cover them. The right side of his face is bruised and cut. And in his hand is a gun, the Ruger Blackhawk. She looks down at it. He looks down at it.

Sort of half lifting it from the wrist alone; "I thought he might be here. You're naked!"

She chuckled. "Yes. And stoned too D. I'm a happy girl. What kind of gun is that?"

"A Ruger .357 magnum, you'd better put on some clothes, sweetie. Can I look around?"

"Yep, yep, yep! So, what happened, Dally?" She calls at higher volume from the cupboard as he goes to look in the other room.

"I got shot," it comes back as blandly as if he were telling her he'd just bought some stale cheese down at the corner shop.

"Shot?" She stops putting on her shirt a moment.

"The gun was filled with blanks," he says matter of factly as he opens the door to the bathroom in the other bedroom. Leaning slowly around the doorjamb he finds it empty. As he straightens back up he catches a glimpse of himself in the bathroom mirror and lets out a sigh. Fruitlessly he dusts something off his soiled shirtfront.

"Sherman?" She's pulling on jeans.

"No," he says loudly, then "You haven't seen him?" as he comes back into the room.

"I haven't seen him. Is he okay Dalbert?"

"I have no fuckin' idea, Rebecca. There are too many people in this game, baby girl. Have you got any aspirin?" He looks down at himself in a quasi daze. "How the fuck am I going to explain this one?" He scoffs and shakes his head. Looks at his watch. It's 2:30 a.m.

"I've got crystal meth."

"Rebecca, girl, I'm a cop. The Babylon, seen." He tucks the gun into his pants. "You're not supposed to fuckin' offer me amphetamines you know, sweetie." He's not angry at her; but he is angry and perhaps fed up.

"Yeah but you know what D, it works a lot better than the bloody aspirin." She smiles broadly, her pupils dilated. "I better get some Dettol too, that cut looks nasty."

"Now, that, that's the fine fucking work of your friend Sherman;" he touched it and winced.

She returns, with the Dettol and some cotton balls.

"Hmmm. Ouch, Ouch! Gently, nuh." He's flinching as she puts the disinfectant on his cut. "God, look at my clothes." Sitting on the bed he can see himself in another mirror.

"Is he going to be alright?"

"Sherman? I don't know. I jus' don't know. I might want to kill him myself." He winces again as she touches his cut. "Look at my fuckin' shirt. I, I don't think that the guy who shot me knew that the gun was loaded with blanks and, well, he took Sherman with him."

"Fuck!" She shakes her head looking down at her toes for a moment and then seems to get lost in them and the colour of the nails. She drifts away and then slowly looks up at Dalbert. "What's this on your forehead?"

He touches it and winces. "Powder burn, blanks fire the wad of paper that's in front of the powder. If you're too close you get hit with it; it's hot, it burns."

Almost sober now, her eyes tear up.

"Yeah, yeah, I know ... I know, scary. I need to change my clothes."

"Are you going to save him Dalbert?"

"I'm goin' to try, sweetie." He shakes his head. "I'm pissed, angry as hell; look, if you hear from him at all you call me, seen?"

"Yeah, yeah...can I come with you?"

"No, no you'd better stay put, he might call. It's getting rough rough out there now, girl." And then he smiled at the thought of it. "Rough, everybody's gonna start laying their cards on the table; there's a lot of money at stake here. Who gave him the gun?"

"Mr. Shapiro."

"And the car too. Okay, okay. Look, Rebecca, you stay put, you hear. I'm going to go and change. Don't look so girl, I'll call you and let you know what's happening along the way."

Shapiro's lights weren't on when Dalbert rang the bell. He didn't wait for an answer but wandered off to the back of the house. A series of instant-on security lights followed his travels. When he reached the back veranda the light on the stairs was on.

A man was standing in the foyer, but it wasn't Shapiro.

Suddenly a disconnected voice over an intercom spoke to him.

"Detective Hannah are you here to see me at 3:00 in the morning?"

Dalbert looked around for the intercom.

"A little to your left, Detective, on the wall next to the door."

"Thanks," he mouthed, raising eyebrows.

"Yes, I am here to see you," he said pressing the talk button. Looking up and around he spotted the small camera and stared blankly at it.

"Why?"

"Questions."

"Ahhh! Mr. Sherman?"

"Hmmm."

"I'll be right down, Terrence and Paul will see to your needs. Terrence is the fellow you can see through the doors; Paul, who you might have missed, is behind you with a spectacularly large gun and a fantastic 'Starlight' third generation night scope that cost me incredible thousands of dollars."

Dalbert took out a cigarette and lit it casually.

"You'll have to excuse my pyjamas, Detective, I wasn't expecting more company for the evening."

Dalbert was amazed by this odd man.

"Can I have the boys get you something to drink? I'm having an orange juice and champagne." In a very effeminate gesture, fingers extended rather than cupped, he lights his cigarette.

"Mimosa? I'd love one, wait, no, how about a Bloody Mary?" Deciding to test the service.

"Spicy?" His tongue came out as he exhaled, the smoke curling back up into his nostrils in a French inhale.

"Naturally, please."

"Your face?"

"I had a shaving accident."

"Now why don't I believe you – did our friend Sherman do that? He's just not as pathetic as we tend to think of him – while you're busy solving gruesome crimes I think our friend Sherman will be finding our missing jewels and more importantly missing documents, ah." He leaned in to watch Dalbert's reaction as he said it, then ran a hand across his bald-head and sat back, retreiving the cigarette from the ashtray as he went.

"Documents, hmmm, yes. Yes. So, what do you know about documents?" Dalbert shaking out the match he'd just used to light his own cigarette.

"How bout some music?" Dalbert said. These two were playing games with one another. He looked at Shapiro, the womanly lips, the Capote-like manner.

Paul turned on the stereo after the wave of indication from Shapiro.

"Funny that!" said Dalbert because the song he'd been mentally singing was playing on the radio, on the 'Zee' – channel Z, Z-99, the local American style top 40. "So you were telling me about documents, Squire?"

"Only rumours detective – but they seem to be making a lot of people nervous, ah. What do you know about them?" He touched himself on the face.

"I'm only interested in dead bodies Mr. Shapiro," he said, contemplating the end of his cigarette.

"Somehow I truly doubt that Detective. Ah, here are our pick-me-ups. How interested are you in Ishmael Greene, Detective?" The cat scratched at the glass door.

Dalbert sipped his Bloody Mary, licked some lime juice pulp off his top lip, and looked at the cat. "Was he one of yours?"

"Oh yes. But, you know Dalbert, I think more to the point you should be interested to know whose he was before he was mine? Who sent him to kill Mr. Sherman in the first place? Dontcha just wanna know Dalbert, really know. I mean, you know, before he became one of mine. Or do you know that already?"

"Perhaps my government sent for him. Is that what you're trying to say, Boss Man?"

"Did you do away with him, Detective?" He leaned in, let the cigarette smoke expell itself from his mouth.

Chuckle. "I'm a police officer Mr. Shapiro, it's not my style." Cold flat stare. Then he looks off across the pool, pass the spot where Elmo Gaunt had sat dead, out at the North Sound.

Shapiro chuckled to himself at that comment.

"See now, that's not quite true, 'cause that's just the police's style. Maybe not usually the style of the police here, but you're not from here are you, Detective?" It certainly wasn't a question. "And maybe it's not the style of this place either, I mean not usually. Sure there're a few vindictive politicians, but that's everywhere isn't it? Everywhere there are those who can be corrupted in that kind of way. But this is bigger than that. Come on Dalbert, you can tell me, come on, was it really the government?"

Dalbert paused, ran a finger around the rim of his glass. "I don't know that answer. Do you?"

"Oooh, see now my friend, I believe that you do, Dalbert. But no, no frankly, I don't; which I find somewhat surprising in itself – see, I know a lot of fucking people in this little town, Dalbert, a lot of people. And let me tell you, when I can't get an answer to something like this it makes me think that the answer must be a very, oooh, well, a very troublesome one. Know what I mean?" He sat back and drank the Mimosa, signalled Paul for another. "You haven't drunk yours."

"Why exactly are we having this conversation, Sport?" Dalbert's attitude had lost its deference, you could always tell when the word Sport was added to the vocabulary makeup of one of his sentences.

"Well," Shapiro leant in, elbows on knees, he ran a finger down his chin and then made a flourish with his hands. "I'm just trying to decide what exactly it is you're working towards."

"And me, me I'm tryin' to find out who has Sherman and why it is they felt brave enough to try and shoot me full of holes. You know?"

"And you were wondering if it was me?" sitting back.

"The thought did cross my mind." He tapped the crown of his head.

"Ahhh, well, let me just make this clear right now, you know, for the record…you're wrong my friend. If I'm guilty of anything it's that I tried to, like you did, to, well, to control Mr. Sherman, casually though. But I lost him, you know. We've both been using him toward some end or the other I think. But, I, for the life of me, just can't quite grasp whom you're really working for, Detective? What's your end in all this Dalbert?"

"Perhaps I'm working for myself eh, Mr. Shapiro. Hmmm? Life's very quiet around here. Maybe I'm looking some excitement. Why don't you tell me what your end is? Surely not jewels…you already have those." He stirred the drink with a finger, smelled it, sucked it, then took a sip.

"Do I? Perhaps it's self-preservation I'm after then."

Dalbert chuckled, twice. "Then perhaps you'd better be quick. I mean if you were to miss the prize what then, ah? How safe you think you'd be, eh?" And Dalbert stood to leave.

36

In the Ptolemaic model of the universe the Primum Mobile, that part of our world that is beyond the stars, was turned by the hand of God himself; and I felt like that right now, like some unseen force was revolving a universe at which I was the very centre. I woke sitting up in a chair in the middle of an empty, dark and very silent room.

I came to slowly. My head hurt in extremes. My eyes felt dry and sandy and there was something pushing my forehead down around my eyebrows. There was a little light filtering under a door. And I first saw it like the light at the end of a tunnel; perhaps the Sendall Tunnel, of home, which joined the Carenage with the Esplanade, in St. Georges. Home. Why was I thinking of Grenada as home all of a sudden?

My arms were numb and the back of my knees felt on edge from lack of water; I was very thirsty.

F. Scott Fitzgerald said something like *'in the real dark night of the soul it's always 3 o'clock in the morning'* – it was that now, both literally and figuratively. Fear and cold sweat crawled all over my skin. I squirmed in my chair.

This is when life passes through one's mind; you begin to think about the whats, the whens, the wheres. To ponder God and love and hate and hope and fear; and fear, yes fear, fear, fear – scared shitless cold sweaty dry-mouthed fear. Life and fear co-mingle in your body; you clench your teeth and breathe through your nose and your eyes bulge a little and dart in short glances from one spot in the room to another.

And you remember (with a certain amount of vague hope) times when the impossible in life was solved; like that time when someone opened the door into the bathroom in which you found yourself trapped as a small boy. Or when some kind hand lifted you through a shattered window, from where you were half buried under 3 feet of bauxite dirt behind where your mother was pinned to her seat by the steering wheel of the now mostly crushed rental car. Of course, in hindsight, these events seem small and insignificant, but at the time they are the deep, meaningful, grasping-at-straw moments of life.

So hope glitters briefly, like a dying torch, and then is resolutely crushed out by the fear and the wishing that you could have done and said something differently yesterday when you were less close to your own inevitable demise. And suddenly passivity sets in, because fate has sealed your nonexistence. But you talk to Todd with your mind and send the telepathic message that you love him and always will. And Rebecca is there and you tell her that it really is love that you're feeling and you wish you had more time to spend with her. Time to learn her body and her moods and the varying tastes of bits of her flesh and the pink skin smells peculiar to that spot behind her ear on a Thursday evening in November.

And you think you hear the sound of people elsewhere and you think of calling out and then are scared of what you'll find and so you keep quiet and hope that the footsteps don't come your way.

Then a memory, some unimportant memory of something that you never realized was all that special or meaningful in your life, like the smell of Grenada after the rain, the taste of crab back and the smell of guava stew. You remember the smell of Grenada after the rain, the taste of crab back and the smell of guava stew. Picnics with Aunt Mary on the Garrison Savannah in Barbados while cricket played. You remember the first time you ate Peking Duck, at that restaurant off Queens Boulevard, whose name you don't remember, with a girl you think was named Sue, but you're not sure. But you remember her big round brown eyes and how her hair always smelled clean. You remember the sun going down off Grand Anse beach and the time it went down all vibrant orange when you were at the US Open in Forest Hills watching Jimmy Connors play an early round match.

And here is where you realise the duality of what you are; some sort of social schizophrenia from which you suffer as a child of multiple worlds where your personalities entwine to make you something other than what you were and different from what you would become.

It came to me slowly then that I was just sitting in the chair, that I wasn't, well, attached to it. And that the noises I thought I was hearing weren't from within the building, but from inside my head. That I still couldn't hear anything beyond a hum in my head and the occasional distinct wave of sound. I stood. My world went woosh! I sat back down.

Slowly again I stood. I coughed and heard it muffled and distant like someone coughing two doors down in your apartment building. I walked to the light.

I'd been in the unfinished office at the back of an unfinished shop, still under construction. The bare concrete floors with half-finished partitions and electrical conduits and plumbing pipes were sticking up from the floor like so many severed arteries during a heart transplant; the smell of cement dust, almost like the odour of hot pavement after a brief rain. I came to rest my hands against the large dusty glass pane at the front of the shop; it had a red and white sticker on it that said ALT. I could see cars passing up and down on the Harquail Bypass, the local version of an expressway, a two-mile stretch of highway running from the West Best Road section of Georgetown to the Industrial Park next to the Owen Roberts International Airport. It was raining still.

Then, in the reflection on the window I noticed a piece of paper around my neck... I lifted it up to read it. It was hand written and looked like it said '*paoO oq oj uoo5*' and for a minute I thought it was in Russian, just for a minute until I remembered to turn it over and try again.

'*Soon to be Dead!*'
Why? Why? And why? And what the fuck did they know? And who?

On Dalbert's desk, when he walked into the station at 5:00 am, was a further report on the gun from the Elmo Gaunt shooting and the phone call list that Tut had been working on and a note from Eloise. Dalbert parked his car in the front lot. He waited a moment for two on duty officers to meander away; the station was on half staff at this time of day. When the girl at the reception window in the lobby turned to grab a bag of cookies he grunted a hello, waving his badge in her general direction. She buzzed him in making a comment about his grumpiness, he replied lying about being sleepy. He dashed up the stairs putting his plastic ID tag, which dangled on a piece of sports nylon, that said Nike, in purple and white over his head.

He just didn't feel like answering questions about the state of his face till he'd come up with a good story. Actually he'd thought of dropping out of sight, pretending he was dead, but then changed his mind. 'Fuck them, if this don't shake them up nothin' will,' he said out loud to himself.

Police in New York had traced the weapon…he flicked the piece of paper…the .38 that killed Elmo Gaunt, from the gun store to one Dorothy Lieberman whose husband had bought the gun in 1984. He had died in 1986, presumably leaving the gun in his wife's hands. So there the trail ends, ostensibly, as Mrs. Lieberman had gone missing two years ago in possibly mysterious circumstances.

She was a widow, without children.

Dalbert sat at his desk and opened the bottom drawer, took out the Appleton and poured himself a glass. The office was empty, except for the musty smell of age and the faded photos of various members of the Royal family 20 years out of date. He turned the snow globe over and watched the snow fall on the moose from Moose Jaw, Saskatchewan.

The phone call list, now with all the names attached, held three very interesting bits of information: there were six calls each to Effrain Shapiro, to the Edwards' house (where Karl and Ava were staying) and to an unlisted number in New York City (presumably Franklin Carpenter). There were two calls to

Franklin Carpenter's Cayman apartment (where Sherman had been staying). Was he looking for Sherman or for Carpenter? All the calls were made in the two days before Agent Froeman's death. A time when Dalbert had presumed that Agent Froeman was still in the Bahamas. What had he found out in the Bahamas? And why was he back here in secret? He picked up the phone and rang New York; his own phone was big and black and 20 years out of date.

Eloise's note gave the height of Gaunt's killer: between 5' 11" and 6' 2".

"Oh yeah, the Lieberman case," came the New York cop voice down the line. "The suspicion was that she was jacked by some real cool cats, a mother-son team, Gretchen and Hubert Moll, nothing ever proven though. But they tried cashing some of the old girl's cheques, after her death, that were most likely forged."

Dalbert laughed.

"What was that?"

"Nothin', nothin', just something funny on this end. Look, could you do me a big favour and sen' me a fax or email of the details including any photographs of the Molls that you might have...please." He gave the New York detective his personal email and fax numbers. "And can you confirm an unlisted number for me?" He read out the number that he presumed to be Franklin Carpenter's. "Your phone company guys wouldn't give me the time of day."

"Yeah sure, sure, no problem, anything to help. Say, how's the weather down there?"

Dalbert took the rum in a single shot and then searched his desk for a cigarette. There was none.

"Grace, it's Dalbert… Why you sound so woman? …Look, don't bother answer, I was just lettin' you know I is alright, just workin' is all."

After which he hung up quietly. He had a change of clothes in his car and so had not gone home at all since yesterday sometime. He went now to the bathroom to wash his face. Then looking at his watch decided it was time to leave before the morning shift came on at 7:00. He stopped to look at a small poster above one of the cabinets; *'sexual harassment is absolutely not tolerated in this office; it will however be graded!'*

As a West Indian he couldn't really understand the concept, there was always 'graphic' sexual interplay between West Indian men and women. West Indian society was warmer and more open than that of the States or England and especially Canada. It's full of all that Bacchanalian bounce and verve and love and passion.

There are two 24-hour gas stations in town. He went to the Walkers Road Texaco and bought a pack of Rothmans cigarettes, a Caymanian Compass newspaper, a spice bun, two Pepsis, a slab of tin cheese and a box of matches.

"Wha' 'appen to your face, Supa?" one of the men asked him.

"Fell off my horse!" he answered pronouncing it 'arse'.

He ate his breakfast, smoked and read his newspaper on an empty beachfront lot that overlooked the Sand Cay off the South Sound coast. On the second page in the top left corner was always a section called 'Police Report – from police incident reports':

A George Town man was arrested by West Bay police officers for being drunk and disorderly. He was locked down until he became sober, say police. There was a time when this was all it ever said – times change.

Now dead people are litterin' the pretty beach.

Very little noise had been made about this spate of crimes in which he was now semi-happily embroiled. The press was keeping quiet – lots of stuff was kept quiet in a place like this. In a small world you don't want to cause too many waves, one or two, step on too many toes and three, there's that pesky problem of a newspaper maintaining work permits for its workforce. The Cayman Free Press was anything but free and Dalbert knew that as much as anyone else.

Dalbert reclined his car seat and went to sleep.

I was barefooted and didn't know where to go. I was deaf and tired and hurt and lonely and scared. I sat on the curb wall outside the shop. It was all very quiet!

The rain stopped and all was damp.

Effy Shapiro's eyes were closed, his head back, he idly shook a fresh Mimosa. He opened his eyes, first one, then the other and straightened his head. He exhaled, puffing out his cheeks as he did.

"Paul," he called without much effort. "Paul." He tried again louder.

Paul appeared.

"I want to find him, find Sherman. Let's get some people on it, quickly, quietly."

Dalbert opened only one eye. There was now a vague lightness to the edges of the darkness. He closed his eye and picked up the cell phone, and dialled a number.

"Tony, is Dalbert." He paused a moment to let the name sink in. "I need you to pick up a car, is a white Range Rover, is out at Beach Bay…the condos out there. Pick it up soon nuh and drop it by the station please."

He tossed the phone on the seat.

A traffic light that I could see turned from green to bright red.

Rebecca rolled over in her sleep, snorted, gave a little moan and continued to sleep. The TV screen was blue in the background, the TV making a soft hum.

Ava sat in the corner of her bedroom peeking out through the edge of the window. She looked mad, not angry but on the edge of some sort of mania, a breakdown, a crash, a burn-out, a fizzle…clutching her knees and rocking slowly back and forth and muttering to herself.

Karl read a book by dim light on the veranda. He loved mornings. He had slept well, gotten up, exercised, showered and come to sit quietly with a cup of coffee, a book, and a cigarette. The sound of the sea was soothing, and the breeze through the screen cool. The sun would be up in about an hour.

Franklin, who had not gone to the company apartment, sat erect on the end of his bed in his suite at the Hyatt. He looked at his watch. Laid out beside him on the bed that he'd already made was his phone, his briefcase, his clothes, his tie; on the floor at the end were his shoes and socks. He was watching CNN Headline news. Waiting.

The sun came up!

37

I was walking four steps behind a lunatic, who was, I think, ranting something about talcum powder, but having lost my hearing I can't be sure. The strange thing for me was that in America you don't often see this; well okay you see it in Manhattan, but you don't see it in Queens, and never in Flushing or Kew Gardens Hills. But out here the lunatics walk the streets right next to the normally corrupt.

I was a bit dishevelled, barefoot and just a little bit smelly. The lunatic was in fact better dressed than I was. There are cruise ship tourists all over the streets. Just off the shore I can see four ships; eight thousand people are on the roads around me right now. I blend.

There's a fat, white, and spottily red tourist leaning against the Elmsley wall talking on a Motorola walkie talkie, probably to his equally fat and splotchy wife, who is off somewhere over-spending their credit card on jewellery that she doesn't need.

He's also smoking and I bum a cigarette. He ignores me as he hands me one – as if he finds the thought of conversation and contact, with the 'obviously local', distasteful. The traveller who wants to see the world as long as it looks just like the America he left behind.

The smoke goes down good. I can feel the nicotine. Aaaah! I roll my neck around. I close my eyes.

When I open them I see a stray dog. This is just about when the reasons why come clearly to mind. Whoever, quote unquote, rescued me last night, shot Dalbert, bang bang bang at very close range more than just a couple of times.

Dalbert's dead and I'm walking around, Dalbert's dead and shot with a gun that has my fingerprints all over it.

Ergo I've killed Dalbert.

I threw up then, right into the sparse oleander hedge of the Elmsley Memorial Church.

I tell myself then that I have to get to Beach Bay, retrieve the jewels, get the documents. Have to! They might be my salvation.

Is it better to be deaf or blind? You ever have this discussion? I'm sitting on the front steps of Elmsley Memorial Church looking at the tips of my fingers. I feel them, rub them together, cup them to my face and smell them; they're very sensitive right now, my entire skin is. Did you know that your skin is your body's largest organ?

I can't hear and so to compensate I can feel. I'd much rather be deaf than blind... I can answer that right now, positively, emphatically: Had the experience, climbed the cliff, dove off the tower, bought the T-shirt at the bottom of the ride.

I'd miss great music. Yes, that I'd really really miss.

Life without music.

Life without freedom.

It looks like it might rain again.

Am I walking to Lower Valley? Where am I going? Which is when I see the Range Rover I'm looking for rolling down Cardinal Avenue, on the back of a flat bed truck, in the half shadow between the buildings like some beautiful Technicolour slow motion shot. I laugh and shake my head and walk off down the street in pursuit.

The Range Rover did a loop around the post office and I cut along beside the Royal Bank building and caught up. I'm moving fast – maybe not exactly panicked but then again not exactly in full control of my faculties.

The Central Police Station in George Town has no vehicle impound; they just park the cars beside or behind the building.

A horn blows; and I know that a horn has blown, I feel a reverberation deep in my ear, I don't hear the sound really, but I feel it. People look at me, or is it just my imagination? I'm dirty.

I stand by a shop across the road and stare at the Central Police Station and I watch them, him really, unload the Range Rover. I breathe deeply, once, twice, close my eyes and count to three, four, five. Okay, okay, let's do it, let's go, be the ball Sherman be the fucking ball. And while the guy's unhooking the chains I cross the street.

"Yao!" I say to him as I pass. "I supposed to get something out de car." I try my best West Indian accent and it comes out sorta 'Jah-merican'.

He says something that I don't hear. Breathlessly I open the left rear door and do my thing, reach up under the seat to retrieve the stash, as if it's the most natural thing in the world.

I've run almost the whole way to Rebecca's house; that's three miles. Passing all that colour again: the silver buttonwood, the coconut, oleander and varigated double red Hibiscus; leafless plum trees, vibrant tropical cherry. It's hot and it's humid and I've been lazy for three weeks. I'm breathing heavily and sweating and my head's hurting badly again. I don't even stop to remember the visual joy of a grove of coconut trees.

I scramble along the back of the building. *'Everybody knows that the dice are loaded!'* I feel like a character in a story by Borges – a guy who is caught up in irony without knowing it; a story by Borges except without knives, at least right now; a lot of machismo but no knives.

I lie down on Rebecca's patio and catch my breath. The tiles are cool on the back of my neck. I'm panting. My side hurts. I've lost my sunglasses and the sun creates an orange glow on the back of my eyelids.

I know surely, as I'm lying there with my eyes closed, that when I get up and knock on her back door it's going to fly open and the police will be blazing guns in my direction. And in a hail of bullets my body will pick up and fly backward, crashing into the chain link fence behind me, leaving a stain of blood across the linked wire. I will flop lifeless and akimbo onto the dirt…dead, and because I'm deaf it'll take place silently and in slow motion.

'Knock on the door, Sherman, get up and knock on the door, Sherman. Be a man Sherman, be brave, be cool, be Super Dude. I don't want to knock on the fucking door; you knock on the door if you're so brave.' And so I lay there on the tiles for a while longer with my panic keeping me company.

I was motivated by the rain, which started again just then. And I see myself like Butch Cassidy and the Sundance Kid going out the door into that courtyard full of blazing guns.

Rebecca wasn't home, but the door was open. I love this town, one of the few places on the planet, much less in the Caribbean, where you can be safe (if your name ain't Elmo Gaunt) leaving your doors open. Sure, petty theft happens (and brutal murder), but truthfully, not much. Not much.

Inside I have a cold shower. It's one of my favourite things. The guy in the mirror afterward isn't me. I swipe away the condensation on the glass and look at him. He's tall and tan with dark hair and my eyes, he has my eyes, well, he has a tired, colder, harder version of my eyes. But he doesn't look like me. His face is bruised and distorted, his ear is red and swollen and he looks old. His hair is longer than mine and he needs a shave.

By the bed's a joint, waiting in an ashtray that's made up of glass beads of many different colours – rolled and ready. I light it and smoke. I like the bed, all that dark mahogany in the soft orange glow. The walls are wine coloured. I look around the room, check in the drawers and on the various table tops. I'm examining some of the minutiae of her life. The trinkets that indicate the subverted personality, like an enamel matchbox with a primitive hedgehog, candles that don't drip and don't smell, but are varied colours. A set of antique counterweights in the shape of elephants, that were used 50 years ago, by some errant Cambodian to balance his scales for opium sales.

I hold in the smoke from the weed, let it out slowly; sniff at the exposed smoke. It's cool in the room with the air conditioning running and I'm naked. The red on the walls lends to the tone of lascivious indolence.

I'm a pot (fucking) smoker!

The phone is ringing, I can see it, feel it and somewhere way down deep like the tinkling of distant wind chimes I can hear it. I may get back my music yet!

This is right where I'd go downstairs and get the papers and the jewels and the money, that I'd found under the seat of the Range Rover where I'd hidden them, out of my trousers pocket. Stop briefly to find something to put on, there's a baggy pair of cotton track shorts with a string tie big enough to fit me, then I'd hide the money and the jewels in the bottom of her Tampax drawer in the bathroom, second down on the left. Come back and I'd lay the papers out on the bed and read them.

I'd do all this if I had them, but I don't! They weren't there in the car, they're gone.

38

"**Eloise, can you get VICAP, Scotland Yard, Interpol, I don't**
care somebody, anybody and get them to sen' us a copy of fingerprints for a Gretchen and Hubert Moll to your computer? They
were suspects in the Lieberman case in New York year before
last?" Dalbert's standing next to Eloise in her lab, he's leaning
back against the counter, that she's sitting at, looking at the photograph of the handprint that was on Elmo Gaunt's neck. In his
other hand is a box of Rothman's cigarettes that he's playing
with.

"We can call them, ay. You've taken up smoking again?"

"I have. Thanks girl. Look, I'm going to go get some sleep,
I'll call you later, alright?"

"Ay."

Dalbert made one more call from the car before he turned off
his phone. He called a man named Oney (called that because he
only had one arm), and he put Oney on the job of finding Sherman.

"Oney, there's four people to watch for me, ah Chief.
Franklin Carpenter stayin' at the Hyatt, the beachfront rooms,
4444. A '*modder*' and son called Hans and Ingrid Dahlem, they

in the Edwards house in South Sound, you know on the beach front just down from Caribbean Paradise? An' Rebecca Starr, you remember her, Chief? The tall white girl you see me with last Christmas.

"And put the word out for the bwoy Sherman, seen. Anything, anything, especially Sherman, you send someone come find me. I going home to take some sleep." His accent had become more deeply West Indian, Jamaican really.

"Where's your mother?" Franklin 'nervous hands' Carpenter said to Karl as they broke away from a tongue-ful suck-lips boy on boy kiss.

"She has locked herself in her room, Franklin. I think she's having a crisis, perhaps even nervous breakdown." He smiles as if her discomfort gives him pleasure. "I'm glad you've finally come." They hold hands.

"Yes."

"Come in, come in, we will have a drink. Coffee?"

"Mmm! A drink I think. This is nice, this is very nice." Franklin looking around slowly walks straight out onto the veranda.

"Well, you know Mumsy always finds the great spots. You look very handsome, Franklin!"

"Yes." He straightens his tie. "It's all Armani. He always makes you look good. I wouldn't like coffee, I would like a Virgin Mary, please, extra spicy." He says it slowly as if he's mentally testing his answers before he speaks them, tasting them for mental acuity. He glances at his watch. "You'll bring me up to date?"

"Yes, yes, sit out on the veranda, it's very cool there, I'll bring drinks."

"This view is great;" like a careful man on a witness stand. "So?"

"Well, so, as you see, mother's in a bit of a panic." He lit himself a cigarette, then stopped, standing in the opening between the veranda and the house so that he could look at his lover. "Things have not gone well…at all. Perhaps your friend Sherman isn't as inept as we might have expected, maybe, yes?"

"What's happened?" Franklin is displeased.

"Two things: There's, well you spoke to him, this Detective Hannah, our own island-style Columbo, you know like the TV detective, but black and, and bald. And your Sherman; I believe that your Sherman might be playing us with the help of Effrain Shapiro."

"Shapiro? Wasn't he Bryce's fence?"

"So they say." He brought the drinks. "But you should know this… Bryce was working with you, this is something you should know."

Franklin scoffs at the 'this's something you should know'. "No, no, not at all." He sips the Virgin Mary. "You ought to know me by now, Hubert; unlike you, I just don't like to get my hands too dirty with these things." He crosses his legs and dusts something off the seam of his pants. Then, where the trousers pool at his crotch he flips one ridge of fabric first one way and then the next; without his tie he needs something to fiddle with.

"I've tried to stay as far away from our friend Bryce as possible, I didn't even know he lived here." He sips the drink again. "Hmm, perfect, you're hired, you can make my Virgin Marys anytime." This drew a smile from Karl.

"I only ever fed Bryce client information that he needed to pull a successful job. And even that at a distance. It went through two exchanges.

"He then handled everything in between that and my collecting 50% of the net at the end of the job; which of course he kindly placed in an account in the Bahamas for me.

"All very hands off, but, well you just gotta love that tax free, Hubert. Just imagine how my fucking father-in-law would feel about all this." He actually chuckles as if that thought is the best part of it. "Come...and kiss me!"

You can sum up Franklin Carpenter in two words, Amoral Narcissist. But it's perhaps more than that. Like a five-year-old with a missing chromosome, he is completely egocentric, self-indulgent, and lacking in that one little gene that renders emotional accountability. He and Karl might have been very much alike, except that Karl craved warm affection and so could experience a slight modicum of caring. He cared for Franklin, oh, he could kill him quite easily, but he cared for him, he might actually miss him if he had to choke him slowly to death. For Franklin, there was only Franklin. But Franklin was weak.

He sticks his tongue in Karl's mouth when he kisses him.

"I doubt that it's little Mr. Sherman giving you the trouble, Hubert. Someone else for sure ... but whom?" He nods, looks over his shoulder and then standing, steps to the screen so that he can look outside. "Sherman's a slacker, not a bad guy, a slacker; that's why I chose him. Christ, he's a fucking photographer, not an investigator, Hubert. He's a softie...he sleeps on the sofa in the other room while his wife fucks here new lover. We'll have to take a look elsewhere, maybe a closer look at Detective Hannah and Effrain Shapiro?"

"Oh, you can forget about the Detective Hannah." Karl smiles broadly, proud of himself. "I killed Detective Hannah last night with a gun belonging to your Mr. Sherman. I killed him and then dumped the unconscious Mr. Sherman in town."

"Hubert, you really are a devious little fucker! Who else have you killed?"

"Well, I would have liked to have killed that horrible private investigator that Mother always has around, Elmo Gaunt, but someone beat me to it. She doesn't know he's dead yet, and I wasn't planning on telling her. She wanted him here as back-up. But of course, you were right that he might have interfered with our little plans, and as luck had it someone else killed him for me."

"God, you're an awful bastard, Hubert. Where's Sherman now?"

"I expected that the police would have found him by this time. I don't know." He detaches a piece of the Casuarina needle.

"Well, darling Hubert, why don't we start by finding this out."

39

"Your house is tapped," I whispered as I lifted Rebecca's skirt. She's changed her hair again, gone blonder. I like it.

"Bugged?" She wrote haphazardly on the pad I'd given her, while with the other she was undoing my trousers. Just a small yellow pad; lined. She was breathing into my open mouth.

"Yes." The word sort of stretching out, as I was sinking to my knees.

"Oh," was the reply that I missed.

"I'm going to need some stuff," I mumbled on penetration. I'd missed that moment, that moment when my cock told my brain that this really was Rebecca. It's always as if I'm shocked by what I'm feeling.

"What…what kind of stuff?" Looking around her shoulder and easing up on her toes, she held up the pad. I closed my eyes, opened them again to focus.

"Stuff." I said noncommit-ally over the squeak of her fingers kneading the edge of the dressing table.

"Stuff?" she sort of exhaled the word, closing her eyes.

We were glad to see one another.

I felt safe again. I'd lost half of my fear.

Cuddled against warm pliant flesh, I could forget for a moment that people were trying to kill me. I could forget my bruised face and battered body; that I, and no one else, was being set as the scapegoat for the largest crime wave this little country had ever known. Rebecca was glad to see me. I haven't quite got it yet, not love really, but comfort she'd said, she wanted something nice in her life and I was the nice. Yet, it was probably love. Maybe.

There's this movie called 'Wait Until Dark' – with Alan Arkin tormenting a blind Audrey Hepburn… I feel like this now. I think that I feel a lot more like that than say like Uma Thurman in 'Jennifer 8'. The Audrey Hepburn, Alan Arkin thing was just so much more sinister. I wonder if Dalbert feels at all like the Andy Garcia character?

A Shakti is a sexual initiator, a partner who helps you experience the power of sex as a vehicle to higher consciousness; we're doing a lot of fucking and I'm getting high on it. What consciousness I'm getting to I haven't decided yet, but maybe I know myself a lot better now than I ever did. I lie here and wonder if I'm medicating myself with sex, if this is my way out of my fear. And is it such a bad way to medicate yourself?

I ran a hand down that slope, the one that runs hip to ribs, as she lay on her side, a 'Long Tall Sally' of a girl, and closed my eyes. I was sad-happy. That post-coital return to reality – and mine was sad and scary. I wanted to just stay here and love her.

She reached out and touched my cock! Kissed my mouth. I felt a stir of pleasure along the flesh between my scrotum and my anus. Cupping my cock she took a finger and ran it along the urethral slit in the head and placed a small dollop of my clear cream ejaculation on her tongue. Fuck!

A little moment later I thought of Todd. I remembered reading to him in bed between his mother and me, lying just as Rebecca and I are lying. I missed his smile, the way that he smelled, the way I felt every time I saw him at the end of a day. Then I wondered what it would be like to have children with Rebecca. They'd be beautiful, I think.

"Do you like children?" I asked.

"Yes," she said and touched my face, gently stroking my bruises, as if she had been thinking the very same thing. "But I don't like Christmas!" as if it were really in context with the question.

She rolled a joint and we smoked it together all intertwined, calf on thigh, chest on tit, head on shoulder.

Rebecca'd been in love once, in the proper squidgy sort of fashion that we all think of love when we think of love. I phrase it this way because she talked to me about it in a very removed sort of third person way; as if she were relating the story about some semi-distant relative about whom she could really give a rat's ass (to use one of her favourite expressions). And she told me that he'd died in a car accident between himself his car and a tree. They'd had an argument. Perhaps she blamed herself deep down in the recesses of herself where she usually didn't walk the paths to smell the miasma of hidden pain and guilt. So we are two people broken by circumstance, me by an unfaithful wife, a slacker's constitution and an accusation of murder. I feel as if people are staring at me and saying well, anyone's capable, even Sherman, he could be a killer.

I am becoming angry and distrustful!

I could almost kill now, I think, maybe.

Making a list and checking it twice.

"Thank God Dalbert's not dead." I light a cigarette in the bathroom, in the steam, with the shower running. I might have wanted to add the word 'yet' here, but I don't remember.

"Lucky! He's bloody pissed though!" She drew two stars next to the word pissed.

"I bet, but he ain't dead." She reached out for the cigarette and I gave it to her.

I explained to her the story of finding the documents and the money and the jewels – fortunately we're not both deaf as this would take some writing.

"He came here with a gun. He's probably not quite sure how involved you really are." Of course the last bit she sort of put down in a vowel-less shorthand. She touched my broken face. "Do you think Dalbert took them?"

"Maybe, maybe." I held up my hand for the cigarette; she took a drag! "I'm just not quite sure about our Dalbert, you know."

"Thank God you're not dead." She looked away, blankly for a moment; then she put the cigarette back into my mouth. I watched the way her mouth formed the words; "Franklin Carpenter is here," she wrote as she spoke it.

"Yep, yep." I nodded cause I already knew. "Dalbert told me. Christ!" Shake my head, swallow hard, think fast, shake the head again. "I don't think they want me dead, they want me alive, they want to blame me for everything. Me, the fucking scapegoat!

"You have a Radio Shack here?" I asked over the sound of the shower; white noise, pink noise, blue green or grey noise, to interfere with any listening devices in the house. I run the back of a hand across the soft tan of her stomach.

"Yeah, sure do." She took the cigarette back out of my mouth and kissed my cheek.

"Locksmith?"

"Of course." she whispered in my ear, but held up the word 'yes'.

"Good camera shop?"

"Duty-free." She licked my neck, and held up the word 'yes' again.

"Okay, okay, here's what we do, we need to go to Radio Shack, we need to go to a good baby supply shop, we need to go to a camera shop, a good camera shop. Then I need to find like a locksmith's van and a telephone company van, where I can get the things that I need, not much stuff."

"Van?" Stepping back, she rests a warm hand on my chest, pinning the pad to my skin.

"Yeah van, I'm going to need to steal some things, I didn't exactly come prepared for my kind of work you know!"

"Steal?" She's flushed, her nipples erect, she writes it in big letters.

"Steal, yes. Can we get a van of our own? A panel van, to beg, to borrow?"

"Sparky." I kiss one nipple as she writes using the top of my head for a rest.

"What?" I look up, my hand in her panties.

"Sparky, a mate of mine, Sparky has a cool van." Her eyes are closed.

"Sparky, you have a fucking friend named Sparky?" Exhaling coolly, it's becoming humid and hard to breathe in the bathroom. I sit on the closed toilet seat.

"Oh yeah.

"So Sherman, sweetie, babe, chappy chap!" She rests a hand in my hair, tilts my head so I can see her mouth move. "Am I going to have to wait all day or are you going to eat my pussy again sometime soon?" which of course is right there at eye level behind a thin veil of mist and fabric. Yum! And on the yellow pad she's written 'eat pussy!!!' Below this she's drawn three arrows pointing downward and four question marks to follow.

I reach out and touch the sheer curtain of nylon behind which the shade of hair waits like a window onto a whole new world.

"**What if they're watching?**" She writes furiously fast.

"And they probably are. You go out the front; I go out the back... I'll meet you out back off Walker's Road. They probably won't follow you down the side road since it's a dead end."

"You mean these houses right back here?" Mouthing the words, she jerks her finger and I get it.

"Yes!" I reach out and tug at her hips. We kiss wetly.

The quasi-ambivalence is gone. We're hot for one another. Stiff cocks and wet pussies!

"I need, I want to call Todd." I'm breathing through my mouth.

You can do anything to me Sherman I like it all!

"We'll find a safe phone." She's kissing me again and writing against the wall behind me.

I've come to a cultural realisation that I couldn't have before!
I think of Dalbert as a Beenie Man song. And so, you say to me, 'Hey but Beenie Man is all about sex and money, about being the DJ Don man. And is that really what Dalbert is all about?' And of course the answer is no, not really, but I cant help but

think of him in those terms... I see him walking down the inner Kingston street, nicely dressed, shaft-like, in the movie about his life and the Soundtrack is playing Beenie Man rhythms.

'I got my gun, I got my vest, mash up any contest!'

Right now, as I'm coming to this revelation, I'm curled up uncomfortably on the back seat of Rebecca's car, staring at the ceiling and thinking. Thinking of life and love and hate and of the things I need and want. And where I am and where I'm going and what's going to happen when I get there. And what Todd might be doing right now and whether he misses me or not and then I get angry.

And would my father be proud of me now?

Rebecca says something. I don't hear it. But I see when she turned her head and her mouth moved.

I look at her profile, and wonder what she meant by *'anything'*. What are the things I could do, would do, want to do to her, what are the fantasies? Tie her up? Paddle her? Drip hot wax on her nipples? Fuck her in the ass? I have trouble even thinking of that for a moment and saying it in my head. I embarrass myself, but it comes back and the second time, I'm not so embarrassed, but then I'm thinking of it as having anal sex with her and don't think of it as fucking her in the ass.

She says something else again and I say, "What?"

Silence, scribble and try not to crash.

"I'm parking in a car lot and going to leave you and walk to the bookshop. The van will be next to you. White, key in it."

"Okay," I answer. "Okay. So where am I going?"

"Radio Shack," she scribbles.

"Does that say Radio Shack?"

Yes, she nods.

"I don't know where that is."

"I was joking," she writes. "Go back to the apartment, park the van on that back road and climb the fence."

"Where'll you go?"

"Work, but I'll meet you at home later."

I would be useless right now without her and want to thank her, but can't yet. And then the car drives into shadow and I can see the concrete roof above. We're in a covered parking garage.

"I'll get a Radio Shack catalogue for you," she writes and then kisses me.

I like it when she kisses me.

If this was a movie this is where we'd see Rebecca make the phone call, the one that goes:

"He wants to set up a bugging operation." She would say into a phone somewhere out of the way, glancing furtively around as if she might be watched.

"What?" would come the indistinct voice from the other end.

"He wants to set up surveillance and wiretaps and bugs. He wants to steal a panel van."

"What'd you tell him?"

"I told him Sparky had a van."

"Why don't you just let him run with this a bit, keep him occupied, keep him out of the way a little longer. Who've you got that can baby-sit him?"

"I don't know."

"Okay, so if you were really going to help him do this, who'd you use?"

"Louis."

"Can you trust Louis?"

"Yes."

"Then put him to work...we need another 48 hours, maybe 72."

"I'll call Louis."

About a mile away Dalbert opened one eye. Grace was standing at the end of the bed wearing her sensible dress and her sour-faced, disapproving expression.

"What happen to your face?" she asked. She was wearing a straight-hair wig, which was slightly twisted and just didn't suit her African face.

He sat up in the bed, then swung his feet off and stood up, naked.

"I fell down," he said as he walked away toward the bathroom, rubbing the back of his bald head.

She averted her eyes, holding her Bible tightly in her hands. There was a moment there when she looked like she might soften, a flash of the old her, but Dalbert missed it and it only crossed her face for an instant like a passing shadow. There was the booming sound of him urinating, and her shoulders became less rigid, her face lost its tenseness, her grip on the good book eased. Then he flushed the toilet and her rigid God came flowing back into her, driving out the momentary devil of soft human acceptance.

"A woman name Eloise just call, she say you are to call her." It was obvious she disapproved of a woman having called.

He walked back out of the bathroom, still naked. "Thank you," he said sadly and went to choose some clothes before going to shower.

40

I'm calmly perturbed.

I wonder if Rebecca's got a Qualude around here somewhere, some kind of a downer that'd just adjust my nerves. I'm taking to drug use quite well, don't ya think? As if I were born for recreational drug use! But I can't call her. I want to call her but even if I could I couldn't, how'd I know who was on the other end of the phone line?

Here's the 'been to Radio Shack and looked in the catalogue' list:
Optimus am/fm/tv sound receiver/transmitter
Infrared headphones
Optex wireless security transmitter/receiver (2 pc)
Cordless telephone batteries
Multichannel microphone receiver and 170 mhz wireless clip on microphone (9v batt.)
Room to room audio/video sender 2.4 ghz
Multichannel scanner

Next to this last one I put a couple of stars. I can smell Rebecca wafting on the air from upstairs where she's changing. Then I draw a bracket around the list and write Radio Shack in the margin.

This is a 'make do' list; back in New York I had my own kit: laser microphone, parabolic microphone, bugs (maybe 183 mhz, WFM), bigger RF transmitters, repeaters, multi-channel distribution modulators blah blah blah; NLJD detection devices and stuff like the Tektronix oscilloscope – my own counter-intelligence. I had my 3M field phones, yellow and blue, with clip in poppers (so that I could trunk into a phone line), tone generators with right angle clips to help a dude make phone calls somewhere secure and untraceable.

Plus the man's gotta have cameras; 35 mm Nikon with 20 mm f/2.8, 60 mm f/1.4, 105 mm f/4, a Watec 902A camera attached to digital recorders, Fuji 4700 digital with 16 bit card for short video etc. etc.

She's brought me some brochures from the camera shop so I continue the list:

Polaroid camera, 35mm version

Nikon D70 digital camera

Canon A 630 digital camera with the 1 gig card for video

I can hear what I think is the music that's playing somewhere in the deep recesses of my ears.

Video with capture kit

Distribution modulator (to manage multiple cameras)

Pick gun

Pick set

I light a cigarette and exhale the smoke.

Field phone
Spread spectrum transmitter
TD reflectometer
Endoscope camera.

I write 'phone co.' next to this and underline it three times.

I can't do the talk like the talk on the TV,
but I can do a love song like it's meant to be.

I like Mark Knopfler.
Soon to be dead, the sign they'd hung round my neck, I don't want to die.

It's like a pop when it happens, you know like when you need to equalise the pressure in your ears and you do and they go pop – it was like that. Well like a combination between that and that sound your stereo makes when you turn on the equalizer and it goes pop with a slight static squeal thrown in. My head did that and my hearing came back on in instant stereo. I'd been gradually getting back some hearing, then it started to fade in and out, and then getting better and better. I'd started to hear more and more noise since yesterday, but then as if some bubble burst inside my ears I felt the pop and the sensation of liquid running down the back of my sinuses and into my throat. I can't begin to explain the feeling of relief or of the nasty sensation of fluid running down the back of my throat.

Rebecca came down the stairs and found me sitting there crying, not bawling, but crying, soft tears dampening my cheeks.

"Tell me what I'm going to do?" I asked Becca-Rebecca.
And she just looked at me a moment and then went back to rolling the joint.

"This' a little out of my league Sherman." But we weren't talking about the predicament, but about Todd and Marjorie and marriage and divorce and love and hate.

I hate my wife today.

"I don't want to go home Rebecca. All this, this ain't me, but it could be," a half laugh. "I'm no island boy, that kid's long time dead, man, long time fucking dead." I take the lit joint from her and smoke. Aaah! "But I could be, you know. I want to eat curried goat or crab back or chicken souse or stewed conch ..." I get up and walk to the window, lifting two of the blinds with my fingers so that I can look out. The sun illuminates my hand, a golden yellow and a stratosphere of lint glows; "I want this life, I don't want the mall on Sundays and my choice of 12 movie screens under one roof." I pause and smoke for a minute. There's a small yellow and black bird hopping back and forth in the branches of the Ficus tree across the way.

41

"You was looking for me?" Dalbert, to Eloise.
"Does your wife always sound so miserable?" Eloise answered.

"My wife is always miserable." He paused a moment then added, "her God demands it of her."

"What?"

"Never mind. You were looking for me?"

"Yep! The fingerprint files you asked for came in, ay."

"I'll soon come."

"Story?" Just as Dalbert hung up the phone Detective Superintendent Macmillan came to sit on his desk.

"No story yet, but I'm working on it." Dalbert put his hands behind his head and stretched his neck forward, rocked it side to side. He was still sore.

"I hear you've been asleep for two days. How's your face?"

"Is alright," touching the still tender spots.

"You fell down they tell me?"

"Tripped on an electric cord. In the dark you know. Tryin' not to wake Grace. " Dalbert looked into his drawer as if occupied.

"Ah, is that so? Whose Range Rover have you got impounded out front there?"

"Range Rover?" sharpening a pencil.

"The white one, they tell me you had it brought in…from Beach Bay maybe?"

"No, no I just did a favour for Effrain Shapiro, you remember him?"

"He's mixed up in all this Sherman thing, isn't he? I'm sure I saw his name in the report. What are you not telling me Dalbert?"

"First you, why don't you tell me what are you not telling me?" Dalbert looked up and smiled.

"Have you got any more of those lovely cigars?"

"Yes."

"Come let's walk and go have a smoke!"

"Dalbert, do we have to go through this all again?" Macmillan had changed from the khakis of that day on the beach to the usual uniform of white short-sleeved shirt and tie with navy blue trousers and brown brogues.

"What all again?" replied Dalbert, examining the end of his cigar.

"The ballet that we keep dancing about your friend Mr. Sherman? Bring him in Dalbert."

They were walking on the lawn of the Glass House, the government office building next to the Central Police Station. A green lawn, dotted with trees, one a beautiful Barrington Pod Tree, surrounded a bronze mushroom of a building, all smoked glass and bronze coloured steel. They stopped under the shade of the Barrington Pod; a large tree with deep green leaves the colour of rubber tree leaves.

"Oh I will." He chuckles, shaking his head. "As soon as I can get my hands on him, Sir."

"Better you get your hands on him than someone else." A nod's as good as a wink to a blind man.

"What are you saying?" Dalbert stopping.

The D.S. took two more steps, stopped but only half way turned back. "A delightful cigar, as good as a Cuban."

"Dominican leaf I believe. What are you not saying to me?"

"I'm saying this's a good cigar and that's all." Smile.

"Oney what you got?" Dalbert had gone straight upstairs to his desk and made the call.

"She been done plenty visitin', that boy name Louis Brandon been with her for lunch."

"Louis, the battyman [the homosexual]?"

"Yeah, an' she was been drivin' in a bus that belong to one Sparky, like a delivery bus, [which he pronounced 'delib urry' bus]. She pick that up and then drop it back off later by the bookstore."

"Sparky. But you haven't seen Sherman?"

"No."

"But he's with her?"

"Lotta action for just one girl."

"Yep, he's with her." Dalbert nodded to himself. "Where they been?" he asked. Then "I wonder what they up to."

And Oney began to give him a rundown of what his boys had seen and heard. Dalbert was abstractly doodling on his desk pad as Oney spoke, when he caught notice of a muscular man of about forty years with little to distinguish him except his erectness like a ballet dancer. And something around his eyes and the way he stood, stopped and moved. There's a specific difference between the British SAS trained spook and the American equivalent.

The British version looks much more like the jogger with three kids who lives next door – no specific haircut, no fashion, no dark glasses; handsome but plain; athletic but not V shaped, square necked muscular. This guy was wearing blue jeans, a dull red cotton shirt, a black belt and brown shoes with socks that didn't match. No clichés but infinitely more dangerous because of it. The SAS man's eyes passed over Dalbert, but you knew he'd already seen everything that he wanted to see, and then Macmillan came striding by purposefully in his stride and the man turned and left. Dalbert wondered if the unstylishness was a part of the disguise.

"Dat Franklin man and them peoples in the Edwards house, they know one another," Oney continued and it wasn't a question. "That Franklin man he come there and stay, he and the boy there seems like old friends…real ole friends."

"Really!" Dalbert lit a cigarette, looked at the end as he exhaled. "Oney, check and see if that delivery van still by the bookstore!"

Dalbert glanced at his watch.

"What the rass are they up to Oney? Eh, what?" he wondered out loud, more to himself than to Oney and you couldn't have been sure exactly who he was talking about.

Dalbert logged on to his email. There waiting for him was an email that he had looked at earlier from SIG-SAUER Sweden with a report on the two weapons that Desmond 'Bad Man' had been carrying when he was killed –

The two SIG Model P239's Ser # ——— *and Ser #* ———
*of which you are inquiring about were part of a very larger shipment
made in February, 1998, to the Israeli Government.*

It was short and sweet. Or not so sweet when you thought about it. What in Christ's name was a Jamaican national in the Caribbean doing with two weapons that had been destined for the Israelis in the Middle East? And was that how Shapiro, being a Jew, had found out about Desmond in the first place?

What exactly was Franklin Carpenter's role in all this?

Nothing in from New York on the phone numbers. He decided to type an email to the detective he'd spoken to as a reminder.

It was all getting very complicated. He glanced at his watch. He made a call to Scotland Yard, asked for an Inspector Everton Desnoes.

"Desi is Dalbert." Both were expatriate Jamaican policemen working for the Queen on different ends of the post-colonial empire. "Desi, if I email you some pictures, can you run a face ID for me?" After a long pause, he added, "very quietly. I mean very very quietly ah, Star!" (Star is a Jamaican proto-nickname, like the American 'buddy'.) Face ID is a very popular system in England, where it is hooked to cameras that are all over cities like London. What happens is that the Face ID computer scans a database of known faces looking for corresponding faces in the crowd that the cameras are watching. The camera can be programmed to scan for a particular face, a general composition or just to cross-reference a scan area with all the known faces.

The system is therefore loaded with the known faces of operatives and policemen, as well as criminals. When an operative's face is spotted the computer doesn't show a record, it simply says *'Face ID confirmed, supervisory password required (agency X)'.*

So what Dalbert was asking was for Desi to feed the system with two faces (to do a backward search so to speak). To plug in one, the new face around the precinct, the SAS face, and two, Wesley Snipes' face and see if they belonged to an agency and which agency they belonged to.

"Wesley Snipes? You want me to load a picture of the real Wesley Snipes in the computer?"

"Well, I don't exactly have a picture of the other guy, do I? Hey, and do me another favour, pretty please," Dalbert added. "There's a back door approach on a man named Franklin Carpenter. I'll send you all the details I have... I jus' don't want the request to come from me, seen. Anything and everything that you can give me." His Jamaican accent was now tinged with just a touch of the Queen's English.

"Is there something I should know?" Desi had asked.
"Yes, I'm quite sure dere is, Star," Dalbert had answered.
"But whatever it is my friend, I don't even know it yet!"

Then he called Eloise.

And then he went to see her:

"So, Eloise, darling, baby, tell me something. I mean, look, here we have suspect number one." He swivelled on the stool and then came back to face the table and rest his hands on two documents. "Hans Dahlem aka Karl Courie aka Hubert Moll." Eloise came to hover next to him.

"His fingerprint on Elmo Gaunt's neck, right? At least, it would seem so. It's an imperfect print...partial. But some key swirls match, right. Anyhow, he's here, this Karl-Hans-Hubert fucker is here. A print that looks like his is here, a gun that's tied to him is here and he knows Gaunt, who's dead." He holds up the photos and then drops first the fingerprint then the digital photo print of Elmo Gaunt's neck onto the countertop.

"We have circumstantial evidence tying him to the gun that killed Gaunt, right. We have eyewitness reports that put him at the house, where Froeman was killed, several times in the days before the killing, right. He's six foot even his file says. So we have suspect number one."

"I thought your Sherman was suspect number one?" Not looking up from the scattered papers.

He turns to look at her. "For some of us. There was that stuff in Gaunt's room that pointed at Sherman. He's six foot one, and left handed," and he smiled. "But! But but but!" He holds up his hands. "Let's not forget that you said that it was likely that whoever killed Gaunt didn't kill Froeman or Desmond Greene. We think that our friend Hans killed Elmo Gaunt."

"You said it yourself, ay, Sherman's six one, and left handed." She had a point.

"Yes, but we know Sherman didn't kill Gaunt. He'd have to be an idiot to kill Gaunt and get caught like that."

"But we guessed that already, Dalbert."

"True, true. Yes we did. Anyhow, Gaunt is, sorry, was an associate of, of this Hans and his mother. We never found the Froeman weapon, right, the possible frying pan but we have all, I don't want to call them clues, we have all this innuendo, these hints, that lead us to this Karl for the Froeman thing." Dalbert paused here and shook his head. "But he's not fuckin' right handed."

"True, but remember this isn't an exact science, Dalbert, it's all just practised bloody supposition ain't it, ay." She smiles.

Dalbert smiled back at that. "Neither of us really believe that, do we, Eloise baby. So what then? Presumably someone's trying to show us this Karl-Hans-Hubert as a suspect for Froeman, but cause he's left handed we know it's not him."

"Did that someone leave that gun at the Gaunt scene as a plant too?"

"I'm confused." Eloise looking up at the ceiling as if thinking.

"Me too, me too. Sherman's left-handed so he couldn't have killed Froeman, ah?"

"Desmond Greene, no murder weapon found either, but we do know that it was a double edged knife about four inches long," Eloise added.

"Yep, and we know Desmond and Froeman were killed within two hours of one another."

"Maybe less." Eloise added.

"Yeah, maybe less, but this's a small, small island, girl. I can be from George Town to West Bay in 20 minutes, 15 at that time of night an' the two of them were dead in half dat distance apart."

"Sherman's tied to the two of them, is that what you're thinking? Again he'd have to be a complete idiot to have done that killing and then call me. I jus' don't know. And why would he kill Desmond, his protection?" He rubbed his eyes with the heels of his palms.

"And he's left handed. Maybe someone wants us to think that they're partners, ay? Sherman and Karl? What about the mother?"

"Ava, Ava, now that's a good one." Dalbert paces. "I wonder whether Franklin Carpenter is left-handed. But what about the bastard that tried to add me to the list of the dead, and it wasn't

Sherman? I mean unless he had an accomplice who likes to hit him real hard."

Dalbert with a finger in the air. "And, and I don't think it was Franklin Carpenter, he'd only just come in, too fast for him to reconnoitre and be ready." He sees in his mind a picture, through the car door, of the man standing in the rain holding Sherman's gun in his left hand.

"Someone beat up Sherman – was that the same man who tried to kill me? What was it he called him? 'A Wesley Snipes lookin' mother-fucker'!" He leant a head against the autopsy room window.

"The two guns that Desmond Greene was carrying were Israeli government issue; why wasn't Sherman's gun loaded with real bullets?"

"Are you talking to me or yourself Dalbert?" Eloise asked, leaning back in her chair.

"A bit of both Eloise, sweetie. Where were we?"

"Nowhere yet, ay."

"True, true, come come let's we go outside and smoke, maybe that'll clear our minds."

"So who's the fourth person?"

"Fourth person? I suppose you're going to tell me, ay?"

"I don't know. Sherman's one, The Couries, the Dahlems, the Molls whoever they fucking are this week and their friend Franklin 'rassclate' Carpenter are two, Shapiro, Effrain Shapiro, three…who's four? Who's four?" He lights another cigarette, paces, turns, throws up his hands. "Who?"

"Maybe the man Franklin's playing more than one side?"

"Maybe." He didn't look unconvinced.

"Maybe it's the police? The government?" Eloise is sitting on a bench against the wall outside the morgue. The world is silent except for the distant hum of a generator somewhere.

"You think? No, no, people keep sayin' that." Dalbert shook his head. "But no, someone would have said something, seen. I would have felt pressure." Then as if thinking about the possibility! "Well, maybe… Macmillan jus' said somethin' cryptic to me…and then a new face, British Intelligence maybe. But no, no, I just don't see it, I'm pretty sure…" and he just lets it trail off. "What else have we got?"

"Evidence?"

"Nothing much Dalbert. All the scenes were very clean. We have the pistol that killed Gaunt, the things in Gaunt's room indicating your mate Sherman…no fingerprints at all except for that convenient one on Gaunt's neck. The two different cigarette ends at the crime-scene, but we weren't able to decipher anything from them. We have the eyewitness reports tying that Karl chap to the house on Boggy Sand where agent Froeman was killed, ay. We have the guns that Desmond Greene was carrying, that in this circuitous way, ay, come right back to your Effrain Shapiro. We know that whoever killed Desmond was a highly skilled man with a knife. And that's it," she concluded.

"We've got the phone call log for Froeman's phone."

"We don't have the New York numbers yet though."

Then after a pause where no one spoke, Eloise continued, "Our favourite boss, Macmillan, is giving you a bit of push, cryptic conversations, strange documents, calls from the Governor's office, the disappearing bodies, lack of evidence, confusing evidence left at scenes, like the guns. There's the pressure to take down this Sherman lad. Sounds like a lot of bloody action to me, ay."

"Very subtle. But let's face it, Sherman does look well and fuckin' good for it if you don't have all the pieces, you know."

"Point. So why haven't you passed Macmillan all the pieces, ay? Why, because you know, Dalbert, subtle or not something's still there, ay. Something real fuckin' subtle ay. The Crown?"

"Britain? Why? What makes you think so, just because it's all so subtle?"

"Exactly because it's subtle. And then the new face."

"What's the Crown got to do with it all, jewels…"

"And documents, you don't know what's in the bloody documents. And lest you forget we're still a British Territory, ay."

"I don't get it." He shakes his head.

"It sounds like the documents might be a key, ay. So, where are the documents?"

"I don't know sweetie, but me, I think Franklin Carpenter's the key. Let's go see who I can go t'row a scare into now."

But what he really wanted to do was to go put some polish on the Aston Martin, to sit in the cool quiet of the warehouse and listen to the engine purr, to dream his little dream of freedom. He looked at his watch to see if there was time enough to just go and sit and smell the leather, knowing full well that there wasn't – dreams tend to require a certain amount of money to fulfil them.

42

Franklin and Karl were sitting on the patio in the shade near the pool.

The wind came across the slightly rippled water and whispered in the long needles of the Casuarina trees that lined the shore. There was what might be called a deafening silence to the spot – a silence that wasn't a reality – the sea and the whsssh-ing of the Casuarinas, the rattle of the Seagrapes were cacophonous.

In what seemed to be the distance, because the breeze was carrying the sound away, were the tones of easy jazz.

Dalbert liked jazz. He slipped off his dark glasses, purposefully folded them slowly, and put them in his top pocket.

The two men were side by side facing outward, seaward, drinking what looked like Bloody Marys, chatting and smoking. They couldn't see him unless they turned. He lit a cigarette, thinking to himself, how elegant they both looked. He checked his own Egyptian cotton shirt that was a delicate blue and the consistency of a silk, if silk could be as heavy as cotton, and dusted the Connolly chocolate leather 'car shoe', driving shoes, with his handkerchief.

Dalbert coughed as he stepped around into the full light of afternoon. Both men turned and Karl nearly fell off his chair, stood, straightened himself, carrying his pack of cigarettes as he went, and smiled.

"Detective, how are you?" He bent around his lighter, then straightened his head and exhaled. Just a moment for composure. "I, I haven't seen you for so many days I was beginning to think that you were dead." He bent and put lighter and cigarettes back on the small table. He was wishing that he had a large sharp knife. In his mind he had a momentary flash of the sound and sensation of killing with a knife. That sucking tension as the body tries to hold onto the blade you've just thrust deep into it and now want to take back out so you can stab it again and let the dying bastard bleed all over the floor.

"No, no Mr. Dahlem, very much alive, just a little bruised." He unfolded the dark glasses and put them back on; dappled sunlight mottled the patio. He glanced around slowly, feeling for the can of mace that was in his pocket. He'd decided against bringing the gun. Never bring a gun to a catfight. He ran a hand back over his baldhead.

"I see that. Accident?"

"I fell over my own two feet," he lied.

"Mine are always so firmly in my mouth I never have the chance to fall over them." Charming smile. "Detective Hannah, have you met Franklin Carpenter?" He stepped aside a little to fully expose Franklin, who then stood.

"We've spoken on the phone, Detective." Pausing before coming forward to offer his hand.

"Yes, yes we have. I didn't realise that you both were, ahm, acquainted?"

"From New York…same social circle," Karl added, seeming to enjoy the intrigue of the moment. "May I fix you a drink, Detective? No wait, it was Inspector, wasn't it?"

"Yes, but Detective is fine. And yes, I'd love something cool to drink. Are those Bloody Marys?" He spoke carefully without falling into saying 'Sport'.

"Yes."

"Then one of those will do me fine." He glanced at his watch, indicated himself a chair and then sat down.

"Good choice, Inspector, Hu…, Hans makes a fine Bloody Mary," taking the next seat. Franklin was wishing for a gun, a nice, say, Walther PPK in .380 calibre with the ½ inch barrel extension to fit a little eight inch noise suppressing silencer and perhaps someone nice and cold blooded to shoot it for him. He didn't want to get blood on the Armani.

Karl went inside to mix the drinks. He stood in front of the bar trolley that sat just inside the living room. He opened the ice bucket and inside was a .38 special, he looked at it a moment. He put the lid back on. In the utensil drawer of the trolley was a four inch long double edged knife. Karl touched it, then closed the drawer and went in the kitchen for ice. He opened the freezer and there on the shelf was a machete.

"Ah, the choices," he mumbled and shook his head.

"So Mr. Carpenter, you've come to join our little party?"
"Well…may I have one of your cigarettes, Inspector?" And it becomes like a game: 'show no fear' was what it was called. Adversaries, circling one another.

"Thank you Detective, your first name is Dalbert, yes? Do you mind if I call you Dalbert?" He exhaled. "Well yes, yes, I thought that I'd better, considering the trouble our man Sherman has got himself into. We have a corporate presence here to protect and that's not a matter for playing games with."

"Yes." Karl reappeared to hand Dalbert his drink. "Thank you. So, Mr. Dahlem, your mother?"

"Unwell Det…sorry, Inspector. She's prone to migraines. She's resting now."

And then as if on cue she appeared in the doorway.

Time will tell on you, you old Jezebel. So how long will the wicked reign over my people.

She looked like a ghost – pale and hollow, with dark rings around her eyes and a certain distant madness to her expression. And she was naked and stooped, the broken example of her other self.

They all stood. Clive, the dog, trotted pass her onto the patio, stopped and sat to scratch himself vigorously.

"Karl, Karl baby are you there? Hubert, where's Hubert?"

"My father and my brother," Karl said softly to Dalbert, then, "Mumsy, Hans is here, come relax," as he dashed towards her.

"Hubert, Hubert, ah, my handsome lovely boy. I need you, Hubert, mummy has peed herself." Her hair was dishevelled and her eyes were insane.

Karl ushered her back into the house.

"Well, yes. So, on that note, Inspector, shall we sit?" There was an uncertain half hesitation, from the lingering moment of embarrassment, then both sat.

"And perhaps you can fill me in on what you know now. My last report was, I believe, that our Mr. Sherman had run away and that he was a murder suspect. Is that still the case?" in that slow studied way of his.

"Oh yes, he's run away...but no, no I don't think he's much of a murder suspect." Then a long pause. Then, "Anymore." And Dalbert left it at that.

"Does she often behave this way?" Dalbert turning in his chair to look at the door through which Karl and Ava had gone, half lifting a hand to point to their departure.

"I couldn't say." Franklin, not completing his turn to the door but faking it – obviously immune to the suffering of others.

"Strange," Dalbert said, then turned back in his chair to look at Franklin.

Clive came trotting back from somewhere, his hairy padded feet all sandy, a very satisfied look on his face.

"So you no longer think of Mr. Sherman as a suspect, then?" changing the subject back.

Madness is always a difficult reality to discuss.

"Well, you know, it's an investigation." He half looked back at the house again, troubled by the past scene. "New things come to light from time to time." He continued uncomfortably then tapped the cigarette on the gold box.

"Yes, yes, certainly. Like what?"

"Well, like traceable weapons, like fingerprints, perhaps some DNA results from hair samples, blood serology, things like that. Crimes always have evidence, Mr. Carpenter: a missing frying pan found, the height of a shooter calculated. But, of course all that may exclude Mr. Sherman altogether." Smile knowingly. "There's still certain evidence linking him to the crimes." He flourished, as if throwing Franklin Carpenter a life-line onto which he expected him to cling.

"I see, yes, a process isn't it. Do you think he might, ahm, well that he might have been working with Bryce?" He smoked more slowly but spoke more quickly than usual. And then he stood and walked, his back to Dalbert, to the edge of the patio.

"I don't know, say…" He turned partway back, speaking sideways at Dalbert without looking at him. "Maybe he was feeding him, Bryce, our corporate information. We have investigators looking into just that possibility back in New York," Franklin continued. "We think we may have found a link. I'll know in two days; and will have a report ready for the police here and in New York." It was a monologue full of pause and effect, with the cigarette used as a tool of punctuation and the patio as a stage. Finishing, he had his back to Dalbert, who still sat in his chair.

"I haven't seen any evidence of that yet." Dalbert stood and walked up next to Franklin. "But I wouldn't doubt that Bryce was working together with someone in your company. I don't doubt that at all." Dalbert had his left hand in his pocket, his chin slightly tilted up and to the right as he brought his cigarette to his mouth in the way that Noel Coward was always pictured doing.

"You have evidence of that?" Franklin was not looking at Dalbert. Both were standing on the low wall at the edge of the patio, smoking affectedly, like actors on a stage.

"I might make some up." He chuckled. "Don't worry, just a police joke," he added.

"Ahh." Franklin, not enjoying the humour.

Karl paused only a moment in the living room. He looked back inside as if troubled about leaving his mother unattended.

Then, he lifted the lid of the ice bucket and wrapped his fingers around the gun, took out his hand and opened the drawer, touched the knife and then saw the ice pick. He smiled and touched his tongue to his lips. He slipped the ice pick up his long sleeve so that the haft was facing downward and he could just let it slide down his sleeve into his hand.

"Is she okay?" Dalbert asked as Karl finally came back out.

"No. No I don't think so, Inspector, mother is a manic-depressive," he took a deep breath and exhaled; "a complete fucking lunatic actually." He had a glass of vodka on the rocks in his hand and took a long sip.

"Ah!" Dalbert, not knowing quite what to say.

"How is your drink?" The hand holding the ice pick was bouncing nervously against his leg.

"Fine."

"I presume this was not for a social call, yes?"

"No." He feels suddenly nervous between the two of them. It's that sensation you get when the dark closes around you and you're alone and you begin to wonder if vampires really do exist or werewolves or small, sharp-teethed, dirty, little evil demon nasties.

"No, I really came to ask you some questions, fill in a few blanks you know, Chief." Dalbert pivots away, to get his cigarettes and put some distance between them. Franklin and Karl turn from their places by the edge of the patio to face him. He lights up and faces them across 10 feet of no man's land.

"Eyewitnesses put you at or around a certain house on Boggy Sand Road in the days leading up to a murder. You and your mother were both with Chris Sherman on the night of this murder.

Chris Sherman finds himself in this same house with the murder victim."

"Is there a question in all that for me, Inspector?" And he let the haft of the ice pick slip three inches down the sleeve.

Franklin moves a little. Dalbert watches him, shifting his weight.

"Were you at this house?"

"Which house?"

"The Griffin and Dunne house on Boggy Sand Road, Boss Man? The grey one with the all-glass front window."

As if he's suddenly made a decision, he lets the ice pick slip out of his sleeve and steps forward.

Dalbert, sensing something, tenses. His hand tightens on the can of mace, and he starts to pull it out of his pocket.

Karl passes him and blatantly sets the ice pick on the table next to Dalbert's cigarettes before helping himself to a cigarette.

"I like that house, I like Boggy Sand Road…we had this discussion previously, if you remember. We used to stay there when we came to Cayman, mother and I; maybe it was nostalgia, you know. And well, you know, the beach, it is quite nice." A smile, a taunt in the eyes.

"Yes, yes, you said that you'd been here before," as if taking notes on a mental piece of paper. "Your mother was with Chris Sherman after the Henzel party?"

"Yes."

"She left with him?"

"You know the answer to that question, I believe, you did ask it once before." His left hand in the armpit of the right, the right arm crooked, the wrist limp, but bending first to bring the cigarette to the lips and then returning – flexion and extension – for the exhale.

"Yes, yes, I do, an' I did. Just clarifying things, you know, since our last chat. You see how this looks, you're attached to the house, you're attached to Chris Sherman, Chris Sherman is attached to the body."

"Accomplices."

"Exactly! Exactly!" Wagging a finger, and now, as if feeling completely in control of the situation he sits, picks up his drink and sips it. Picks up his cigarettes. "I've been tryin' to quit." Then "What do you know of a man named Elmo Gaunt?" As he sets down the cigarette pack and picks up the ice pick.

So here are the choices: think fast and lie, kill somebody quickly, or say 'what the fuck' and tell the truth.

"I see where you go with this, Inspector. You've perhaps checked immigration and you find that mother and I have not been to Cayman Islands before as Hans and Ingrid Dahlem. But perhaps you find that we have as Ava and Karl Courie. And perhaps you know that Elmo Gaunt is" (chuckle) "was an associate of Ava and Karl Courie...yes?"

"Yes." He taps the ice pick on his thumbnail.

"Then yes, we do know him!"

"Did you kill him?" Set down the ice pick, pick back up the cigarettes.

"Now, Detective, please, I would hardly like to answer yes to that now, would I?"

"Probably not." He taps the cigarette on the thumbnail. "But I thought that I might try you know, Sport." Lights the cigarette, inhales, exhales, smiles. "Why aren't you travelling under your real name, Sport?" Dalbert again from left field after a brief pause. Sets down the lighter, picks up the ice pick again.

"Anonymity." Karl seems not in the least disturbed. "We are actually legally entitled to the names Hans and Ingrid Dahlem.

Our names were legally changed in Austria as a precaution in a case that you're really not entitled to know about." Smile. "I can show you the legal documentation, which you may feel free to check."

"Ah, and are you entitled to the names Ava and Karl Courie?" He feels the end of the ice pick, sharp!

"You've been doing homework, Inspector. The answer to that too is yes." Smile again – and certainly his brain is quietly going over the ways in which he would like to flay the skin from Dalbert's body while he were still alive.

Dalbert looked at Franklin, who, looking bored, was sipping his drink. "Oh don't look at me, Inspector, I've only got the one name."

"Yes. But you see now why your Mr. Sherman begins to look a lot less like a candidate for the electric chair, seen. Well, that's me done, so, I'm going to go now." Dalbert stood, then he stopped, hand hovering above the glass he'd just set down and slowly straightened up. "Mr. Moll what do you know bout a woman in New York named Anita Liebermann? I only ask this 'cause the gun that killed Elmo Gaunt was originally registered in her name."

"I thought you'd killed him?" Franklin said staring in the direction that Dalbert had gone, leaving only the bad taste of his presence in their mouths.

"So did I." He swallowed the vodka in one shot.

"Well, Hubert, darling, he looks awfully good for a man with thirteen bullets in him."

"Fourteen…" and picking up the ice pick he stabbed it into the table.

"Well, then, next time eh!"

"Obviously… I'd better go check on Mother."

Mother's dead, who's got the will?

Karl lifts her from the bathroom floor where he had left her earlier and into the bed. There's a small trickle of blood down the back of her neck, from a wound behind her ear. A small wound made by the ice pick that he'd stuffed up into her brain, while he held her close against his chest, rocking her back and forth and whispering 'Who loves ya baby' to her softly.

He places her on the bed that he's already turned down and pulls the cover over her as if putting her to bed. Her blood gets on the pillow.

"How is she?" Franklin asks when Karl reappears.

"Hmm? I gave her some Valium, she'll sleep," he lied.

43

"So, who do you think you want to bug?" Becca Rebecca had asked me earlier.

"Dalbert, definitely Dalbert." I had to pause to think about that, not about Dalbert but about who might know more than I did about this little predicament.

"I want to bug Dalbert, but that's going to be hard. I'm not talking too loudly am I? I feel like I'm talking loudly today." I breathed out heavily, I'm nervous. "And Franklin's here, our fucking boss!" I was a bit disdainful. "Franklin Carpenter, I'd like to bug Franklin... I'd like to annoy the fuck out of Franklin actually 'cause I'm sure there's something that bastard's not telling me about all this. I'm sure."

Of course I was discussing this then as if I were living in a perfect world where the job would be easy and the consequences nonexistent.

"Shapiro, cause I just can't fucking figure him out. Can't figure him out at all. Do you know where Franklin is?" I'm angry and I'm speaking tougher than I really am.

"He's staying at the Hyatt, he called this morning, said he'd be in the office tomorrow..." Something's obviously bugging her. *"How are your ears?"*

"Sharp noises bug me."

"I'm going to ask my doctor about it."

"Okay, what's bugging you?"

"Gee, fuck, I don't know, matey," she shakes her head. *"What do you think?"*

"I don't know."

"This is bloody crazy, Sherman. Let's not do this." She paused a moment, *"Crazy!"*

"I can't do this without you, Rebecca." Pleading.

"Fuck." She grabbed the pack of cigarettes and stormed off, did like a circle of the kitchen and came back. *"We can't do this Sherman."*

"They're going to kill me."

"Who?"

"If I knew that I wouldn't be half as scared."

"I gotta go take a walk," she said and shook her head at me.

Here's where in the movie version we would see her make the call to the indistinct voice again – the call filled with second thoughts and doubts about moralities.

"I don't know about this."

"You don't have a choice, just do it, deal with it."

It took her ten minutes to get back. *"I have an idea,"* she said. *"I think. Louis."*

"Who's Louis?"

And she smiled ever so mischievously. *"A friend."*

"Do you really really want to bug Dalbert? Really?" She asked again. And then when I nodded, said, *"I may need to*

do some drugs soon." Eyes open mockingly wide, eyebrows exaggerated.

She smells just right. In a French movie called <u>After Sex</u>...
'Men' the actress had said *'smell of geraniums'.* Rebecca smells of tropical rain; that spicy pimento and bay leaf smell. I know that I will remember her smell long after she has left me. And I know that she will leave me. That's inevitable.

She stood there yesterday, just stood, in front of the stereo; you'd almost call it lazily. Relaxed, with her hip popped out to the left...she was in panties. Just ordinary panties. No bra. I couldn't see her breasts, just her back. And in that one subtle laconic stance she said it all.

In her eyes you can see *'the been there done that and swallowed the evidence'.*

"Why are you here?"

She's lying on her front and I'm lying on my back, the air conditioning has just booted up and I feel the cool air wafting across my chest and my cock and my thighs and my toes.

"What was it you said... *'I believe fate has brought us here'*?" I asked.

"I'm just a prisoner of your love." She rolled onto her side. "But that's it, isn't it, that's it. You love me and that's nice for me. You're soft and sweet and untainted."

"All the things you're not?" Trying to read her mind.

"All the things I'm not used to," she corrected me. "You are good for me Chris Sherman."

"And I bring out the mother in you." I don't roll onto my side – I want to, but, I don't. I don't want to look into her eyes.

She smiled and touched me twice, ever so gently and I felt my cock stir, the physical manifestation of which was a violent penile lurch.

"Oooh!" she said. And touched me again. Like a performing animal the cock repeated the movement, less aggressively this time as it had hardened a notch. "How lovely. All this is so serious matey; you like fucking me, Sherman?"

"You are like a drug to me," and I swallowed hard and coughed so that I had to look away.

"I like fucking you Sherman. You're tender and you take direction well." She smiled at that. "I want to tell you I love you Sherman. I want to." She stopped then and stared away. "I want to," as if she were sad.

"I like being here. I like being loved by you." I like to hear her talk like this. "I feel so much better since I met you Sherman." Such a nice smile. "I'm…shit, how to explain it. Christ I don't know, but look at me I'm smiling. You know, the other day when you were gone, when you were hiding, I felt that I had lost goodness – I met my old self again in a few lines of Crystal Meth." She continued, "I'm your drug, you're my therapy. I don't need to find happy when you're here, Sherman. And I like to fuck you."

And we made love again, softly, two people hiding from the world and from themselves.

"I've got to find somewhere to put you," Rebecca said later, meaning somewhere to hide me.

"Present," she says and lays a .38 snub nose police special without the hammer on my chest. It's cold and very heavy. I'm always amazed by the weight of guns.

Why is everybody giving me guns these days?

44

A day later I'm living in new digs near town. And that same day I'm going around the roundabout at the end of the Harquail bypass, I'm looking for Radio Shack. And I've missed Radio Shack when I see the locksmith shop. I pull in. I'm driving Sparky's van and so I take out the key and go to get it copied. I look in one of the company vans that's parked out front.

What I'm looking for is right on the seat…a grey steel tool box, no lock, with the word LAB written on it in big Caterpillar yellow letters and another tool box right next to it.

I look at my watch as I leave and realize that it's nearly lunchtime and maybe if I wait they'll drive out for lunch and I can have my shot at boosting his gear.

I sit, sipping a coffee from the Texaco gas station and waiting. And while I wait, I think about horses for some odd reason. I haven't ridden in years. I loved horses when I was a '*bwoy*', we used to ride all the time in Grenada. I don't think I've ridden a horse in 20 years. I'd like to ride a horse today. It seems like such a perfectly cool breezy day, good for horse riding or golf.

And then, suddenly, I see two Cable and Wireless guys abandon their telephone van on the side of the road and go into the locksmith. And it must be my lucky day. I follow them inside, but everybody's busy and from inside you can't see the vans and so I turn and walk back outside.

I boost the locksmith kits as I pass the open window and stop at the Cable and Wireless van...

I could get a field phone, I could get a couple of sets of Clip-ins – I might find some spread spectrum transmitters and, oooh yeah, maybe a Dracon master hunter. I wanted a couple of other bits and pieces, but it would be a rush job, so I would just have to grab some quick stuff and a tool belt and make a dash back to the van.

In for a penny, in for a pound – Just do it! And I do.

Louis, I was told, could do anything. Louis is a Caymanian. Well, actually he's got one Caymanian parent, mother, who grew up in Jamaica and one Jamaican parent, father, who grew up in Cayman. He's a tall, stocky, olive-complexioned guy of 35 with Dolce and Gabana eye-glasses, Bally moccasins, Hugo Boss ensemble and a fantastic scent which he tells me is Shishedo for men and only available in Canada. I thought Louis was gay when I first met him. But turns out he's just immaculate, articulate, elegant and effeminate (and well perhaps sometimes he might bend both ways just a little, if only occasionally).

(If we're talking axiology here, what's Louis's value to me? Well in this story Louis becomes my bravery.)

"What do you need?" was his first question.

"A cigarette."

He offered me the pack, Malboros. The nail on the little finger of his left hand was just a little longer than the others, all beautifully manicured – 80's coke fashion.

"I need a couple of directional or parabolic microphones," I tossed out, exhaling smoke skyward.

"Oh, go on," he scrunched up his nose at me. "Give me something hard."

"That's not hard?"

"Easy!"

"A laser microphone?" I tried.

He checked his nails. "You know, you're not really testing my abilities here."

"I want to put a bug on the Governor and at least two in the Central Police Station."

He looked up at me then and just smiled happily at me.

45

I glanced at my watch as I knelt in front of the door. I could pick almost any lock with a diamond tip pick – it's called that because of the shape of its head, faceted like a diamond (or a trapezoid really) with an opening where the last facet would go against the handle. Between that and a simple Shepherd's crook (you get the picture) 90% of my lock work possibilities were solved. If I came up against a dead wall I would normally resort to the pick gun. I was at the top of Elizabethan Square, an office building in downtown George Town, styled like an Elizabethan or Tudor building encircling a central courtyard with shops facing both inward and outward. I had climbed the stairs just to the left of the lobby of British Caymanian Insurance. A half floor behind me was a door with no name on it, nothing but a peephole – which made me nervous. But Louis was standing behind me making me brave.

I sweated a little. My hands were shaking, but still, in 23.6 seconds we were out onto the roof of the Elizabethan square. The air was fresh. The sky was sunny.

There was a large green bank of Trane air conditioning units, which was good, because we were dressed like local A/C technicians in uniforms Louis had begged, borrowed or stolen; I never asked which. They even had the orange Trane logo on the shirt pocket (Louis can do anything).

I took a moment to look around; there was something that looked like a camera to my left, it was on the other section of the roof that looked down across the police station's back lot. I put my pick set back into my bag next to this cute clear green sheath about the thickness of a credit card that held the newest example of Swiss Army Knife technology.

I studied the camera – it wasn't focused on us, and it wasn't on the enclosure below. It looked like it was looking back at another camera across the way…odd.

I walked along the bank of A/C units as if they were my only concern, looking out the corner of my eyes at what I needed to see. It was hot up there and I was sweating. My mouth was dry. Louis was whistling somewhere behind me. The bank of A/C units was divided into 2 groups of three and I moved between them. Taking out an electric screw driver I unscrewed one of the panels so that I could use it to block the vision of the other camera across the way on a radio tower on the far side of the station just inside the back lot. That one seemed to be watching this roof, specifically the camera to my left. I didn't get it – two cameras, one watching the other.

My breathing was heavy. I sat down with my back to the nearest unit trying to get into the thin, half-wedge of shade that it cast. My eyes hurt and there was a dull ringing in my ears. I stretched my neck and had a distant urge to throw up.

"Okay, okay – let's go look at the other location."

The next stop was easier. Piccadily Parkade, sixth floor. You just take the elevator up; no locks, no security.

Out in the bright sunlight I closed my eyes for a moment, felt its warmth. From up there I had an unobstructed view of several buildings – Christ, if I wanted to do some listening in this town it would be so easy – The Maples and Calder buildings were probably out of range, Queensgate Bank too; too much space, noise and heat distortion in between. But, I could probably listen to most of what Royal Bank didn't want me to hear, Bank of China, Barclays, Scotia and I've definitely got a great line of sight on the window that Dalbert sits next to. Middle floor, third from the left. There's a television antenna up on the roof already, and a Cable and Wireless Cell site; the laser microphone wouldn't stand out amongst all that…camouflage.

I walked to the far edge of the building and looked out at the harbour, Hog Sty Bay. Louis stayed by the door; he was slowly revolving, looking around.

There are three cruise ships at anchor offshore – the Carnival Destiny, God she's big. It's beautiful, it's warm, the sea's so blue and sparkling. Light twinkles and dances off it like a disco ball. I don't want to come down off of this roof and back into reality – like all those tourists wandering the streets below who don't want the holiday to end, who don't want to go back to their credit card bills.

I lit a cigarette and leant against the wall. Slowly I smoked. My ribs hurt.

Down below preparations are being made for Pirates Week, public works is dropping off some barracades. It'll kick off tonight at seven with a fireworks display and then a street party and dance. Tomorrow will be, the Pirates landing, a street parade and then another dance. The streets will be packed with Pirates and debauchery.

When I turn, Louis is standing there by the door of the stairwell, his hands cupped together at his crotch, waiting, unmoving, patient... well dressed.

"So?" Louis asked.

"Perfect, I'm worried though that the camera on the radio tower on the far side of the station is watching this camera here." I tapped the little drawing I'd done.

"That's not a camera." Louis, casually as if it were an unimportant tidbit of information.

"What is it then?"

"They're for laser transmissions, data stream transmission via laser. All the government offices are linked like that."

"Ahh."

"Are you sure you want to go up there?"

"Sure enough."

I feel myself slowly deflating; back in the van I start to relax from my head to my toes as if I'm doing some Yoga exercise. I actually feel the tension flowing out of me and my scalp is left tingling with its passing. I close my eyes for a moment and breathe – 2, 3, 4 – inhale, exhale.

"Are you really going to do this?"

Was I really going to do this? Go James Bond? Yes, hell yes, maybe. The evolving me is going to do this; I'm, what is that word that they use: empowered. I'm making things happen, kicking off my shoes, letting my hair grow out, taking it easy and kicking some ass. I might even grow a little goatee on my chin with a soul patch just below my lip. Fuck you! I am man, hear me roar!

"I'm going to have another look upstairs."

"I've gotta go," says Rebecca who had just arrived at the van with some lunch. "Louis, can you give me a drive?"

"Sure. You okay, Buddy?" he asked me.

"Yeah, yeah fine, thanks. I'm okay. So, we'll start to do this tomorrow, huh, while everyone's occupied with Pirates?"

46

I walk from the shade into the light; from the lower, covered level of the top floor out into the sunlight of the top floor of the car park. I stop and revolve slowly scanning the skyline. I hear a cough and slowly turn in its direction – Wesley Snipes is visiting. I start to back up.

"You don't listen so well." He's lost the bad West Indian accent.

"Are you going to hurt me again?"

"I might."

"See, I was afraid of that." And I reach around my back and pull out the .38 that Rebecca gave me.

And in reply he reaches around and pulls out a larger gun, a 9mm that looks like a Glock, I think.

This is right when the car drives up the ramp. It's one of those new Lincoln Navigators in a wine red with all that shiny chrome that really sells them. This is a cool car and 'Effy' Shapiro is driving it.

"Hello!" he says.

And I think to myself *'always bring a big Ford to a gunfight!'* The car is between me and Wesley now.

"You don't mind if I take him away, do you?" Effy says to Wesley as his window finishes going down.

"Oh! I can always find him later," says Wesley. He doesn't turn more than a fraction as he hears Paul, Effy's 'muscle', open the door from the stairwell that's above and behind him. "A friend of yours?" He jerks a head to indicate Paul, who hasn't walked into sight yet.

It's a bit of a tense little moment.

"Yes, yes." Effy raises an eyebrow, bites his bottom lip and nods slowly. "Fun, fun, fun! So no need for any gunplay then, ah? The wrong people might get hurt." He waves a hand, palm vertical, from side to side.

Wesley's a professional and I see him calculating the odds of the little challenge and somehow I believe that he feels fairly confident that he can kill Paul and Effy and me. But still he simply smiles and says, "Yes."

"Get in," Shapiro says to me. Then. "Quickly, Sherman, before he changes his fucking mind."

I get into the car.

Shapiro backs up slowly so that he doesn't have to take his eyes off our Wesley Snipes.

Paul backs slowly towards the exit door to the stairwell.

Wesley doesn't move, but he seems very relaxed.

We leave the sunshine and enter the shade. Wesley waves, a short wave, a sort of flick of the wrist that brings the palm around.

"Your lucky day!" Shapiro backs up to where Paul has just come out of the stairwell door.

"Yeah, yeah, my lucky day. Have you got a cigarette?"

"Paul, keep your eyes open," Effy says as he pulls to a stop at the exit. "Stay around for 5 minutes or so, okay?"

We're driving, neither of us speaking, and I'm left with myself again: *You've navigated with raging soul far from the paternal home, passing beyond the sea's double rocks, and you now inhabit a foreign land...* It comes to me, something I'd read inside a collection of Camus; he hadn't said it first, it's Greek (or something), originally. Anyhow...

Sometimes you feel that way; like you're so far away from everything that's normal to me – imagine Captain Cook and his men finding the absolute abnormality of Australia; a reality completely different from anything they've ever known. Hah, I'm sitting in this Navigator with my feet up and the window open and it's like I'm living the life of some odd antipodal antithesis of myself as I smoke and I listen to the radio chitchat.

And I suddenly don't really want to be doing this; I'd like to be lying on the beach somewhere relaxing, burying Todd's legs in the warm sand and watching him giggle as he pops them out, the sand first cracking and then giving way, his skinny legs with the large kneecaps breaking free. Then standing there, his body coated like a sugared doughnut with crystals of sand.

'I could film this,' I suddenly think. 'A young man's struggle for his truth!' I consider...this would be great. I sit up and look for the camera.

'How'd I start it?'

'Where the fuck have I put the camera?' And I say it a bit loudly in my head, like I'm internally angry or something. 'Ah.' I remember it, I get a picture of it, under a shirt that I've taken off and Stanley's <u>Into the Dark Continent</u>, which I'm still trying to read.

I see it in my room in the new digs that Becca baby found for me, just down and around and across from the Blue Parrot, which is fast becoming my favourite Caymanian landmark. A friend of a retired friend of an acquaintance's boss' wife's sister's house. It's a nice, small, plain, concrete box house, like 60's Hollywood Florida. It's got a gorgeous overflowing Poor Man's Orchid in the front yard all full of constant purple colour.

I close my eyes and breathe deeply; my nose feels dry.

I really do have to get back to reading that book.

"Any idea who that guy was?" invades my daydream.

I turn to look at Effy Shapiro quizzically. "What?" Because I'd been in deep thoughts.

"Who was he, that guy?"

"He looks a lot like Wesley Snipes," I say.

"Now, friend, tell Uncle Effy what's the likelihood that Wesley Snipes is trying to kill you on some fucking rooftop in Grand Cayman." He strokes his cheek, pulls at it really with the friction of two fingers

"I don't know – but you have to admit he looks an awful lot like Wesley Snipes. I mean, it could happen, right? Suppose that the movie star thing's just a cover." I smile because I know I'm chatting shit. "How'd you come across me?"

"We've been looking for you. Wanted to find you before Dalbert did."

I'm thinking that I'd write the screenplay…calling it what? 'Looking for Dalbert?' Who'd play Dalbert?

Delroy Lindo of course.

47

"I found dat man Sherman," Oney said to Dalbert. **"We was** followin' the next man, Shapiro…anyhow, long story, I report dat later…dey gone up to Shapiro 'ouse."

"Cool. Look, Oney, keep a close eye on dem for the next little while please."

Dalbert looked at the messages on his desk, shuffling and reshuffling the pink slips. There were two that Grace had called and one from Eloise. He tapped the two from Grace.

Dalbert exhaled – let the air run wild from his body, expelling the duppies (West Indian ghosts) that had gathered in his corners during the day. He stood and went to the filing cabinet by his desk and pulled out the file he had on Stewart Bryce.

He had read it a few times, thought about it when he walked, talked, went to the bathroom. Thought about it when he went to the Bahamas right after Bryce had been found to have a house in Cayman. Thought about it differently on his way back to Cayman.

He stopped a moment and his fingers walked across the tops of the file folders. Reaching his destination he tapped it twice and then pulled out the file on Franklin Carpenter as well.

Sitting heavily in his chair he looked around the room as he slid open his desk drawer.

It was 7 p.m. The day shift was over and so the room was pretty quiet.

He poured himself a nice tot of rum.

He still hadn't called Grace and (fucking well) wasn't planning to. A long sip of the rum (the smell, the warmth, the bite, the exhaling breath) and he leaned back, rested the glass on his forehead and closed his eyes.

Sitting up suddenly he picked up his phone and dialled the immigration department at the airport.

"Tamara baby, how yu do? Listen baby girl I need a favour…"

A plane passes over and it's very loud, and it's then that Shapiro pulls over and turns to me and says, "Where are the documents Sherman?" It's very matter of fact, if tinged with a shade of exasperation. And I don't like the look on his face.

"Documents again, I don't know about any documents. Why'd you give me a fucking gun that was loaded with blanks?" I suddenly blurt out bravely.

He doesn't even look at me. "So you'd feel safe but you wouldn't kill anybody by mistake." He scratches his temple with the back of a finger. "Anyhow, stop changing the fucking subject. Did you find something at Bryce's, Sherman?" This time he turns to me.

"I did, I did."

"Bryce was my associate."

"Yes."

"He had other associates," as if he knows something, as if he's asking me a question, as if he's asking me if I know something. He's looking at me, and his long chubby fingers are quietly tapping on the wheel.

"Who?" I swallow a little hard.

He doesn't answer that question. "Since you've popped up, life's been quite tense around here Sherman," and he seems to like that judging by the smile. "And I think that it's got a lot to do with some missing documents." He smiles again. "I suddenly get the impression that the documents were Bryce's safe ticket. They might've been my safe ticket too."

"Meaning?" I'm curious.

"By osmosis, you know." I picture him, Shapiro, wearing a hat, a fedora with a large brim. He isn't wearing one, but I see him that way. "His safety trickles down to be my safety. He's dead, and I'm not so safe anymore." We're stopped at a light and slowly he runs fingers across his forehead, eyes closed.

"I thought you said you weren't the type that they killed."

Shrug. "I could be wrong. I have a feeling that's why you're not dead yet, Sherman…they're not sure if you've found anything. Have you found anything?"

And I don't know what to answer. And the way he speaks makes me nervous.

I hesitate and then he says, "Sherman, Bryce and I were friends, not just associates, but friends. We trusted one another." And perhaps I get the implication.

"Yes and no," I said and then added quickly, "I found what might be them, I hid them, they're gone from where I hid them."

This is where I start to get an image of me dashing, frantically nervous, out to the car in the rain at Beach Bay; of opening the right rear door and stuffing the documents up under the seat. And then the rain diffuses and I'm in the sunlight, remembering me scared and shaking and approaching the Range Rover in the police parking lot. I'm freaking out inside, that much I remember clearly, as I open the left rear door and reach up under the seat and find nothing. And then I bolt.

Right side in, left side out. Fuck! I'd looked in the wrong place.

"That might be why Wesley Snipes was going to kill you. Maybe they've recovered the documents and..." Effy stopped. Maybe I was white and sweating. "You okay?" he asked.

"Yeah, yeah." And I'm not really paying any attention. "Sorry, sorry it's been a lot of shit going down. I'm... Effy, can I get out here? Right here, can I get out right here? I feel like throwing up."

"It mightn't be safe."

"Effy, I don't have anything. If I have something I'll talk to you. I'm going to get out here, okay?"

"Okay." He's unsure, I can see that, and so am I, I'm unsure, very unsure. But, but, but I have to get out of that fucking car and do it now.

They've already blockaded Cardinal Avenue and are setting up a sound system on the back of a flat-bed truck. The party starts here.

48

How was I going to do this?

I'm back, standing across the road from the police station. But, and this is a big but, the Range Rover's not out front anymore, it's out back, behind a tall fence and a gate. I lean back against the wall. It's four something in the afternoon. The traffic's building already. 4:35, it's 4:35.

The gate into the compound is open, but it just seems too public right now, very public.

I think that I'd better go call Rebecca, then remember that she's probably still meeting with Franklin. I decide that I'll make my raid after dark, hoping for the distraction of tonight's festivities. (Maybe I can get Louis to do it.)

That's when I see Wesley Snipes strolling in the bright sunshine from the direction of the Glass House, the government offices, and walk in through the front door of the police station.

I just close my eyes and breathe deeply.

4:45, Oney calls Dalbert at his desk.

"We lose the bwoy. He get out of Shapiro car an' we lose him in town!"

"In town? What time is it Oney." But it's not really a question 'cause he's looking at his watch. "Listen, put two boys on the street and see if you can come up with him." He leans over to look out the window. "I'm gonna go take a walk around too," he tells Oney.

There's a stall on the waterfront selling Pirate paraphernalia. It takes me fifteen minutes to walk there. Authentic bandana replicas, you know, for you to tie around your head so you really look the pirate part. T-shirts, that look like a shirt with a jerkin, a vest: genuine pretend, cotton and colours. Cut-off trousers with tassled bottoms, all black and white striped of course, true to the style of the times, I think sarcastically.

So here I could be, for the price of a few shekels, the comic book version of the pirate. I buy a bandana and a red cloth for a sash and a plastic sword. Gotta look the part. I'm of course thinking disguise here. It'll be dark soon. Gotta look the part.

Next door(-ish) is Mr. Arthur's shop. I go in and buy a pack of cigarettes.

Do Pirates wear Ray Ban sunglasses? Do they smoke Benson and Hedges Gold?

5:15 and Dalbert is standing in the shade of a Chefalaro tree at the corner of the Scotia Bank building on Cardinal Avenue. The crowd around him is growing.

Leaning around the corner to avoid the breeze as he lights a cigarette he sees Wesley Snipes moving fast along the cloister in front of the post office. He looks away not recognizing him, then looks back.

"Who the fuck else could it be D," he says to himself, and watches intently from his 'hide'.

Wesley pauses and starts to cross the street. Minister Jefferies is coming the other way, crossing from the direction of British Outpost. They meet on the island in the middle of the road. Standing in the sparse shade they speak briefly, as if not speaking to one another and then part ways, Wesley going off in the direction of British Outpost and Minister Jefferies heading down toward Coffee and Bite. Dalbert glances at his watch.

Dalbert wonders if he should follow Wesley.

His phone rings.

"Yes."

It's Oney.

"The girl, Rebecca, it seems is meeting with two men, one the same Franklin, one unidentified." He gives Dalbert a brief description, which doesn't instantly ring any bells, but gives him a strange feeling of premonition anyhow.

At 5:35 the people are thronging the streets as if going home they might suffer the potential to miss something, ooooh, exciting! But nothing's happening yet, except the testing of the odd instrument on the back of the flat bed trailer that's facing the waterfront. It's a mass lurk. A few thousand people in party limbo, like that 30 minute wait after you take your first Viagra.

Rebecca's carrying Louis' phone for safety sake – no traces, at least that's what we think. I call the number from a phone booth that's tucked away in the courtyard behind The Landmark, under the cover of the Craft Market restaurant, and get his Cable and Wireless answering service.

There are a few other Pirates skulking aimlessly, nothing to pillage, nothing to rape yet. A distinct lack of debauchery...yet!

"Hey, it's me, I'm… I'm in the middle of something, I'll, I'll call you later. Everything's okay though, don't worry. I'll look for you by Paradise for the fireworks." I lied, just in case. "It's ahm," turning over my right hand to look at my watch, "ahm, 5:45."

Dalbert's cellular phone rang moments after I hung up.
"He called her on Louis' phone." It was Earl. "I hope if I get fired you're gonna pay my salary."
"Yeah, right. You didn't find him though?"
"Not enough time."
"She didn't answer?"
"No. But he did say he'd meet her by Paradise for the fireworks"
"Okay, keep in touch."

Karl's feeling lonely; Mumsy's dead, Franklin's out and about at a meeting with his office. Karl's standing looking in through the plexiglass bubble of a little yellow submarine that's sitting on the land near the south terminal of the port. He turns to look at a group of Pirates passing by.

There's a black tall ship up against the North terminal dock.

On the finger pier at the North Terminal, fireworks are being set up.

He's wasting time waiting to meet Franklin for the fireworks. He hated wasting time, liked to do stuff, even if it was watching television – he tells himself that television is doing stuff.

He's got to go home and get rid of mumsy's body.

Anyhow, all work and no play makes Karl a dull boy. Besides, who wants to sit around a house with a dead body?

He'd turned the A/C really cold, didn't want mumsy rotting too fast.

His phone rang.

" Hallo?"

"Hubert, I've just had a tip that our friend Mr. Sherman might be onto something. I think he's in town."

"There're a lot of people in town, Franklin."

"Well, he's there, and if he's there, he's after something."

"I'll have a look around."

Karl slapped the phone shut. And thought: 'Fuck off'. Franklin darling was up to something, he was sure of it, not sure what, but something. He looked at his fingernails a moment, then looked around, then stepped off, heading in the direction of town.

Shapiro pulled the Suburban to the curb at exactly 5:45. Paul stepped out, looked at his watch.

"You start here," Effy said to him. They'd pulled over at the War Memorial clock outside the Legislature.

"Why'd you let him out of the car?"

"I don't know… I'm going to go park on the other side and work my way back. You check Rachaman's Pub and I'll check Paradise after the fireworks start."

Behind the Craft Market Cafe, through the Kirk Freeport staff parking lot and out onto Elgin Avenue, people were setting up food stalls. The smells of West Indian cooking and the chatter of West Indian voices filled the athmosphere. Rice and peas, with scotch bonnet pepper and coconut milk, sal' fish and ackee, fry fish, jerk chicken and jerk pork; the smoke from 15 fires and the steam from a dozen pots of cock soup and pepper pot soup and 'Manish' water (goat's head soup).

The sun was setting.

I stopped a moment, as if my feet just came to rest, in the middle of the street, amongst the press of people, brown people, black people, the odd white face. The safety in numbers thing was doing it for me. There was an empty spot on the curb and I moved to it and sat down there with the odours and the sea of moving legs.

"You want somet'ing fe eat baby?" I hear a voice and look up into a smiling round black face. "Nice rice an' peas an' oxtail?"

I smile back. "Yes, yes, why not." I pat my pocket. "How much?"

"Free tonight for you baby." She laughs. "I like you pretty face. You drink a cold Red Stripe?"

I nod.

It's the way of this world sometimes.

Two stereo systems were competing, with conflicting reggae tunes. A big fat mamma was bopping to the beat of JC Lodge singing 'Telephone Love'.

I turn around and there's this terrific orange to the sky out pass the harbour. I'm watching it, my mouth open in awe of the moment, and then I see Karl cross the street at the corner, a hundred yards away, walking along the harbour front, and I shrink a little by pulling my shoulders in, as if that'll make me disappear. He doesn't see me anyway.

If I'd known that the whole world was on the streets with me, I'd have gone home to bed and surrendered.

I take out a cigarette and light it and slowly revolve, like a diver in open water, circling his vision to see what's around.

The smell of the food, the music, the moment.

It's a beautiful day.

Long may it last.

Carpe (fucking) Diem.

Dalbert leaves the corner with the Chefalaro. He heads (the wrong way) up Cardinal Avenue, pass Kirk Freeport, the Wedgewood gallery, the Coach shop, toward the sea.

Effy's parking the Suburban behind the Hard Rock.

Paul stops to look around, as if confused, look left, look right, doesn't know which way to turn first.

Karl leans against the railing and looks into Hog Sty Bay. He closes his eyes for a moment and just stands there (contemplating murder?).

49

At 7:15 they cue the music that you can't hear unless you're standing on top of the South Terminal, and the first fireworks burst into the air over the harbour.

Wow!

The way the water in front of the finger pier is illuminated is fantastic, and just at the edge of all the light a group of boats are lurking, milling like sharks at the edge of your vision. This must have been what an old sea battle felt like. The smells, the reverberation, the water, the sound, the smoke, the ships lurking and milling, waiting their turn to engage.

I duck away and head for the police station. I figure this's the time of maximum distraction, and I've got 25 minutes of sound and fury and pretty lights in the sky. I love fireworks.

Dalbert turns from his walk along the fence in front of the seawall, where earlier Karl had stood. He pushes through the crowd behind him. He crosses the road and stops for a moment in front of the window of Artefacts. The fireworks are reflected in the glass, as he bends to light a cigarette and then turns to lean against the glass. He looks left, right, slowly scanning the crowd.

Karl, sitting by the bronze and green fish that adorns the garden planter in front of Columbian Emeralds, tries to make himself inconspicuous.

Wesley Snipes is on the roof of the Piccadilly Parkade, looking out at the flashing light.

One of Oney's men is coming along by the post office when he sees me angling across the street in front of Anderson Square.

"Mr. Dalbert, this be Reggie, I see your man," he says into the cellular phone.

Dalbert, loathe to leave the light spectacle, pushes off the wall, closing the phone. He looks both ways again and turns right. He looks back as the next boom heralds the next fireworks.

Karl sees Dalbert head up the street and gets up, throws down the cigarette.

He stops to look at the white and blue china platter in the window of Artefacts and touches the glass.

There's a magnificent volley of pink and white. Boom! Boom! Blossom of burning colour!

Up in front of Harbour Center, Rebecca steps out of a new black Jaguar, pauses a moment, and then shuts the door to join the crowd. The Jaguar drives off.

There's a pair of dogs, both with all four legs, rummaging through garbage behind the 'Subway Sandwhich Shop'.

Dalbert's phone rings.
"He dressed like a Pirate and headed down by the police station."
"Reggie?"
"Yeah."
"Cool, sorry the noise of the fireworks, did you say he's headed for the police station dressed as a pirate?"
"Yeah."

Shapiro steps out of the crowd, his eyes following the black Jaguar. Then he turns toward the direction that Rebecca went. He stops, and looks back in the direction of the Jaguar.

Dalbert's phone rings again.
"Uhhuh?"
"The girl's here now." It's Oney this time. "So's the bwoy Karl from the Edwards house, and Shapiro. The bwoy Karl is 'bout 50 yards back of you."
"Well Oney, the town full tonight."
"Look so, my frien'. Don't worry my bwoys will keep an eye on you. Be careful, seen."

The gate into the back of the station is still open. There's a group of police people standing in the parking lot looking up at the fireworks. I'm hoping that the whole station is as relaxed.
I'm moving fast. I walk right pass them and say, "Good evenin.'"
"You not watching the fireworks?" an uniformed woman asks.
"Work," I say.
"Too bad," she answers.
I walk around the corner and in through the open gate.

Dalbert's running now, not too fast, but running.

Karl looks at Dalbert picking up the pace. "Fuck, running," and lopes off too.

Wesley Snipes crosses the rooftop to the side overlooking the police station. He doesn't make me out from that distance.

The door's open and the keys are in the car. I hear a distant boom and the massive ball of light is reflected in the glass of the Range Rover. I think, wow, how beautiful.

I make a sudden descision.

Dalbert arrives at the corner in time to see the Range Rover driving away.

"Fuckin' rassclate!" he says and shakes his head.

Then picks his phone off his belt.

"Oney, Oney, I can't fuckin' believe this...you wouldn't believe it. Oney, find me the girl, an' don't let her out of your sight."

He turns suddenly and sees Karl duck away around the corner of the Cable and Wireless office.

III

50

I think I know who killed agent Froeman, I think I know who killed Elmo Gaunt, I think I know who killed Desmond Greene!

And now I'm just a little worried.

I'm sitting here on the floor of the borrowed house with a bunch of jewels scattered around me holding down several of the discarded pages of the documents which I've already read.

It's 8:48.

Off to the side is the counted pile of money from the three rolls: a million dollars U.S. In this day and age one million isn't what it used to be, if you just stick that in a bank, it's only about $40,000 a year in income – not much to live high on.

I'm getting this sinking feeling that I'm not going to get it. I unload the .38 that Rebecca has given me and slowly load it back. I wonder where she is right now, but don't bother to call out just yet. I hide it under a pile of paper.

Al Green is making me feel sad in a happy kind of way… 'I'm so tired of being alone.'

The documents before me, some of them…others tell an altogether different story that we'll come to soon…are the partial minutes of meetings between regional heads of government and business from Antigua and from Cayman and from Jamaica; drugs, money, money laundering…meetings with foreign bankers and local lawyers and businessmen from here and there.

There are names and dates and the things that were said. This must be the stuff that came out of Luthra's desk in Antigua.

This is somebody's safety net and somebody else's huge fucking mistake. People were getting killed for this.

The other documents, the ones that tell the other story, are a paper trail of stolen jewels and their conversions to cash flow. There's itemised documentation of the various involvements and complicities of Franklin Carpenter, along with tapes of conversations, deposit slips and dates and account numbers. Every transaction with Effrain Shapiro is recorded, not only ones for the Cayman Islands but in six other places as well. There are similar notations on other people, citizens, whose names I do not recognise. Over there is a pile held down by three jelly-bean-size emeralds that holds indications of the friendly services of certain local government officials and the odd police officers; with photographs.

The pile next to that, under two cashew-nut sized diamonds, relates to other governments for which I have no immediate concern but which might come in handy if I ever get audited by the IRS. Next to that, all by itself, garnished with a lovely Ruby, is a particularly nice piece about Minister Jefferies… I wonder if he will really care. What was it he said to me?

'*The people expect you to be corrupt, Mr. Sherman. As long as you serve their needs they have no quarrel with how much you steal. Perhaps they feel it is inevitable and therefore forgivable. People have been beaten, people have been killed, women abused, men raped, money stolen and no one cares as long as they have their social services."*

"Socialism for the masses, opulent consumerism for their leaders?" I asked.

"When Castro isn't on Cuban TV he wears Armani and lives like a king."

"And you wear thousand dollar shoes?"

"Twelve hundred dollar shoes." He'd smiled.

There's a third set of documents. An anatomy of the many lives of Stewart Parkman Bryce; and as a small byline, some on the life (and death) of one Grendall Charles Vosgien – same age, same size, same colouring…earlier death! Mr. Vosgien provided the dead body (replete with erection) in Miami.

Stewart Bryce was still alive.

Stewart Bryce wasn't dead and he was going to be wanting his stuff back.

And I had his stuff. I flipped the cylinder of the .38 back into place. And I called Effrain Shapiro, just to hear him scream down the phone line.

51

"**I was wondering when you were going to show your face,**" Karl said, half stepping from where he'd been standing in the shadows, onto the pathway at the Laguna Del Mar.

The man he spoke to turned abruptly and the light ran across his face.

"Hubert, how are you my boy? Scared me! Where's mumsy?" Stewart Bryce, stepped into the half light, looking very healthy for a dead man!

"She fell on an ice pick!" He replied almost as if he were joking. "Nice shirt, Stewart." Reaching out to dust something imaginary off the shoulder.

"How'd you find me?" He looks at his watch.

"It's 9:30, in case you're interested. And I found you the same way that I found you before... Franklin." He lit a cigarette, the dim yellow glow of the flame putting half of his face back into shadow.

"Franklin's here?" He looks around.

"Not anymore. He rushed down as he was worried that you might have left something behind that implicated him." The exhaled smoke danced in patches of light.

"I did." He chuckled.

"He doesn't care anymore."

"He's dead?"

"Fell on the same ice pick!" Was he joking?

"Sad, I saw him this afternoon and he looked so well. How'd you know I was here?"

"Hunch…many dead people that I didn't kill. So, did you have a nice meeting with Franklin this afternoon? And that woman, Rebecca Starr? Oh, don't look so shocked, I had a long chat with Franklin about 2 hours ago." That smile again. "He wasn't very talkative at first."

"Are you carrying a gun, Hubert?"

A question he doesn't answer. "And then there was much evidence tying me to this Sherman. Is this Sherman working for you also?" He looked away and up. "When he wasn't fucking my mother, that is."

"Ahh, Hubert," Bryce swallows hard, takes a very deep breath through his nose. "I shall miss her, I liked your mother. It's a bit public out here, Hubert, shall we go inside?"

He pulled the door shut.

"Do you like my new hair?" It was shorter and darker.

"Takes 20 years off of you." Karl looking around the room.

"Don't you think? Can I get you a drink?"

"Yes."

"But you did kill Elmo Gaunt, Hubert?" It wasn't really a question; and then the clink of ice in a glass.

"No. I didn't leave the murder weapon in the pool either. Nice touch that though!" He stops to look at that usual pastel condo art that adorns the wall. The kind they put there just to make the place look un-lived-in.

"You didn't kill him." A statement filled with quizzical disbelief as he stands there with two Scotches in his hand.

"No."

"Yes, you fucking did."

"Okay, yes I did." He makes a little flourish with his hand and then his voice changes; softly, with care he says, "Mumsy always said, '*Deny everything*'."

"Thank you." He takes the scotch from Bryce. "You know, Bryce, I studied up on you when Franklin first gave me your name. Lover's chit-chat; he wanted to brag, I think."

"I never figured you for a fag, Hubert."

"Call me Karl, please. Oh, I'm not faggot, Stewart – Franklin's a faggot. I'm an opportunist. So, where are the documents?"

"I was going to come and ask you the same question. I left them in the apartment for safekeeping. I was hanging around till all the fuss blew over."

"Sherman!" they said in unison.

"Don't try and fuck me, Bryce," Karl said quietly as Bryce handed him another drink. "I'm wanting to kill you already. We are partners here, yes? I want you to understand this well. I'm going to want money, lots of money and lots of protection and I will kill for it."

"Oh come now, Hubert. You can't really fault me for not trusting you and your mother, can you?" as he flopped into a comfortable armchair, stretched his neck and sipped his drink.

"Honour amongst theives." Karl rolled a cigarette around in his fingers. "I *will* kill you this time."

"Why don't we just say that you'll try, Hubert. Can I have one of your cigarettes? Now, let's discuss the near future, Karl."

The house is dark and musty when Karl arrives back home. He can smell the death in the distance.

"Don't you look the lovely couple," he says to the two bodies lain out side by side on his mother's bed. "I will have to get rid of the both of you shortly, before you begin to rot." He sat on the bed and leaned over as if to examine Franklin. "You, my friend, Franklin, are a bit rank already."

52

The phone numbers from New York, the Face ID information from London and the lists from immigration are all waiting for Dalbert when he gets back from a quick supper. He looks tired. He is tired. Tamara has done the immigration list in alphabetical order, as he'd asked. It is 35 pages long. 'Christ,' he thinks, 'do that many people visit this fuckin' place?'

He hasn't put an APB out on Sherman. He does have Oney's boys scouring the place for Rebecca.

"Hard thing D, one white gal in all this party." Oney had said.

Dalbert can hear the noise of the dance starting up; actually it's just the talent competition right now.

Within 20 minutes Dalbert is sitting on the hood of Minister Jefferies BMW outside Maxin's seafood restaurant on the other side of town. The alarm is ringing and a robotic feminine voice is calmly repeating, *'You are too close to the vehicle, please move away from the vehicle'*.

"Inspector Hannah, you're denigrating my cool ride with your hot backside. You wanted my attention?" Minister Jefferies, looking ever the cool and dapper gentleman about town with sexy young women.

"You're not dressed as a pirate, Minister." In the not too distance the sound of the street party now in full swing. A group of drunks pass by on the main street hollering loudly.

"Not my scene, Inspector." He smooths the chest of his two hundred dollar shirt.

"Your date, Big Man?" Dalbert indicated the blonde peering through the window.

"Lovely, isn't she?"

"This man belong to you, Chief?" Dalbert held out a photograph of a Wesley Snipes-looking mother-fucker' that had just been sent back to him by his London contacts.

"Hmmm, I don't recognize him; he looks like Wesley Snipes though."

"His name is James 'Punky' Edwards. An ex Vincentian-American bad boy, now cool operator, does the occasional work for the U.S. government in West Indian situations. Word has it that you brought him in after Shaprio bought Desmond Greene out. So, I ask again, does this man belong to you?"

In the background, appropriately is the Shaggy song; 'It Wasn't Me.'

"He does. Has he become a nuisance?"

"I don't know, who has he killed?" Dalbert is unwrapping a pack of cigarettes.

"No one that I know of. Do you mind?" asking for a cigarette too.

"Well then, suppose I ask you off the record," he holds out a cigarette for the minister. "Is there anyone he's killed that you don't know about?"

"That I don't know of?" Exhaling the smoke and contemplating the question.

"Yes, that you don't know of. Hmmm, like, say, Desmond Greene?"

"I would say that, ahm, that I don't know that that man, in that picture, killed Desmond Greene."

"Thank you. Well, then now, Squire, let's say this, if you don't know that he's after killin' Sherman, call him off."

"Who's going to call off the Queens representative?" Jefferies smoking elegantly.

"The SAS agent? He got back on the plane this evenin' when I explained the situation to him." Dalbert's still sitting on the car. "He was sent here as an independent observer, so to speak, rumours reaching Whitehall's ears. He was just supposed to quietly assess the course of justice."

"And if justice wasn't served?"

"He'd have to kill some people," he added sarcastically.

"And he was adverse to that, Dalbert?"

"No, I don't think he was at all." A small chuckle. "Then Macmillan finally stood up to be counted."

"Ah. How nice, you actually have friends?"

"Some people, I think, believe in duty and honour, Minister Jefferies. Some people put these things above personal gain, sometimes." Rolling his right hand from the wrist as a punctuation. "Maybe" …and now he opened both hands wide…"Because these are the things that make them the men that they are."

"I presume we're talking about Macmillan?" he said with a wry smile. "You do understand that the information that this Sherman may have in his possession is damaging to this government."

"Plausible deniability, isn't that what the Americans say, Chief?" He switched his nicknames. He had a plethora of them.

"The members of the public who know that governments are duplicitous, you like that word, already know about the dishonesty, don't they Minister. Those who don't are just pretending."

It almost seemed as if the conversation was over, then Dalbert started again. "Is the information that Bryce held about you of, oooh, say a much more personal nature?" Dalbert asked, continuing.

"Presumably." He seemed to be enjoying both the conversation and the cigarette, as if the game of brinksmanship was as normal as chess and that 'mate' didn't actually cost lives.

"Ah well then you should know that Bryce isn't dead, he's alive and he's here. He came in two months ago, just as this all started. He came in first by private plane to Little Cayman under the name Grendell Vosgien. Then he came here on the Island Air flight. I 'aven't found him yet, but I'm beginnin' to get very close. Call off Wesley Snipes, Minister. When it all goes bad, I'll take care of the information 'bout you."

"You are too kind. What'll it cost me?"

"I haven't decided yet."

As Dalbert started away, Minister Jefferies called out.

"I already knew he was still alive, Inspector. It's he who said I should hire your Wesley Snipes!"

Dalbert was tired, but too close now to stop. He looked at his watch. A fleeting thought of Grace passed his mind. He opened the desk drawer and poured himself a rum.

He closed his eyes and felt the St. Ann's breeze in his hair and the tremble of the Astin Martin beneath him.

My eyes can only look at you.

53

"Fuck!" I say out loud.

And I hear the lock turn in the door.

I touch the gun and call out.

"Who's there? That you Becca?"

"Yes," she calls back. "I need to pee, I'll be right back."

I look at my watch; it's 11:00.

Rebecca comes into the room. "You're having a party?" She's barely dressed and I look up and am immediately horny. "Wait a sec, you found it!" There's surprise to her voice. "That's a fucking diamond, right there, and a... Jesus Christ, Sherman, that sapphire's as big as a fucking egg!" She sort of flops down in a daze. "Are these the documents, Sherman?"

"Yes, yes they are." But all of a sudden I'm not interested in documents, I'm interested in fucking! I'm interested in that dark patch of fuzz beneath the fabric of her panties. I'm interested in eating her raw, in tasting her pink sticky moistness. And I do, I do, I push her back and she goes. She knows what I want and raises her hips so that the panties come off and she opens her legs for me and smiles.

"Sherman," is all she says.

And then I lick her from anus to clitoris before burrying my lips, my nose forging its way through fantastic fragrant electric pubic fuzz.

Her stomach is convulsing with the waves of her orgasm when I notice that Bryce is sitting in a chair on the patio quietly smoking a cigarette and looking right at us through the open door. He's sitting relaxed; he looks at his nails then back at us. Only a mosquito screen between us and him. He's sitting in the dim yellow light cast by the mosquito bulbs on either side of the door.

I can hear the running water of the fountain that's in the shade garden in the background and the occasional hollow song of the bamboo wind chime. My fingers and mouth are covered with the smell, the taste, the wet stickiness of her, my shirt is off and my cock is making my pants feel very very good. I no longer wear underwear! I sound happy, and I was, but I'm suddenly not anymore.

Dark clouds rolling in and I'm standing out in the rain.

"Oh fuck!" I say and sit back.

"Hallo, Sherman." His voice seems to ring in my head. I want to hyperventilate.

Rebecca sits up.

"Rebecca," he says, and I realise that she knows him.

"Stewart." She stands and doesn't seem nervous to be naked in front of him. Then looks at me and says, "Sorry Sherman. I tried not to, I really tried." And then she leaves the room.

But stops by the door and says, "Really sorry, Chris." Just before her beautiful ass disappears from sight.

Funny that's just what that bitch Marjorie had said to me the day I found out that she was leaving me for fucking Jack. 'I'm sorry, Chris.' Then paused long enough to light a cigarette with perfectly manicured fingernails showing. 'Really sorry, Chrisy.'

'Well gee fucking thanks, that just makes all the bloody difference in the fucking world, thank you very fucking much, doesn't it. Aaaaaaaargh!'

"I come as a surprise, do I?" he said to me, still sitting in the chair.

"No, no, actually you don't." I sound angry. "Rebecca," a slow nod, "Rebecca on the other hand comes as a total fucking surprise." I shake my head. "But then I should have known, ah? I mean this is me right, Sherman. Shit! It's not like me to get well laid. And as it turns out the two people that have been fucking me have been friends of yours. I should keep you around." But I want to kill you, I think, but don't add.

"Ava," he says and seems sad.

"Ava," I nod.

"Can I have a gin and tonic?" he asks, but I don't really think I have any choice. "Ava's dead, Sherman. You should know that. Karl killed her." I'm in the kitchen finding the gin, and he's still talking. "You should know that as well. He's also killed Franklin Carpenter. I tell you these things so that you understand, Sherman. With me, life might be lenient for you, but Karl's a stone-fucking killer, Sherman. Karl's going to want to kill you." I don't like how my day's turning out. "The facts are these, Sherman, can I come in? I can see that you have my stuff all over your floor." I notice that he has a very slight stutter.

I don't say anything, but he comes anyway. He slides the screen back and stands in the doorway. "You see, well you know, Franklin and I were in business together. Franklin was worried that the reinsurers were getting suspicious. So we were closing shop."

"Why me?"

"Because, I guess, but really because you were the only West Indian on the SIU payroll."

"O'Malley?"

"Yes, O'Malley worked for us too."

"What's his fate, run over by a fucking bus or something?"

He shrugged and pulled the screen door closed, standing on the other side of it as if seeking its protection like the mesh veil of the confessional that seperates the penitent from the priest.

"Karl and Ava?" I asked.

"Really just Franklin playing with me. He tossed them at me in Bahamas, they were tied in with a banker named Luthra from whom they wanted something, at the same time I wanted some documents that were useful to me – Franklin was fucking Karl or Karl was fucking Franklin...doesn't really matter at this stage."

"Honour amongst theives, ah!"

"Franklin was a self-centred snake."

"And you're just a saint," I say sarcastically.

He turns away a moment and looks at the fountain. "Maybe so, Sherman."

Then he turned back and he smiled that charming smile of his. He was infinitely charming, even now. "My suggestion is that you take the money I'm going to offer you. And I'm going to offer you a lot of money, but I'm not going to negotiate. You take the money I offer you, you take the passport I'm going to offer you, and the plane ride that goes with it and you leave this place and forget it, forget me, forget Karl. Can I get you a bag to put that all into?" He indicates his stuff.

Rebecca walks back into the room then; dressed again, and smoking.

I'm a sad case because all I can think is that she still looked fuckable! I wanted to hate her, but looking at her all I wanted to do was have sex with her.

"And forget Rebecca." I added.

He shrugged watching her walk by.

She didn't look at me or at him but went to the kitchen.

"Rebecca likes you, Sherman." He sat down in his chair again and sipped his drink. "Don't feel sorry for yourself, boy. It's all a matter of self-preservation; Rebecca did what she had to do to survive. She may not have liked it, but it's better than being dead, isn't it? Think about it, Sherman, what would you do to survive? Look at her, Sherman, she's sad. She likes you, Sherman, you're under Rebecca's skin, my man. She almost didn't come through for me. Sure, in the beginning it was easy, all fun and games. Getting Louis to distract you for a little, that was easy. But then, when I called on her today, she almost didn't come through. But, we go way back. We have a history. I can be a dangerous man Sherman." Yeah, as if I was doubting it.

"What about Shapiro?" I asked, changing an uncomfortable subject.

His face was odd then.

"What about Effrain?"

"You're cutting him out."

He seems to be thinking. "We weren't partners, just associates."

"And friends?"

"And friends," he added, and then I understood. Karl would be killing Effrain Shapiro soon.

"Who else will Karl be killing tonight?"

"Karl'll be killing Dalbert because Karl wants to kill Dalbert."

"So why not me?"

"Because I like you. Rebecca likes you."

That's when I shot him.

I shot him dead. Right through the screen, in the sort of cowboy Western lingo of these things, I just shucked out the old .38 that Rebecca had given me (and which was sitting under a pile of paper). I palmed iron in one fluid motion, raised it, aimed it as an extension of my arm, exhaled, leant just a litle forward and fired. I felt it buck.

Top dead centre! Aim for the big bits, the parts you can't miss.

Blood was oozing onto his white shirt when I shot him again. I stood and walked almost to the door while he looked at me incredulously, dying, slowly. By now he was feeling the burning hot sensation of the bullet's passage, not the pain yet, but a sensation of heat. And I shot him again, closer now, and the chair went over backward with him and his head made a horrible crack as he hit the concrete.

Rebecca didn't scream. She didn't move.

There were two neat holes in the mosquito screen.

I opened it and walked outside. Bryce was dirty; his clean clothes were smudged with dirt and blood. He'd spilled his cigarette ash on his shirt. A splotch of blood was on his cheek. And I stood over him and shot him four more times.

Violent death sort of disassembles people.

Rebecca was still just standing there in the kitchen, looking fuckable but pale and nervous, like necrophiliac fuckable. Her hand was wrapped around a glass that she wasn't drinking from. Motionless.

I walked pass her and then back out with a clean shirt, a reloaded gun, and the digital video camera. Her other hand was gripping the counter.

My fingers now smelled of more than her pussy; they smelled of gunpowder and of death.

I went to the phone. There was no answer at Shapiro's home or his cell. I get the feeling that he's already dead. Paul's probably bleeding on the floor of the Suburban.

I filmed Bryce where he lay dead. I film him with the Canon A630 digital camera.

An odd disconnected sensation when in contact with the dead; you notice quickly that you can't make conversation with them.

Rebecca has come to the door behind me. Finally brave.

"Is he dead?"

"Where will Karl be?" I ask.

"At the house in South Sound. Bryce was to bring a boat," she answered, not looking at me; she's looking at Bryce.

"Chris."

"Hmmm." I don't want to talk now.

So I left her standing there, looking pale. I wanted to ask why, but didn't. I wanted to know stuff, but I had a feeling that stopping, I would never go again. That I would break down. Stop and melt and cry and weep and dissolve.

It'll still be two days till I say I'm sorry.

54

"How nice, two for the price of one." Karl seems happy that he's got me bound and gagged. I'm upset that I've only just recovered from my last beating. I'd come to have one last little play with the sharks, but the water'd been chummed and the sharks were in a feeding frenzy when I got there. I'm lying half on my back, my bound hands getting in the way of being flat. I close my eyes, wanting to cry because I'm going to die and because I'm bleeding.

I'd come in round the back with the .38 in my hand, wasn't sure what I'd find. Not even sure why I was doing this, playing the lone ranger.

Just that I was angry about people playing the political game with me. The easy answer was still to let Sherman take the fall. Sherman was the easy patsy – I didn't bite back very hard, I'd be an easy loser – so maybe I just wanted to bite back.

The house had been black and dark and just that whisper of wind in the Casuarinas as he stepped up onto the patio.

Clive didn't bark.

The back door was wide open...

I'd stopped to smell the sea and the sand.

Effrain Shapiro looked a bit worse for the wear, battered and bleeding, and white like a sheet that's been drying in the sun. I'm trussed up like a chicken for roasting. The duct tape around my mouth is making breathing and swallowing difficult. My hands were sore and beginning to swell where the duct tape was cutting off the circulation. Shapiro's sitting in a chair. Our eyes meet. I nod at him. Effy's face twists to show what must be a smile under the duct tape.

"How nice, a loving reunion for you two," Karl's sitting on the bed looking out the window. "Fucking idiots." He reaches out and runs the back of a finger across Shapiro's temple. Shapiro just looks at him, hurt but calm. "Your friend sold you out to me." He bent next to Shapiro's face and licked his ear. "Yes, your friend Bryce sold your soul to me.

"I'm the clean up crew you see."

I'd stepped in through the open patio door. The house had seemed quiet, deserted. I'd lowered the gun.

"I wouldn't try to move if I were you." Karl had just been quietly sitting there in the darkness in a dark outfit, hidden, like a ninja.

After Karl had tied me up, he'd casually gone outside, crossed the road and killed the man Oney had watching the house. He brought his ear back for me..

"A present for you, my friend – the man across the road. Your friend Dalbert should be here soon." He threw the ear so that it landed on my face, I squirmed, scrunching my neck and wriggling my head to dislodge the dead flesh. "Then I can finish up and get the fuck off this rock."

"Predictable." Karl lit himself a cigarette. "I look good in black don't I?"

Effy's missing one of his thumbs; he's very pale now, a cold sweat on his forehead.

"I've been reading Louis L'Amour, you know." Karl's talking to me. "And I'm always fascinated by those bits about how the Apaches would torture a man for days before killing him." He chuckles. "Unfortunately I don't have time." He glances at his watch. It's 3:08am. "Our mutual friend Mr. Bryce is to bring a boat around for us." He walks to the window and looks out. The sea is flat and the moon is shining a wide swath across its surface. It's a beautiful night. "Your girlfriend's going to bring the jewels. It's such a beautiful night. We'll dump your bodies out at sea. I'd like to fucking dump your friend Dalbert alive." He rests his foot on my chest. "But I can't take any chances now. Roll over." He was screwing the 8" long suppressor onto the Walther PPK.

He looked out the window, then back at his watch.

"Time!"

Down with the moral majority, I want to be the minority.

"Bryce's dead." I suddenly blurt out. "Yes." It's more a croak than anything else because he's moved the foot to the middle of my back; my arms are stretched out in front of me.

"Shit."

"I have the million in cash and the Hudson House jewels," I grunt.

The gun backs up an inch or two.

"You're a bit of a godsend, aren't you Sherman? Always surprising me, something absolutely likable about you. Your friend's dead." He straightens and waves the gun to indicate the room in general, but he's still standing on my hand.

"Have you said goodbye to mother?" He lifts me up and turns me to the bed. The room is full of bodies. "She's naked," he says as if this might be enough sexual enticement for me. "Would you like to fuck her one more time? She won't be as, as warm as usual, but just as willing." He laughs.

"Shit." And I throw up, hearing Blondie's Ave Maria playing around in my head as background music.

"Now see, that's just fucking nasty, Sherman."

It's a 1985 Buick Regal station wagon.

"Convenient for bodies," says Karl. I'm untied and rubbing my wrists, he's tossing the money and the jewels that he's taken from my car, into the back of the wagon.

But we've got no bodies. '*No point in dumping you now.*' Karl had said as he pressed my fingers around the grip of the Walther. He then made me hold the pruning shears he'd used to cut off Effy's thumb. '*Nice of you to provide the alibi.*' Throwing down the Walther he'd taken the .38.

Held up with your own gun, see that just sucks.

"Well let's not bother to wait for your friend Detective Dalbert to show up. Your fingerprints are all over everything, it'll be damn hard for him to convince the world that you weren't the fucking asshole. Maybe I'll dump you at sea...but I like you Sherman, you're an annoying little prick, but I like you...maybe I'll let you live."

"It's time to go Sherman."

The moon's up and there's a huge Poinciana tree in the circular planter in the drive.

"Right, well you drive, Sherman." He threw me the keys. "Better for me to keep an eye on you." The smile is so charming it's half hard to be scared of him even as he was waving the gun in my general direction.

"What about your body?" I ask as I'm backing up.

"You'd like that, wouldn't you, Sherman. Too bad you don't have what it takes to kill me," he says.

"You never know. I mean, it's better than the alternative." I say. "Where're we going?"

"There's a boat in Spotts.

When we're on the road again I glance at him twice, then say, "I shot Bryce six times." I'm not really bragging it's just for information.

We don't get to Spotts because just pass the South Sound boat ramp we pass a guy dressed as a Pirate, walking down the middle of the road. Karl looked back and let his guard down, and me, I suddenly swerved off the South Sound Road.

At 50 mph, no matter how you drive into a tree it hurts. But it doesn't stop us. Karl grabbed at the wheel and we take the Sea Grape tree a glancing blow on the right side at the same time as I hit him in the face with my watch. I wear my watch on my right hand, see.

The collision tears up the passenger side and sends us careening head-on into a Casuarina tree – it's a Casuarina stump really, what's left of a tree that was half destroyed in a Hurricane years ago. We bounce off it like we were made of rubber and bang back into the Sea Grape tree. Here we come to a full and complete stop. The car does anyhow.

I'm lucky. Karl, who was distracted by my watch and the pain of broken glass and bending metal tearing at the right side of his body, is not. He's not paying attention and the dashboard kills him.

Blood's on the fitter of my cigarette. I notice I've lost one shoe and I know I'm going to hurt in the morning.

All sorts of things are going to hurt me. So when I think, 'Fuck you' and smile all red and twisted I know how I'm going to ache tomorrow. My heart and my mind and my body are going to scream with pain... I'm going to miss Rebecca, I'm going to miss Todd.

Karl's got a gun in his dead hand.

I've got a million dollars in cash and some really nice jewels and the kind of documentation that can buy a guy out of jail. Anything can happen now, I can make anything happen now.

I, I wanna rule my destiny!

55

Things happened quickly, I made a call to Louis, Louis who can do anything, who made a few calls of his own. I catch a car to a boat, the boat took me to a seaplane. Boom, boom, boom all within an hour.

The hills of Jamaica are so big and so blue after Cayman.

So three hours later I'm sitting on James Bond Beach in Oracabessa, Jamaica. I look around, it's a bit like a construction site rather than a beach.

The seaplane pilot walks up with a cell phone. He smiles at me but doesn't say anything so I simply smile in reply and take the phone.

"You alive?"

"Yes, I'm alive." I say.

"How's Jamaica?" Dalbert asks.

"Nice." I'm a bit nervous, wondering where all this is going to.

"Sorry I missed you," he continues. "Rebecca called me while you were killing our friend Bryce. I didn't get there in time."

"I was moving kind of fast, what can I say. Rebecca called you?"

"Yeah, she likes you, Sherman – we've been working together for a while, you know. She and I go way back. Sorry, Sport you were sort of the bait; I had her working both sides of the fence and you in the middle.

"I missed you at Karl and Ava's too," he continued.

"Well." I shrug. "So Rebecca was on your side; I missed that bit."

"Yes, yes you did. As I said she came to like you, Sherman."

When? But I didn't ask it, wasn't sure I wanted to know at what stage I went from being patsy to stooge.

And then at least one of the questions I didn't want to ask, "Is Effy dead?"

"No, but he is very badly hurt. I hear you found Bryce's jewels?"

"Do I have to answer that?"

Ava, Karl, Franklin, Bryce, Elmo, Desmond, Froeman all dead. Froeman had found the first evidence that Bryce was alive and wanted a piece of the action. He'd wanted in. He asked for in, Bryce killed him. Karl had killed Elmo, his mother, and Franklin; he thought he'd killed Dalbert, twice. Dalbert's lucky. Wesley Snipes had killed Desmond to get at me. I'd liked Desmond. Him and Effy...probably, I mean if you get right down to the psychological mumbo jumbo of it all, I really miss the Rebecca I thought I knew. Whatever, I like Rebecca.

"You can come back here now, you know, Sherman. It'll all be safe and sorted by the morning."

Me, I've never gone back.

In more ways than one.

I left me at the safe end of a smoking gun. Me doesn't exist anymore, Chrisy's gone, man; Sherman's taken his place.

Marjorie begged me to cum on her face as I fucked her, so I did.

She said, '*God, Chrisy, you're so different!*'

I told her, as I fucked her, from behind, again, with her hands tied together above her head, that I was leaving her, that she could have her Jack (bastard!), she could have the house, she could have the dog, she could even have the fucking car. But, I told her I wasn't letting her take Todd, told her that we were sharing him. She didn't care then.

She started to complain after the sweat began to dry on her back, but didn't like the look in my eyes or the tone of my voice when I said to her,

"*Marjorie, I'm a different kind of me.*" *I'd whispered it in her ear, her hands still tied above her head and the full weight of me on her back, my cock flacid now, soft and sticky between the cheeks of her ass.* "*You don't want to fuck with this me, Marjorie. You don't wanna fuck with this me.*" *And I kissed her cheek wetly!*

She shook, vibrated really, with the joy of a little fear as I fucked her again moments later.

'**The rules don't apply to me anymore,**' I think to myself as I drive down the Southern Highway.

The new Land Cruiser is comfortable. Abba's good music for the airy way that I feel.

Knowing me knowing you.

I live now in a place called Belize, down south in a town called Placencia, by the sea. I've grown a beard. I drink a lot more, smoke a little grass with my cigarettes. Or smoke a little cigarettes with my grass. Sometimes I like to listen to Air Supply;
I'm all out of love, I'm so lost without you.

I'm rich and I've killed men. I don't know what exactly this says about me, but it says something, doesn't it?

I got a note from Dalbert the other day. It had a photo in it. I give a little snorting chuckle of joy here. It was of him in his 1979 Aston Martin V8 Osca India, in Chinchester Blue with Magnolia hide interior and 5 speed manual transmission, driving down the Queens Highway between Discovery Bay and Rio Bueno... The Jamaican wind caressing his bald head. I can't see who's shot the photo, but from the smile on his face it's probably not Grace.

Dalbert's retired.

A guy Louis knew cut the Blue India for me; cut it into 30 two and a half carat stones and then with some imput from Effy helped us pawn it and all the rest of the jewels. I could have returned them, eh? The old me might have, but what the fuck, the insurance had already been paid out on them, Bryce was already said to be dead – fuck, if he wasn't before, he certainly is now.

So who was to say that the jewels had ever been found? Not me.

I gave the documents to Minister Jefferies, who flew to Jamaica to collect them. Dalbert came with him.

"No copies?" he'd asked.

"No copies," Dalbert had answered.

There was a lovely blonde, about 19 and all tight and fit, lurking close by.

"She's lovely," I said.

"She is, isn't she?" the minister had replied with this smile that I so enjoyed.

So certain things were taken care of, other things swept under the carpet. The names were changed to protect the innocent.

I made a few million on the deal, even at the cut rates they were offering me.

Dalbert's coming next month for a visit and, we're going fishing, Todd's coming too for his holidays. Marjorie and I have worked out joint custody; in the end it just seemed the better choice, you know. I didn't want to go back to live in New York, in America; it just wasn't me anymore. So Todd stays with his mum during school term and on holidays he comes to me. I miss him when he's not around.

Effy called just to cough and splutter; he's still feeling rough around the edges, and life's hard without thumbs.

I got an email from Rebecca a few days ago. She misses me; I know she does. Not that that's what the email said, it was, you know, just general chit-chat. But, you know, she changed me. Everything else is just the ancillary, the by-product of my life with Rebecca – she as my catalyst.

Like a (fucking) Spanish guitar to paraphrase a pop star!

And suddenly, as I finish writing this – I realise how I'll start my movie. I see it, the perfect image, the empty road, the soft light of dawn; on the right the sea, on the left undeveloped bush. The straight road, and there, weaving the line, the Pirate, a remnant of the previous night's revelry, post pillage, pre rape, drunk and staggering home; out of his place, out of his time…an anomaly!

- The End -

Printed in the United States
129454LV00004B/1/P

9 789768 202543